T0278653

THE *loudest* SILENCE

SYDNEY LANGFORD

HOLIDAY HOUSE · NEW YORK

Library of Congress Cataloging-in-Publication Data

Names: Langford, Sydney, author.
Title: The loudest silence / by Sydney Langford.
Description: First edition. | New York : Holiday House, 2024. | Audience:
Ages 14 and up. | Audience: Grades 10-12. | Summary: Told in two voices,
follows the friendship between queer teens Casey, a singer who is
grappling with sudden hearing loss, and soccer captain Hayden, whose
Generalized Anxiety Disorder weighs on his every move, after they bond
over their shared dream of a music career.
Identifiers: LCCN 2023039041 | ISBN 9780823456246 (hardcover)
ISBN 9780823459315 (ebook)
Subjects: CYAC: Hard of hearing people—Fiction. | Anxiety
disorders—Fiction. | Friendship—Fiction. | Music—Fiction. | LGBTQ+
people—Fiction.
Classification: LCC PZ7.1.L344115 Lo 2024 | DDC [Fic]—dc23
LC record available at https://lccn.loc.gov/2023039041

ISBN: 978-0-8234-5624-6 (hardcover)

CONTENT NOTE

Sign language, like all languages, is rich and layered. While multiple variations exist, both in the U.S. and abroad, in THE LOUDEST SILENCE, ASL (American Sign Language) and SimCom (simultaneous communication—speaking and signing at the same time) are used.

ASL can be different from place to place or person to person due to factors like regional and generational differences or the use of "English" signs vs. "Deaf" signs. ASL also has different grammar rules and syntax from English. This, plus the fact that ASL is a visual language, means any author representing it on-page has some (often tricky) creative choices to make.

In THE LOUDEST SILENCE, the <u>descriptions</u> of signing use ASL grammar and syntax. However, ASL/SimCom that has been translated into English uses English grammar and syntax and is *italicized*. The latter represents an interpretation of what's being signed but isn't a literal translation.

Other D/deaf authors may portray ASL/SimCom differently and those creative choices are also valid!

For clarity, ***bolded and italicized*** words do not relate to ASL; these are emphasized English words.

AUTHOR'S NOTE

Dear Reader,

When I was fourteen years old, I suddenly and unexpectedly lost about sixty percent of my hearing. Fourteen is a difficult age for most people, but when you lose one of your five senses and your world is abruptly and irrevocably changed, it adds a whole slew of complications to an already tumultuous time in your life.

After becoming Deaf-Hard of Hearing, I didn't know where I belonged. I didn't yet know ASL, nor was I raised in the Deaf community, so I didn't feel "Deaf enough" for the Deaf world. Conversely, I wasn't "Hearing enough" for the Hearing world anymore. All of this led to a long grieving period, an element I explore in this book through Casey's character. Casey's emotional arc throughout the novel largely mirrors my own experience, and I hope Casey's and my journey with this particular kind of grief can provide some insight, or even comfort, to others.

While I was grieving my hearing loss, my Generalized Anxiety Disorder reached new heights—something I explore through Hayden's story. Drawing on my own experiences, I've tried to portray what GAD looks and feels like, both to the person experiencing it and to those around them. At times, Hayden's anxiety may seem disproportionate to what he's experiencing, but that's intentional. Those of us with GAD are often extremely anxious about things that other people consider mundane, for reasons that may not be apparent to people without anxiety disorders.

During my first few years of grappling with hearing loss and battling overwhelming anxiety, books provided my only escape from reality. But the more I read, the more I longed to see myself represented. I craved books about D/deaf teens; anxious teens; messy, chaotic, queer teens. I craved more stories about queer and/or Disabled teens with big, complicated emotions—anxiety, joy, grief, love. Teens who form unbreakable and unique bonds. Teens who don't fit into any of society's neat little boxes.

That's when the idea for THE LOUDEST SILENCE first came to me: a story about how Casey—a bisexual singer, a girl whose entire world revolved around sound—would cope with the sudden and inexplicable loss not only of her hearing, but of her music. And about how Hayden—an aro-ace soccer captain with severe anxiety—could learn to embrace his secret passion for the performing arts.

I wrote THE LOUDEST SILENCE for the anxious, lost, fourteen-year-old version of myself. I wrote THE LOUDEST SILENCE for Disabled kids struggling to find representation. I wrote THE LOUDEST SILENCE to help introduce able-bodied readers to Disabled perspectives they may not have considered before. I wrote THE LOUDEST SILENCE to show anyone who has ever felt like they don't belong that someday they will find their place in this world.

From the bottom of my heart, thank you for letting me share this story with you.

Sydney Langford

CHAPTER 1
CASEY

I'M STARTING TO SUSPECT I LIVE IN A COMING-OF-AGE MOVIE.

It's like my entire existence was created in a Netflix writers' room. I'm the confident, determined, averagely attractive teen girl whose world has been turned upside down in a sudden, unexpected plot twist.

Obviously, it's just a conspiracy theory I invented to entertain myself during the forty-seven-hour drive from Oregon to Florida. But the longer I'm trapped in Mom's overpacked minivan, the more I grow convinced my life has been scripted by underpaid creatives sitting around a table and brainstorming unbelievable scenarios.

It's a better explanation than four different doctors saying they don't know why I suddenly lost fifty percent of my hearing four months ago. Why I went to bed one night with ears that worked fine and woke up the next morning to a muffled world—like I was submerged underwater.

It **might've** been the flu. It **could've** been an underlying condition.

Or maybe—just maybe—it was those damn Netflix writers.

"What are you thinking about?" Mom interrupts my riveting inner monologue, her eyes trained on the highway.

"My early-onset midlife crisis," I grumble.

I look out the window at the palm trees that blur against the sky as we glide down the highway. I catch sight of Dad's car in the side mirror and watch as he bobs his head, presumably to the tune of his obnoxious Polish folk music.

Mom ignores my attempt to deflect, intent on having an impromptu therapy session. "Is this about Dr. Riger?"

A groan escapes me before I can suppress it. Fingers bent in a claw shape, I toss a hand away from my mouth, using American Sign Language to show disdain for audiological exams. "She accused me of faking it, Mom. The world became inaccessible overnight, and Dr. Riger had the audacity to accuse me of faking my hearing loss? Why would I do that?"

Mom eyes me after the outburst but stays silent. I think she knows I'm not actually mad at her, even though it may seem like it. The real target of my anger is the ignorant doctor who performed my latest hearing test. I'm also mad that I can't effectively communicate, and I'm mad that we're moving to Florida in the middle of this whole mess. But above all, I'm furious at my ears for deciding to inexplicably crap out on me after a committed sixteen-year relationship.

"I'm sick of tests," I continue. "They all show the same thing. Profoundly *Hard of Hearing*." I say, using SimCom—simultaneous communication, or signing and speaking at the same time—for the last words, my horizontal index and middle fingers pressing together as I tap the air in front of my chest twice, moving my hand from left to right. Sure, Mom's not going to see me signing because she's driving, but using SimCom is good practice for me.

"No more tests. I promise." Mom gives me a sad smile, the kind that makes you feel worse than you did before. I've drilled into my parents that I don't want to be patronized, but they can't help themselves with the sad smiles. "Unless you want a *hearing aid.*" She curls her thumb and index finger around her ear.

Mom and I have had this discussion at least five times now, and every time, I've told her I don't want a hearing aid—getting one would involve even more tests, then fittings, and there's not even a guarantee it would help with my type of hearing loss. Why doesn't she understand that I'm done being poked and prodded?

"No." I stick my hand in front of her and slam my thumb, index, and middle fingers together like a pincer.

Mom drops the subject, and we drive in silence for the remaining hour. I grab my phone and open Instagram to kill time, deflating a little when I see there are zero new DMs in my inbox.

I click on my most recent story—a picture of the WELCOME TO FLORIDA sign we passed earlier—and confirm that all the "friends" I left in Portland saw it. A lump forms in my throat and I close the app.

Seriously, what did I expect? For the friends who ghosted me after I lost my hearing, the people who abandoned me when I needed more support than ever, to suddenly start messaging me again? For my newly ex-boyfriend, Victor, who broke up with me because I was "too hard to communicate with," to stop treating me like a huge inconvenience because I'm no longer able-bodied?

Yeah. It's pretty clear that's not going to happen.

I shake the thoughts away and focus on the cars whizzing by, the tropical flowers and swaying palm trees that line the highway, and the smell of the ocean. The brightly colored exuberance of Miami is on proud display. It's a stark contrast to Portland's weirdness, which I already miss.

The scenery changes as we pull into our new neighborhood. The streets here are incredibly dull and uniform, all white houses with terra-cotta roofs, perfectly trimmed green grass, and minivans parked in pressure-washed driveways.

I find myself thirsty for another glass of the Miami I saw earlier.

Some neighbors wave as we park, and we politely wave back, then make our way inside our prefurnished rental home. The interior decor matches the cookie-cutter aesthetic of the neighborhood's overall design: white, lifeless, and severely lacking originality.

I peer up the staircase that leads to the second floor, then glance back at my parents. *"Which room is mine again?"* I ask using SimCom.

I probably should've watched the 3D tour of the house Mom sent to familiarize myself with the layout before we arrived, but the last thing I wanted to do on the drive was think about my "fun new life in Miami"—as Mom and Dad looove to phrase it, like there's even an infinitesimal chance I won't absolutely hate living here.

"It's the door at the very end of the hallway," Mom chirps. "It's a little bare-bones right now, but don't worry, we'll spruce it up! Make it feel like home."

"Pretty sure all the 'sprucing' in the world won't make it feel anything like home," I mutter under my breath.

"What was that?"

"Nothing." I kick off my shoes, release my sphynx cat, Jell-O, from her pet carrier, and charge upstairs. I locate the small bedroom at the end of the hall and face-plant onto the bed.

Welcome to effin' Miami.

The scorching sun beats down on Mom's van as we speed down South Dixie Highway the next day. I blare HAMILTON at a volume too loud for any Hearing person, hoping to avoid a pep talk from Mom. She glances my way but doesn't say anything.

She'd never admit this, but I think she feels guilty. After all, she's the reason we've moved to Florida mere months after I lost my hearing. The event-planning business she works for opened a new branch here and she was handpicked to run it.

Meaning I get to spend my junior year at a new high school three thousand miles away from home. With no hearing, no friends, and a perpetual sunburn. (I have a sneaky suspicion that even if I use SPF 5000, my pale, Edward Cullen-esque skin will instantly burn here.)

Okay, so, maybe I'm a little upset with Mom. Just a **smidge.**

Mom reaches over the center console and hands me her phone. The Notes app is open, a message typed out onscreen: **I'll be in meetings all day, but I'll check my phone during breaks, in case you need me.**

I sigh, place the phone in the unoccupied cupholder, and return my attention to HAMILTON.

We come to a stop in front of Palmera High School's front courtyard as "Satisfied" ends. I unbuckle my seat belt and fling open the car door. Before I can make my getaway, though, Mom grabs my wrist.

"Did you read my note?"

"Yep." I sigh, looking up at the building.

"Don't be afraid to ask for accommodations if you need them. There's going to be an adjustment period." Mom smiles reassuringly. "But you've got this, sweetie."

I give an incredibly forced smile in return. If I had a dollar for every time she's encouraged me to "be my own advocate" while navigating school as a Disabled person for the first time, I'd have enough for a plane ticket back to Portland.

She holds up her hand, tucking her middle and ring fingers to her palm. *"I love you,"* she signs.

I half-heartedly return the sign as she drives off, then take the world's deepest inhale and push through Palmera High's doors.

I keep my head down as I walk toward the front office, doing my best to avoid being noticed by the other students. I thought pulling my hair into a cute messy bun and wearing my favorite shirt—a crop top with a subtle embroidered bisexual pride heart—would give me a much-needed confidence boost, but now all I can think about is how my hair is a rats' nest from the humidity and my top is wrinkled from the way I packed it for the move. It's less effortlessly chic and more slob-who-just-rolled-out-of-bed.

We're off to a magnificent start.

The woman sitting behind the desk looks up at me through thick-rimmed glasses. "Casey Kowalski?" She smacks on chewing gum between words.

I may be new to this whole Deaf-Hard of Hearing thing, but I can tell I won't be able to understand her when she's chewing gum. It's like talking to a baby—complete gibberish.

"Yep." I mess with the hem of my shorts. "I'm supposed to meet with Audrey Simons. She's my student guide."

The woman hands me a piece of paper with my class schedule on it. Her mouth moves, but the words are blocked by the simultaneous chewing. When I stay silent, she glares at me, lowers her glasses, and points to the chairs behind me. She looks disturbingly like Roz from MONSTERS, INC.

"Wait there," she commands with a grimace.

I take a seat and occupy myself by scrolling through TikTok until, a few minutes later, someone materializes in front of me. I look up from my phone, expecting to see Audrey Simons, but instead I'm greeted by a white woman in her mid-thirties with a blunt brown bob and a wide smile.

"Hi, Casey! I'm Colleen, the school counselor." She extends a hand toward me, and I reluctantly shake it. "Principal Vega informed me you're an IEP student and that you recently became Hard of Hearing."

I blink up at her, unsure how to respond.

My silence doesn't discourage Colleen, though. "I brought these for you. Maybe you can give them a read when you have a moment!" She hands me two pamphlets and a thick binder.

I scan the pamphlets first:

SO, YOU'RE THE NEW KID IN SCHOOL: HOW TO MAKE FRIENDS AT A NEW SCHOOL!

SO, YOU'RE AN INDIVIDUALIZED EDUCATION PROGRAM STUDENT: HOW TO BE YOUR OWN ADVOCATE!

The binder is Palmera's official student handbook, which I assume is full of arbitrary rules about spaghetti straps and dyed hair.

"If you need anything, please stop by my office. I want to support you however I can during this tough time in your life," Colleen says.

"Uh. Thanks…?" I murmur, glancing around to ensure nobody is watching. All I want is to lie low, and lying low doesn't typically include a personal greeting and public discussion of your IEP accommodations from the school counselor.

Colleen flashes another smile and makes her exit.

Forty-five minutes later, I'm still waiting and have missed first period. Bored with TikTok drama, I get up and peruse the bulletin board hanging in the office. It's cluttered with flyers: a school bake sale, dance lessons, the ASL Club.

I take a closer look at the ASL Club's flyer. There's a picture of a white girl signing "I love you" front and center, with a caption underneath that identifies her as Audrey Simons, president of the ASL Club.

Her picture looks overly Facetuned to me, but nevertheless, I'm excited to meet Audrey. I'll finally have someone to use sign with.

The next thing that catches my eye is a flyer for the Rossi Music Studio. I scan the text: VOICE LESSONS FOR ALL AGES, GENDERS, AND SKILL LEVELS! CUSTOMIZED TO FIT YOUR NEEDS!

I'm about to rip off one of the tabs with contact information at the bottom of the page, but I stop myself. My mind flickers to Laurel, my vocal coach back in Portland. I had been working with her for six years, and I really believed she could help me develop a career in music.

But three months ago, Laurel said she had to drop me as a student because she couldn't meet my "growing needs." (Which is code for: "You lost your hearing, and I don't know how to accommodate that.")

The subtlest of ableism. Truly artful.

My world was upended when my hearing deteriorated, but the thing that hurts most is that I lost my voice, my art.

I started singing my own songs almost before I learned how to talk. Music was my only way to explore challenging situations and express my emotions. I shaped my happy moments into verses and hid my deepest secrets in bridges. I wove my soul into the choruses I wrote. My life was a song.

But without sound…I'm not sure how that song can continue playing.

I turn away from the bulletin board empty-handed. My fist clenches by my side as I sit back down, trying to set aside the bitterness swirling in my head.

Audrey Simons shows up, finally saving me from Roz's evil eye. She flips her bleached blonde hair over her shoulder, smiles like the Cheshire cat, waves a perfectly manicured hand, then begins signing at the speed of light.

I stand up, slack-jawed and utterly lost. "I'm not fluent in ASL," I breathe, oddly embarrassed to admit that.

Audrey's smile turns into a deep frown. "Oh. But they said you're deaf."

"I am." I cringe. "But I only lost my hearing four months ago. I'm still learning ASL."

She shakes a 'V' in front of her mouth. *"Do you lipread?"*

Fingers extended, I swivel my right hand side to side. *"Kind of."* I shrug. "Just face me when you talk. And speak normally. Not too quickly, but not slowly."

Audrey pastes her smile back on, but her eyes scrutinize me. "No problem."

Though, as it turns out, it is a problem.

During our school tour, which causes me to also miss second period (I get the impression Audrey is using this as an excuse to skip class), she randomly yells at me every time she remembers I'm Deaf-Hard of Hearing and occasionally makes eccentric hand gestures that even a beginner can tell aren't ASL. I wince as she shouts explanations about how the classrooms have names instead of numbers: Einstein, Aristotle, da Vinci.

Everything about Audrey rubs me the wrong way, so when third period finally arrives and ends the tour, I send a silent thanks to the universe. If algebra gets me out of Audrey's shouting range, I welcome it.

As part of my IEP, all my teachers provided me with work packets ahead of class to assist me in comprehension of lessons, but I'll stand a better chance at catching some of the in-class content if I'm close to the teacher. I walk to the front of the classroom and stake my claim on a desk.

Moments after I sit down, someone stands in front of my desk. I look up to find a pair of fierce brown eyes glaring down at me.

"Hey, new girl. This is **my** seat," the boy's voice booms. Scary for most people, helpful for me. "Move."

He sports a douchebag buzz cut, a silver cross necklace, and a thin black tank top that not so subtly displays biceps he could bench-press a Mack truck with. Ugh. I have a feeling this dude is the same breed of entitled, lunch-money-stealing, desk-claiming jerk that every American high school is equipped with. He also reminds me of my jock ex, Victor (look, I haven't always made smart choices), which automatically makes him one hundred percent more annoying.

"Says who?" I shoot back.

Bitchy Hot Guy taps the desk with a grating scowl. I look down and run my fingers over the desk's DIY engraving.

PROPERTY OF CÉSAR RAMIREZ

"Fairly certain this desk belongs to the Miami-Dade school district, Caesar." I cross my arms.

One of his thick brows shoots up. "It's——"

I blink at him, trying to figure out what he's getting at. "What?"

He repeats himself, but I still don't understand.

"Write it down, if you must." I cock a brow, slide him my notebook and a pencil, and re-cross my arms as he scribbles something in the corner of the page.

He shoves the notebook toward me with all the annoyance he can conjure up.

SAY-ZAR

Even his handwriting is packed with anger.

"Not 'see-zur,'" he spits mockingly. His biceps flex as he crosses his coppery tan arms, mirroring my pose.

"Okay, fine, César. But you're still not getting the desk." I roll my eyes, which only adds fuel to the fire.

"——yuma." I don't catch the beginning of his sentence, but his eyes have darkened, and his jaw is clenched. Clearly, he doesn't like his authority being tested.

"César!" A voice calls out from behind me. I turn to find a shorter, scrawnier boy jogging toward us. He nudges César when he gets close enough. "Leave her alone, she's——" the rest of his defense is unintelligible.

Scrawny Boy pushes a swath of brown curls out of his eyes and steps between me and César. "Sorry about him."

I stay silent as I watch César stalk to the back of the classroom, brooding like a bad-boy stereotype.

Scrawny Boy nervously smiles at me. "I'm—"

His introduction is cut off by—I check the name on my class schedule—Ms. Ochoa entering the room, loudly clapping to get our attention. "Sit down. All of you." Her voice is nasally, but it carries well. I can work with that. Scrawny Boy scurries off and sits at the desk next to César.

"Welcome to my advanced algebra class, Ms. Kowalski," Ms. Ochoa greets, then leans next to me and lowers her voice, which makes her impossible to understand. Not wanting the class to hear whatever private thing she's sharing with me, I social bluff and nod, pretending I can understand what she's saying.

She claps my shoulder as she stands, satisfied by my reaction, then starts talking about quadratic equations or…something.

Unfortunately, when the bell rings, my notebook is empty. I didn't catch anything Ms. Ochoa relayed because of her fast-paced speech.

Trying my best to not act crestfallen, I sling my backpack over one shoulder and head to lunch. My ears throb with sensory overload as I step into one of the busiest cafeterias I've ever seen. Tugging my backpack straps a little tighter, I swallow my discomfort and squeeze into the lunch line.

I glance around the room as I wait in line, my eyes jumping from person to person, but I focus when I make eye contact with Scrawny Boy from advanced algebra. He offers me a shy wave, but his hand is slapped out of the air by César, who sits across from him. There are three other people at their table, but I don't recognize them.

Before I can decide whether or not to wave back, Audrey suddenly appears in front of me.

"Casey!" she shouts, inches away from my face. "The ASL Club is meeting during lunch. You should come!"

That's more a command than a request, as it turns out. As soon as we've both received our trays of unidentifiable sludge masquerading as food, Audrey steers me back out of the cafeteria and into a small classroom I haven't been in yet. The walls are decorated with finger-spelling charts and ASL posters as well as some French and German posters—this room must house all the foreign-language classes. The desks have been pushed to the edges, and a dozen students sit on the floor in the open space, conversing in sign.

It's a nice classroom, and I can picture myself practicing sign here, but the ASL teachers at Palmera are all Hearing, so my family signed up for lessons at the University of Miami—with a Deaf professor—instead. My tutor back in Portland was Deaf, and she suggested I continue learning

ASL from a Deaf teacher since I specifically want to learn Deaf culture and slang and to be a more authentic signer.

"Everyone! This is Casey!" Audrey announces.

"Hello," I sign timidly, balancing my lunch tray with one hand.

A Black girl with wiry curls and cat-eye glasses smiles up at me and her fingers fly through the air at a breakneck pace. I barely catch her fingerspelling her name: *"J-E-S-S-I-C-A."*

The other students introduce themselves, but the only other name I make out, Marco, belongs to a boy who gives off major asshole-supporting-character-from-RIVERDALE vibes as he smirks and speeds through his signs.

"Casey——new members——I think you beginners will really get along," Audrey tells me, some of her words cutting out. She gestures to a group of students in the far back, all of them sporting deer-in-headlights expressions as they observe the rapid signing.

"Oh, uh…nice." I gulp. *"Are any of you Deaf or Hard of Hearing?"* I ask using SimCom.

Asshole-Marco scoffs. "Hell no. I'd go psycho if I was deaf!" He guffaws, clearly thinking that's a totally funny and not at all ableist joke.

I grit my teeth. "So, what inspired you to learn sign?" I narrow my eyes. I have a gut feeling I'm not going to like his answer.

"Looks great on college applications." He smirks. "Plus, ASL class is an easy 'A,' unlike the real foreign language classes."

Ding, ding! My hunch was correct. An absolutely garbage answer!

I look around the room to see if anyone else is offended by his ignorance, but they don't acknowledge it at all. Marco strikes up a conversation with Audrey as if nothing happened, that infuriating smirk still on his face.

Blood boiling, I scoop up my backpack and leave. I'm not putting up with this bullshit. Plus, all the auditory input from trying to track several different conversations has triggered an excruciating headache.

My head pounds as I slam the door shut behind me, angry and exhausted. The hallway is peaceful and soundless, so I sit, trying to talk myself off the edge and lessen my tiredness.

I only get a few minutes of rest before the bell rings. Battling an unresolved case of auditory fatigue, I trudge toward my next class, resigned to the fact I have no hope of absorbing what any of my teachers say for the rest of the day.

Sure enough, when the final bell rings, all I have to show for my first day at Palmera High is a heavy heart and a killer headache.

CHAPTER 2
HAYDEN

MIAMI'S BEST WEATHER IS IN EARLY SEPTEMBER. IT'S THE KIND OF HEAT that surrounds you, the air thick as mirages roll off the sidewalk.

Unfortunately, for me and the rest of the Barracudas—Palmera High's fútbol team—early September means it's time to start getting ready for the upcoming fútbol season. There's nothing like four weeks of fútbol boot camp to make those tropical temperatures lose their charm.

I make my way toward the pitch, weaving past my teammates as they dart around the field, stretch, and lace up their cleats. My pace quickens when I notice Coach Ramirez glaring at me and checking her watch. I'm only a few minutes late, but she demands her players be punctual. I feel like it shouldn't matter if I'm a bit late today, since this month-long skills workshop is optional—our official season doesn't start until October. But when Coach says something is "optional," she really means "not optional at all but I can't legally say that."

Coach raises a judgmental brow. "Get lost on the way here?"

"Lo siento, Coach," I mumble an apology and jog over to where my sixteen-year-old cousin sits on the sidelines, flipping through a smutty romance novella. "Lela, did you take notes during language arts?"

She nods, still reading.

"Could you text them to me?"

"Why do you never take your own notes?" She dog-ears her page and looks up. "What would you do if I weren't here?"

"I dunno." I shrug. "Fail language arts?"

"I am criminally underappreciated," she laments. "I'll send them later."

"Thank you! I love you!" I call out as I head onto the pitch. A few steps in, I spot my younger brother, Dino, doing some warm-up exercises.

"What exactly are you doing?" I ask him.

"Joining practice!" he exclaims, as if it's obvious.

"You're not even on the team, Dino."

He rolls his eyes. "Coach said I can join the boot camp since it's supplemental. Plus, the extra training will give me a better chance at making varsity."

It's almost unheard of for a freshman to make varsity, but Dino is nothing if not cocky. I sigh but squeeze my younger brother's shoulder in encouragement.

Near the center circle, I sidle up to my best friend, Paz. He grins at me and bounces a soccer ball on one foot. "You excited? First fútbol session of the school year!" he singsongs, eyes shining.

"Yeah. Ecstatic." I gulp.

"Hey." Gabriel Cuevas, the Barracudas' goalkeeper, nudges me. "Henry scored a pretty sick goal the other day, huh? Do you think he has a shot at the Golden Boot award this year?"

I pick at a hangnail and avoid answering the question about my other brother.

Enrique González-Rossi: the eighteen-year-old Cuban-Italian American kid who earned the moniker Hat-Trick Henry in high school and subsequently caught the attention of David Beckham himself. Soon after,

Henry was drafted by Inter Miami CF and rose to local fútbol fame. You know, normal teenager things.

Paz jabs my rib cage after an uncomfortable silence. "Golden Boot... yeah... that'd be cool," I mumble.

"Yo, Hayden!" Jacob Miller runs up and joins us; he claps my shoulder as if we're best friends. "How's Henry doin'?"

My jaw becomes concrete as Henry is name-dropped for the thousandth time today. "I dunno, Jacob. You'd have to ask him yourself," I bite.

Jacob and Gabriel continue bombarding me with questions about Miami's Golden Boy; I stare at the artificial turf and try to steady my shaking hands.

Truth is, I don't really know how Henry's doing. We haven't had a meaningful conversation in months. He calls our mom every week, and when she hands me the phone we exchange pleasantries—"Hi, kiddo, how are you?" "Good. You?" "Good."—then hang up. It's nothing like it used to be. We're nothing like we used to be.

Now, instead of taste-testing new recipes for our dad's restaurant, teaming up with me to tease Dino, or commiserating when our parents chew us out for something, he's training (and hanging) with some of the biggest names in fútbol—Messi and Beckham, anyone?—and is apparently too busy to even acknowledge, much less spend time with, his own brother. It's like signing with an MLS team changed his family tree.

I'd be lying if I said it doesn't sting every time his name comes up and I'm reminded that my best friend, my big brother, became a stranger practically overnight.

"Everyone, pay attention," Coach booms, her voice cutting through my wandering thoughts. Her dark eyes snap from person to person. "As you're all aware, the Barracudas have won the state championship for the past three years. And most of the star players who made that happen have now graduated. Including, of course, our former captain, Henry González-Rossi, who went and earned himself a spot at Inter."

Can we seriously not go five minutes without Henry being mentioned?

"You boys have some major shoes to fill, and over the next four weeks, I'm going to get you into shape so that you can actually fill them. I will **not** let you sorry excuses for fútbol players break our streak."

"With the captaincy vacant," Coach continues, "we need to decide who will lead us to our fourth state championship." She steps away from the huddle and confers with her clipboard. "I'll read the names of the top three choices submitted by the team earlier today, and then, by a show of hands, you'll vote for your new captain."

"But Coach," says Nathan Nakamura, one of the seniors, "the whole team isn't here to vote."

Coach glares at him. "Well, if they wanted a say, they should've opted into boot camp, Nakamura. Even Dino came"—she gestures to my little brother—"and he's not an official team member yet. That's the initiative you guys need to be showing. Do I make myself clear?"

Everyone mutters yes.

"Your choices are," Coach reads off her clipboard, "Jacob Miller, César Ramirez, and Hayden González-Rossi."

My eyes bug out of my head when my name is announced. Jacob is a good offensive midfielder and would make a fine captain. And César is a no brainer—he's the best player on the team, and everyone seriously respects him. (Plus, well, I don't want to discredit him, but he also happens to be Coach Ramirez's son. Nepotism is alive and well. That's all I'm sayin'.)

But me? I'm not captain material. I don't even think anyone on the team besides César and Paz acknowledged my existence until Henry became a local legend, and I was fine with that. I don't like being in the spotlight.

I have a feeling I was only nominated because of my now-legendary family connections.

…Maybe *I'm* the nepo baby.

"Now you vote." She begins calling names. "Jacob Miller."

I scan the crowd. Not a single hand goes up.

"César Ramirez." Coach glances at her son, and for a fleeting moment, she looks proud.

I smile at César and raise my hand. He nods at me curtly, acknowledging my vote. Then he looks toward the rest of the team, and his lips curl into a scowl. I'm the only one with my hand raised.

I lower my hand and swallow heavily at the unexpected result, but before I have a chance to dwell on the election outcome, Coach calls my name. My stomach twists into a knot as everyone's hands shoot up. I have no doubt I owe this to Henry's celebrity status.

"Congratulations, Captain." Coach smiles at me for half a second, then sends us off to run drills. Endless drills.

Unease nags at me about being elected captain of Palmera's fútbol team—a position I never aspired to, in a sport I don't want to play—as Dino and I push through the doors of El Pollo Cubano, the restaurant my dad and uncle run on Calle Ocho.

A cloud of cool air smacks me in the face as the restaurant greets me with the powerful scent of cumin and freshly chopped cilantro. I hear the sound of buñuelos sizzling in the deep fryer, so loud it's audible over the music flowing from the speakers.

My dad is standing in the dining area, beaming at the wall where family photos are proudly displayed. "Congratulations, Captain González-Rossi!" he bellows as soon as he spots me, announcing my new role to the whole restaurant. A few confused customers clap.

Crap. Coach must've told him. There's a lot of downsides to your fútbol coach also being your aunt, but the biggest one is definitely that everything that happens during practice is immediately shared with the entire family.

Papá motions me over. My feet drag and nerves bubble up as I slowly walk toward the photo wall. Dino trails behind me.

I freeze as soon as I spot Papá's newest addition to the "Wall of Fame" that's always showcased the three generations of male González fútbol players in their proudest career moments: my abuelo, my dad, Henry…and now there's a fourth frame.

Me.

Every muscle in my body locks up, and my heart beats faster. In the picture I'm in my Barracudas jersey, sporting the world's fakest smile—my solo portrait taken during the team photoshoot last year. Before Henry was drafted. Before I was captain. Before I unwillingly completed the next step toward a family legacy.

My eyes wander to Henry's photo. He's wearing his iconic pink Inter Miami jersey and standing in between Beckham and Messi, grinning. (Because *of course* it's a photo of him in his Inter jersey with the legendary David Beckham and Lionel Freaking Messi.) Next to Henry is Papá's picture from when he was captain of the Barracudas during his senior year, right before he got his career-ending injury.

Lastly, I glance at Abuelo's picture. Behind the polished glass, he's beaming alongside his teammates on the Miami Toros, one of Miami's very first professional fútbol teams. The photo was taken in the seventies, when he was just a little older than Henry and had only recently immigrated to Miami. He left his home country to pursue a dream of playing professional fútbol, and I've always been in awe of the bravery that must have taken. I wish I was even half as brave as Abuelo.

Blurry childhood memories always come rushing in whenever I look at pictures of him: Abuelo teaching six-year-old Henry and four-year-old me how to bounce a soccer ball on our knees; Abuelo chuckling when I said he was the greatest player of all time; his colorful stories about being part of the early days of fútbol in Miami, starting his family, coaching two generations of Youth League fútbol teams; his former teammates sharing their own stories about him at his funeral eight years ago.

I choke back tears as I blink at the photo. Abuelo was courageous and passionate and never gave up on his dreams. He was everything I'm not. Everything I'll never be, because all his bravery and confidence and enthusiasm for fútbol seems to only have been inherited by my brothers.

Papá clasps my shoulder, pulling me away from the photos. "I'm proud of you. And your abuelo would be too—I know he's watching over you." A bittersweet smile crosses his features as he looks at his father's picture. "You're carrying on the dynasty!" he says, turning back to me. There's a joking lilt in his voice, but the statement triggers a clammy, cold sweat that crawls across my skin.

Dynasty. Pride. Captain. Abuelo. Henry. Fútbol. Fútbol. **Fútbol.**

The words echo inside my head. I squeeze my eyes closed and beg my brain to shut up (it's never worked before, but I might as well try).

"Okay, enough chit-chat." Papá interrupts my regularly scheduled identity crisis and I peel my eyes open. "Get to work!" He claps his hands and ushers Dino and me into the kitchen.

After putting on an apron and a hairnet, I seek solace in the walk-in freezer. I cool off next to a rack of ribs and take a deep breath. My peace lasts all of two minutes before Papá comes barreling in.

"¡Oye, mijo! My freezer is not for recreational purposes." He balances a fifteen-pound bag of rice on his hip. "I don't pay you to stand around, do I?"

Papá lightly smacks the back of my head as I exit the freezer and step into the kitchen. I wash my hands before heading over to monitor an industrial mixer that combines ingredients for buñuelos. I stand next to Dino as he assembles a to-go container of ropa vieja.

"How did fútbol practice go, Dino? You still going to try out for varsity next month?" Tío Eddy asks from where he's hunched over the stove, dumping a slew of aromatic spices into a skillet.

I'm pretty sure my family is physically incapable of going ten minutes without talking about fútbol.

"Oh, yeah. César says I'm a shoo-in!" Dino calls out. He slides the sealed takeout bag toward the to-go section of checkout. "And Tía Carmen—I mean, Coach," he corrects, "told me my 'hocus pocus' needs work but that it has the potential to be on par with Henry's."

"¡Que chévere! When Captain González-Rossi"—Papá winks at me—"is drafted to play for Inter Miami, perhaps you'll become captain!" He grins at Dino. "Your destiny will be fulfilled."

I try to ignore the spike in my heart rate and focus my attention on preventing the buñuelo dough from becoming too chewy.

"I mean, we are the 'Floridian Broldans.'" Dino smirks as he assembles an order.

My family has been joking for years that Henry, Dino, and I are "The Floridian Broldans." The nickname stems from the "Brothers

Roldan"—Cesar, Cristian, and Alex—who have all garnered a reputation in the professional fútbol world.

That makes me Cristian, the middle brother and the most attractive out of the three. Though, with my Dumbo ears and braces, I'm hardly the best-looking González-Rossi brother.

"You're nowhere near as talented as Alex Roldan, Dino," I mumble, more bitterly than I intended.

"Boys, don't bicker," Papá chides. "Hayden, check on table six." He hands me a tray of water glasses.

Balancing the tray in one hand, I walk into the dining room and head for the table near the window where my cousins and best friend often hang out.

"Congratulations, Captain!" Lela exclaims, snagging a glass from the flimsy serving tray.

"Yeah, congrats," César snarls. He's usually in a surly mood, but today he has a valid reason. I stole his rightful position as team captain.

"I'm sorry, César," I mutter. He doesn't look at me. "I-I voted for you."

He finally makes eye contact. "Nobody else shared your sentiment."

"To be fair," Lela says to her older brother, "you're already captain of the béisbol team. Don't get greedy!"

His focus snaps to her and he narrows his eyes. "Yeah, but I'm trying to get a fútbol scholarship, not a béisbol scholarship. There's just not enough money in college béisbol to go around, and I need a scholarship or I can't afford to go at all."

I wish I could tell him how this situation has screwed us both over. But instead, I let silence engulf the group.

Thankfully, Paz is unrivaled when it comes to breaking through awkward tension. (Probably because he's usually the one who creates it.)

"Sooo, who's the new kid you saved from Cécé in Ms. Ochoa's class?" He waggles his brows and smooths his crisp white polo shirt. He says it makes him look sophisticated, but we all think it actually makes him look like a forty-something-year-old who plays golf when he should be spending time with his children.

"Dunno what you're talking about," I mutter.

"You liar! The cute white girl with the mousy brown hair that's in desperate need of some layers and highlights? Or maybe balayage?"

"Hm. Doesn't ring a bell. Anyway, three cubanos and a round of tostones?" I ask, not wanting to get dragged into their gossiping. César grumbles his approval. "Great, I'll be back shortly."

But before I can leave, Lela's pointy witch nails dig into my wrist as she grabs hold.

"Hay," she says, blinking up at me. "Aren't you curious?"

I pull out a chair and plop into it. "Fine. What's her deal?"

A grin appears on her face. "Her name is Casey Kowalski. She moved here from the West Coast—"

"Did you see her bi pride shirt?!" Paz interrupts enthusiastically. "It makes sense. I mean, basically everyone from the West Coast is at least a *little* bit bi, right? Hey, don't look at me like that! True fact."

"Shut up, Paz." Lela rolls her eyes. "Anyway, her family moved because her mom got a job here. She's a wedding planner, I think?"

"God, I hope Casey really is bi," Paz mumbles. "Heteros scare me."

César flicks Paz's arm from across the table. "That's heterophobic."

Paz blows his straw wrapper at my ill-tempered cousin.

"Lela," I say, "how do you know all of this?"

She waves a dismissive hand. "I know everything. Ah! She also has a cat named Jell-O, who is the ugliest creature I have ever seen yet has a certain charm."

"Aw, like Cécé!" Paz teases, reaching over and pinching César's cheek.

César slaps Paz's hand away, his nostrils flaring. "Vete pa'l carajo."

"Okay…well, thanks…" I stand up and remove myself from the situation.

César only tolerates my best friend because he knows Paz and I have been a package deal since we bonded over our mutual love of Lizzie McGuire while swinging on the monkey bars in second grade. Unfortunately, they've been getting on each other's nerves ever since.

Paz is truly the Lizzie to my Miranda. (He wouldn't be caught dead as a side character. He has main character energy—according to him.)

Hanging out with César, on the other hand, has always been more of a requirement, since he's my cousin. Recently, though, we've grown a lot closer. He's been filling the suspiciously big-brother-shaped hole in my life ever since Henry left.

"For table three," Tío Eddy hands me a tray with two bowls of steaming ropa vieja. The scent makes my mouth water as I squeeze through the tight passageways between tables. I deliver the food to the Gómezes, an elderly couple who've eaten at the restaurant since the day it opened.

I entertain their questions as they tuck into their dinner. That's the common-courtesy rule with old people. You let them kiss your cheeks and ask invasive questions. Even if your three best friends are watching you squirm while Mrs. Gómez asks if you have a girlfriend.

After we close the restaurant, César, Lela, and Paz eat the leftover buñuelos while Papá and Tío clean the kitchen and Dino sweeps.

Taking the opportunity to peruse Instagram, I type in "Casey Kowalski" with many different misspellings of the last name until I find her. Her account is public and has over two thousand followers. Interestingly, the account is a business account and she identifies herself as a musician.

Her grid is beyond aesthetically pleasing (aside from the pictures of her hideous cat). An even mix of pictures and reposted TikTok videos, all with the same filter added. I click the latest video on her timeline and discover that she hasn't posted since May. Huh.

The clip is a rendition of "On My Own" from LES MISÉRABLES. Her singing is silky and powerful, and I hum along, tapping out the notes on my leg as if I were pressing piano keys.

"Finish the dishes. Don't make me fire you." Papá's brisk tone snaps me out of the trance Casey's singing put me in.

I scramble to mute the video, not wanting him to catch me watching it. I press the Follow button underneath her bio and smile as I hop to my feet, grab the sponge near the sink, and start on the grease-coated pans, humming "On My Own" as I scrub at the grime.

CHAPTER 3
CASEY

"YOU'RE NOT HUNGRY?" MOM ASKS IN SIGN. SHE FLICKS HER THUMB FROM under her chin, then drags a 'C' handshape down her torso.

.   I make tense eye contact with the lukewarm brussels sprouts on my plate and push them around with my fork. Mom frowns. Dad barely acknowledges my distress and continues shoveling Mom's sadistic tuna casserole into his mouth. This is the sort of food white soccer moms give other white soccer moms when a loved one dies.

"How was school?" she asks using SimCom.

"Some of the ASL Club members were ableist, I didn't understand any of the teachers, and some asshole tried to bully me into moving seats," I deadpan. "So, obviously, it was wonderful."

"Just remember we'll only be here for a year," Mom says.

Praise Deaf Baby Jesus. I don't think I could take anything longer than that.

"And you could always transfer to Oceanview!" she adds.

I groan, pierce a brussels sprout, and bring it to my mouth. "Absolutely not."

I have a feeling the only place more soul-sucking than Palmera High is Oceanview Prep, the stuffy private school where Dad now works.

The Oceanview student profile is "entitled rich kid," whereas Palmera's website practically beats you over the head with a "we're inclusive of all students, no matter their race, religion, disability, or sexuality" sledgehammer—a rarity for Florida public schools.

When we were first looking at schools in the area, the prospect of Palmera's voices-off ASL Club game nights and field trips, and their Deaf outreach program, appealed to me, even if their ASL classes didn't.

But my experience with the ASL Club today shattered any hope I had of finding acceptance there.

Dad glances up from his plate for the first time, finally tuning into the conversation. "Speaking of Oceanview," he chimes in, "I made an interesting discovery today." He stands up, grabs his work satchel, and digs around in it, then returns to the dinner table with a crumpled-up flyer in hand. "I saw this in——lobby."

Dad carefully smooths the paper, then slides it across the table: THE ROSSI MUSIC STUDIO OFFERS VOICE LESSONS FOR ALL AGES, GENDERS, AND SKILL LEVELS! CUSTOMIZED TO FIT YOUR NEEDS!

It's the same flyer I saw in Palmera's lobby. Hey, got to give credit where it's due: this studio has great advertising, if nothing else.

"Dad and I looked at her website. She seems nice, Case. Why not give singing lessons another shot?" Mom says.

"You have not sung in months, moja droga," Dad adds. "You must miss it."

I laugh bitterly. It's less about "missing" and more about "feeling an excruciating desire to be myself again." Potato, potahto.

"I know Laurel hurt you," Mom perseveres, tag-teaming with Dad, "but that doesn't mean every vocal coach——a bad match. Sometimes——kiss a few frogs before finding your prince. Or princess! Or…otherwise gender nonconforming child of a monarch," she rushes to add.

I fight an amused smile at her clunky attempt at queer inclusivity. No matter how annoying Mom can be, at least she's an ally.

When I don't respond, she nudges Dad. "Stan?" She jerks her head toward me. We all know he's the one who usually gets through to me when I'm being stubborn.

"Twoja matka mówi prosto z mostu," he says. I barely know enough Polish to greet my grandparents, but I've been raised around Dad's beloved, mostly untranslatable idioms and can recite dozens by heart.

I sigh heavily and he responds with a dopey dad grin. "You never know unless you try," he adds.

I lean back in my chair, eyes flickering between my parents. I'm pretty sure I'm breaking a teenager rule by saying this, but I think they might be right.

Even if the Rossi Music Studio isn't the right fit, what do I have to lose? Nothing.

I've already lost everything important to me.

"Fine," I concede with a grumble. "One lesson. To see if it's really as 'customizable' as she claims."

"Fantastyczny!" Dad enthusiastically claps and gives me a thumbs up. "You will be the next Linda Ronstadt!"

I frown at him. "Uh…I don't know who that is…but I'm going for a Florence and the Machine or Olivia Rodrigo vibe."

The excitement quickly drains from his face. "You have never heard of Linda Ronsta—mój Boże, I've failed you." Dad hangs his head.

After dinner, I help Mom craft an email to the owner of the Rossi Music Studio. I warn her against bombarding the teacher with too much information, but she's type-A to a fault, the rare breed of person who makes spreadsheets for fun. Her first draft is a fifteen-paragraph behemoth that goes into minute detail about my hearing loss. I suggest condensing it into two or three.

We reach a compromise at four paragraphs.

Mom and Dad settle on the couch to watch whatever war documentary he's picked, and I head to my room. I'm about to queue up Netflix when my eyes drift to my trusty songwriting journal, a weathered, yellow leatherbound notebook Dad bought me back in eighth grade that sits abandoned on my desk.

I take a deep breath and flip to "Lionhearted Girl." I started working on this song three months ago, a month after my world suddenly went quiet. I thought writing it might help me process the hurricane of emotions, but they proved impossible to sort through or find the right words to describe. So I never finished it.

FEARLESS BUT BRUISED, SHE IS SOMEONE NEW.

THAT LIONHEARTED GIRL, SHE IS BRAVE, SHE IS STRONG.

BUT HER COURAGE CRUMBLES WHEN THE WORLD HAS NO SOUND.

Before I know it, I'm quietly singing the words and trying to fine-tune the melody, performing the original piece for the very exclusive audience of Jell-O.

When I get to school the next morning, Palmera's lobby is packed with students, most of them sectioned off into cliques. Oh, the joys of high school.

Audrey and some kids from ASL Club are huddled near the front doors, rapidly signing. Eager to avoid them, I duck my head and hide behind my hair to pass by them undetected.

As I fumble with the door to my locker, I spot Bitchy Desk Guy, César, casually leaning against the lockers across the hall. The three girls surrounding him wear identical infatuated smiles as they chatter to him. One of the girls reaches out and lightly touches his arm. His stoic expression doesn't waver as they flirt.

He may be playing it cool, but I bet he's just eating this attention up.

Again, my mind flickers back to my ex, Victor. Star of the football team, meathead extraordinaire, winner of the shittiest boyfriend award. He would act all cool and indifferent to the girls throwing themselves at him, but I knew he was getting off on the attention. I only ignored it because I thought we were "in love."

Until I lost my hearing and he decided I wasn't worth the trouble, of course.

Watching César be all hot and broody and mysterious makes my stomach churn. I don't think I'm ever going to like him, and not just because he was a jerk to me in class.

I grab my American history notes and slam my locker shut. As I'm shoving everything into my backpack, my phone buzzes with a text from Mom.

Your 1st singing lesson is scheduled for next week. September 14!

I shoot back a quick **ok. thanks** before tucking my phone into my pocket. When I look up, there's a stunning, fat, raven-haired girl waving at me from down the hall. I glance over my shoulder to check for someone behind me, but when I turn back around, she's right in front of me.

"Hi." She gives a toothy grin. "Casey, right?"

Up close, she's shamelessly bold and slightly intimidating. Her eyes are dark and piercing, her lips are coated in baby blue lipstick, and she's wearing a black crop top and black high-waisted shorts that accentuate her hips.

"Hi…?" I eye her suspiciously.

"I'm Lela. Nice to meet you! You're——Oregon?"

My mind fills in the blanks of her question. Her voice carries well, but the sound gets lost in the ambient chatter of a hundred other students. In a quiet room, though, I think I'd be able to understand her perfectly. Lela's voice is brazen; it seems like her entire being is brazen.

"I'm from Portland." I realize I've been staring at her. I smooth out my dinosaur-patterned button-up shirt and wait for the next installment of small talk that I may or may not hear.

She smiles wider and messes with her gold septum piercing. "I've heard good things. Mostly about the doughnuts."

I stifle a laugh. Portland is famous for craft beer, an overwhelming number of hipsters, and Voodoo Doughnuts. Not in any particular order.

"Portland——I've always wondered——is that true?" Words fly out of her mouth faster than I can comprehend.

"Oh. Mm-hmm. Totally." I scratch the back of my neck.

She scans me like an airport metal detector, eyes running up and down my body. "Do you want——" She returns to making eye contact.

I try to avoid staring at her lips. When people aren't aware you're trying to lipread, it comes across as suggestive. Although, to be honest, I'd probably still be staring at her lips if I were Hearing. Lela is possibly the prettiest girl I've ever seen.

"Casey?" Lela reaches out and touches my forearm.

"Sorry, uh, what were you saying?"

"Do you want to eat lunch with us?" She jerks her head behind her. The group I passed in the cafeteria yesterday is standing by the staircase. I spot Scrawny Boy and two unfamiliar faces. I remember César being with them yesterday too, but evidently, today he's too busy soaking up the free compliments from his groupies to hang out. Ugh.

I take a slow step away from Lela. "I…can't. Sorry."

Back in Portland, I decided that I wouldn't make friends in Miami. Mom's event-planning company only needs her to stay for a year. Once the Florida location is up and running, we'll be heading back to Oregon. So it would be a waste of time. Besides, the last thing I need is another friend group treating me weirdly after learning about my hearing loss.

A pang of regret thumps against my chest, like my subconscious is beating me up for turning down a lunch offer from a pretty girl and her pretty friends. But it's easier to say 'no' now than to risk getting friend-dumped a second time. I won't put myself through that again.

I feel her eyes bore into the back of my head as I walk away.

But as the week passes, I learn that Lela is not easy to deter. Every morning, I find her by my locker, waiting to pose the same question: "Do you want to eat lunch with us?" And every day I answer, "No."

Instead, I start bringing lunches from home and eating alone in the front courtyard. Sure, it's hot as an oven, and I'm usually covered in a sticky layer of sweat by the time lunch period is over, but it's better than the chaos of the cafeteria or dealing with the ASL Club.

And yet, like the world's most gorgeous and monstrously aggravating boomerang, Lela always shows up the next day and asks again. It's annoying, but her daily appearance is also the only notable thing that happens during my first week of school.

She apparently rethinks her strategy over the weekend, because on Monday morning she appears with a bribe prepared. An iced cinnamon almond milk macchiato with caramel drizzle—AKA: my lifeblood.

No Friends. I mentally repeat it to myself like a mantra. I've held strong this long, and I'll be damned if I let a bribe break me.

"Happy Monday!" Lela grins. "Casey, would you do me the distinct honor of eating lunch with me?" She bats her lashes, which are coated in a neon-green mascara that only she could pull off.

"How do you know my coffee order?" I stare at the drink in her hand.

"I know everything."

"Welp. That's super creepy." I take a step back. "I'm busy today, can't eat with you."

She refuses to break eye contact as she hands me the coffee. "You're stubborn. I'll give you that," she sighs and saunters off, hips swaying as she disappears into a sea of teenagers.

I take a hesitant sip of the sweet, creamy coffee as soon as she's gone. I hate how much I enjoy its cinnamon undertones and caramel swirls. This means Lela won our battle of wills, doesn't it?

God help me.

I push our interaction out of my head as I sit through American history. Mr. Gibson is easier to follow than Ms. Ochoa, aside from his distracting, frantic hand gestures. The man gets entirely too animated about the Founding Fathers.

Come lunchtime, I head straight for the courtyard, but a few feet from Palmera's front doors, Lela ambushes me.

She's leveling up like a damn Pokémon.

Before I have a chance to protest, she links our arms and whisks me into the cafeteria. We stop at a table in the back of the room.

"This is Casey." She gives me a small push and I stumble toward the four boys who occupy the table.

All four pairs of eyes snap upward. César glares at me. He stabs a french fry and aggressively bites it.

Scrawny Boy, the kid who saved me from César, smiles softly. I take in his tragic sense of style. A light pink sports jersey, cargo shorts that're a size too big, and weathered Adidas. Haute couture. I also notice the smattering of freckles on his sun-kissed face for the first time. He wiggles his fingers in greeting.

A Black boy, the third in the lineup, grins. Long, brown locs are twisted around his finger, and his arm is draped over Scrawny Freckle Boy's shoulder. His outfit—turquoise satin shorts and a polo shirt that's giving major midlife-crisis vibes—is also an atrocity, but at least it seems like a stylistic choice. It's hideous but intentionally so.

"Lovely to meet you! I'm—"

Baz. Or Paz. The downside of lipreading is that nearly everything needs to have context. Names don't have context. It doesn't help that tons of letters look similar. Especially Ps and Bs.

"Yo. Dino." This kid looks exactly like Scrawny Freckle Boy, but with no freckles, slightly tanner skin, and a very unfortunate haircut that's halfway between a wolf cut and a bowl cut.

"Hi," I say, devoid of emotion. No Friends plays in my mind.

Lela takes a seat between Dino and César, who glares as I sit near Baz/Paz and Scrawny Freckle Boy.

Honestly, I'm surprised they're cuddling in such a public place. In Portland, queer people and couples are everywhere, but I assumed Floridians—even the teenagers—would be a bit more… conservative.

Lela tries to hand me half of her sandwich. "Trust me," she says, "this is better than whatever you brought. It has two kinds of pork in it."

"Um. No thanks," I reply. I have some perfectly good leftover kartacze and ogórki kiszone Dad made in my lunch bag.

Baz/Paz turns and stares at me in a manner that strikes me as far too intimate for someone I met thirty seconds ago. "Wait, you're not, like, vegan or Peleliu or on any of those happiness-free Pacific Northwesterner diets, are you?"

"Paleo," César corrects. "Peleliu is an island, dipshit."

Baz/Paz hurls a french fry at César. It hits his shaved head and leaves behind a streak of grease. I snicker but rush to cover it with a cough when César scowls at me.

"Uh, no. I'm not," I answer the original diet question. I hazard another glance at César. He scrubs the grease off his head and stares me down.

We hold eye contact for a few beats. Neither of us wants to break first.

Finally, he grumbles, almost too quietly for me to hear, "Why don't——just pick another desk?"

I scoff. I'm not shocked he's still obsessed with his freakin' desk since he's been shooting me dirty looks every time he gets to algebra class and sees me sitting in it. But to actually bring it up again? What's his problem?

"There are other desks in the front row. Why don't you take one of those?" I fire back, crossing my arms.

"Because——my desk in algebra. You can't just waltz into——new school——take someone else's spot."

My jaw clenches and I steel myself. "You're pretty entitled, aren't you?"

"Entitled?" His brows curve into an appalled frown and he sucks a breath through his teeth, calming himself. "If you——give me——desk back and apologize, I'll forget you said that," he says, offering the deal to me like he's being super generous and not a pompous ass.

"Cécé," Baz/Paz interrupts, "you wouldn't even be in algebra class if you didn't——retake it because——flunked last year." César shoots him a death glare. "What? True fact!" he exclaims.

"I didn't **flunk** it," César refutes. "I withdrew."

"Because you were flunking it."

I cackle and César's glare is redirected toward me. "Okay, how about this," I say, "I'll keep the desk but in exchange, I'll tutor you. I love to help the algebraically challenged!"

He clenches his jaw. I guess he's not used to people challenging his bullshit. "You—"

This time his speech isn't drowned out by the racket of the cafeteria, but instead by Lela shoving three french fries into his mouth. She shoots him a withering look and mutters something. He sinks back into his chair, angrily chewing the fries.

Baz/Paz snort-laughs. "Don't worry, he very rarely bites."

"Uhh, well, I'm Aiden," Scrawny Freckle Boy interrupts with an awkward wave. "Sorry I didn't introduce myself earlier." He defuses the tension at our table by flashing a toothy smile; the harsh cafeteria lights glint off his silver braces.

"Hi, Aiden." For some reason, I feel compelled to return his smile with one of my own. Something about his calm aura puts me at ease, which isn't easy to do these days.

His brows knit as he starts to say something else, then decides against it, taking a bite of food instead.

"What do your parents do?" Baz/Paz changes the subject. He leans across Aiden and faces me directly, probably because he's being nosy, but I'm thankful; without realizing it, he's helping me understand his question.

"My mom's a corporate event planner," I explain. "Networking events and stuff. We're in Miami for a year while she sets up a new branch of the company."

"And your dad?" he presses.

I hesitate. Something tells me these guys aren't going to be super impressed that my dad works at a one-percenter prep school. "Uh. He's a Spanish teacher…"

"Ah, ¡no sabía!" Lela interrupts before I can continue. "So you're——" Her speech is lost due to background noise. She frowns at me when I don't reply.

"Sorry. I didn't catch that." I slump in my chair as she repeats herself, still not understanding what she said. I nod and smile, social bluffing.

"That's cool!" Aiden says, eyes alight. "That means we're all at least part Cuban. Dino and I are also half Italian. He's half Ethiopian," he points to Baz/Paz, "and they're half Colombian." He gestures to Lela and César. "You?"

"Oh, you think I'm Cuban…?" I'm lost. When did I say I was Cuban?

Aiden frowns at me. "You nodded when Lela asked——" He turns his head toward Lela, which blocks his lips and redirects the sound away from me.

I catch the general meaning. By nodding, I somehow told Lela my dad is Cuban.

"I'm not Cuban. Uh, my dad's Polish and my mom's mostly Irish." I cringe as they collectively raise brows or frown.

César sits up straighter, indignation burning in his eyes. "I'm sorry… your dad is **Polish**? And he's teaching **Spanish**? In **Miami**?" he enunciates, tone dark.

"He works at Oceanview Prep." My face flushes as I admit my father's employment status.

"Oceanview Pr—" César's sentence is cut off by a deep, cutting scowl. His tongue pokes his cheek from inside and he narrows his eyes at me. "Oceanview hires a Polish guy to teach Spanish to prep school kids in Miami, but **I'm** entitled, hm?"

"Whoa, buddy," I scoff. "You're just a ray of fucking sunshine, aren't you? I do get your point, but to be fair, my dad's spent like twenty-five years studying Spanish instruction; he's not just, like, some random guy who did a semester abroad in Barcelona."

César's jaw muscle leaps and he opens his mouth to respond, but Aiden interrupts.

"So, uh, Casey, do you speak Spanish?" he asks, jumping in to stave off another argument. "Since your dad's a Spanish teacher?"

I shrink into myself. "No. I took German for my mandatory language credits. It's one of my dad's four languages, so I already knew some."

He smiles kindly. "Hey, German is cool."

I have a feeling Aiden has a gift for playing peacemaker in the group. And thankfully, after Aiden cuts César off, Dino starts rambling about sportsball player stats or something. He might as well be speaking an alien language as far as I'm concerned, but I welcome the subject change.

I spend the remainder of lunch break social bluffing. I fake-laugh when they laugh, nod and smile when I don't understand what they've said, and pretend I belong. Honestly, it feels sort of nice to be in a group again (minus César. Obviously.), even if I don't fit in.

I could never be one of them, though. If they knew I was Deaf-Hard of Hearing, they'd reject me, just like my friends in Portland. Besides my parents, nobody in my life has tried to accommodate my hearing loss. Well, it does seem like Aiden intuitively realizes when I haven't caught something and knows to say it again. But I probably shouldn't read too much into that.

As nice as today has been, I tell myself I won't eat with them again. I decide I'll stick to homemade lunches in the blistering heat. I replay my self-protective mantra over and over: No. Friends.

After lunch, I attempt to listen to Mrs. Li during chemistry, meticulously poring over the notes she provided for today's class, but my brain has shut itself off. A dull headache thumps against my skull.

This tiredness, pain, and inability to focus started coming on shortly after I lost my hearing. At first my parents and I suspected a brain tumor. Inexplicable hearing loss plus debilitating headaches added up to something more serious than Sudden Sensorineural Hearing Loss. But an MRI revealed nothing nefarious.

It wasn't until recently that I learned about auditory fatigue. When a D/deaf or Hard of Hearing person has to listen for extended periods of time, it makes their brains work on overdrive.

Eating in the cafeteria meant I had to filter through background noise, lipread several conversations at once, and fill in the blanks for things I didn't catch. No wonder my brain is fried after all that.

My eyes grow heavy as I raise my hand. Mrs. Li pauses her lecture about the periodic table and looks at me.

"Can I use the bathroom?" The words are thick on my tongue.

Mrs. Li hands me the faded sticky note that serves as a hall pass.

I leave the chaos of the classroom and bask in the stillness of the hallway. I know it's only a temporary escape from the exhaustion, but I feel lighter as soon as the classroom door closes behind me.

I sink to the ground next to a garbage can, rest against the cool wall, and breathe in the peace. The weight in my head clears as I take the world's longest bathroom break.

My train of non-thought is broken when I feel the vibrations from one of the classroom doors slamming shut. I look up, expecting to find one of the students from Mrs. Li's class coming to fetch me.

Instead, I see Aiden—who's not in Mrs. Li's chemistry class—at the end of the hall. He's walking in my direction, presumably to the bathrooms located behind me. But then he stops, cranes his neck, and peers over his shoulder. Oblivious to my presence behind the trash can, he begins shimmying his shoulders and tapping his feet.

Despite my sour mood, I struggle to hold in laughter as his impromptu dance performance continues.

He does a full 360-degree spin, then leaps. When he lands, his arms lengthen above his head, first to the right, then to the left. His feet continue to tap down the hallway.

It's poorly executed, but I recognize the dance as an excerpt from the NEWSIES "King of New York" tap routine. Which is my third-favorite scene from NEWSIES. The song plays in my head as Aiden comes closer, still shimmying and spinning.

He sticks the landing of a surprisingly graceful leap and finally notices me. His cheeks turn cherry red, and his eyes widen to the size of Jupiter.

I give him a slow round of applause, finally releasing my laughter. "Better than Ben Fankhauser himself."

Aiden's jaw snaps shut. Then opens. Then shuts. This routine continues for thirty seconds.

I force myself to stop laughing. "That was literally the highlight of my week," I joke, attempting to get rid of this tense silence.

His shaky hands mess with the hem of his pink jersey, then he finally replies, "You must've had a pretty crappy week."

"Oh, the absolute crappiest."

He sits cross-legged in front of me. Another pause ensues as he alternates between making eye contact and glancing at the floor, thinking through whatever he's going to say next. At last, he makes up his mind and asks, "Why do you call me Aiden?"

I frown. "Because it's your name?"

Aiden shakes his head again, brown curls falling in his eyes. "My name is Aiden."

"Aiden?"

"*Aiden*," he enunciates, squinting at me.

It's my turn to adopt the deer-in-headlights facial expression. He's saying Aiden...right? He's not saying Braden. His lips would touch during the 'B.'

His brows draw together and lips curl downward. "My name is Aiden," he repeats.

"Oh, right. Sorry." I paste on a smile. "My bad."

"What's my name?" Aiden (or whatever) raises a brow.

Damn. He knows I'm lying.

I don't reply.

His shoulders shake as he chuckles. He reaches into his pocket and retrieves his phone. After typing a message, he flips the screen in my direction.

My name is Hayden.

Damn. I was *so* close.

He takes the phone back and writes another message: **Do you have trouble hearing?**

This is the very last thing I wanted to happen. But social bluffing isn't a perfect science, and some people are bound to figure it out sooner or later.

Welp. There's no use trying to lie my way out of this.

"Yeah…I'm Deaf-Hard of Hearing. You caught me." I brace myself for the pity smile that usually follows the confession.

Instead, Hayden flashes the same smile I saw in the cafeteria: genuine and not pitying at all. "Can you hear me talk?" He points to his lips.

"Yes, but it's quiet. Normal talking voices sound like a whisper to me."

"Should I speak louder?" Now his voice sounds normal to me, which means he's raised it above a socially acceptable volume.

I shudder to think Mrs. Li's class can hear him but can't bring myself to care. "That's great, actually."

"Cool!" He shoots me a thumbs-up. "Why didn't you tell everyone earlier? They would've talked louder."

"I didn't tell anyone…well, because people tend to think of me as a burden when they find out," I explain. "The human race is a bunch of assholes."

Hayden just nods like his own life experience has confirmed this.

"Hey, speaking of assholes," I say, ready to change the subject from me, "why do you hang out with César? The others seem chill. But **_César_**?"

I don't know Hayden at all, but he doesn't seem like a kid who'd mesh well with César's aggravating energy.

"César and Lela are my cousins. So I don't really have a choice." He chuckles. "But he's not that bad once you get to know him! And we——talk loud——if you——" His words cut out and I frown, eyes trained to his lips.

He reaches for his phone, a considerate smile on his face.

I won't think of you as a burden. I'll talk loudly if you need me to. And I won't tell anyone about your hearing trouble until you're ready.

I try to refrain from tearing up, but my recent track record of controlling my emotions is not superb, so I get misty-eyed. "Thank you."

"You're welcome," he says.

He types something else on his phone but then frowns and backspaces. He types again, then deletes that too. Finally, he puts his phone away with a shake of his head.

I blink the wetness away and clear my throat. I try not to focus on how uncool I must seem, crying in a school hallway like I'm five years old and want my mommy to come get me.

"Uh, while we're on the topic of names…what's the little guy called? The one with the fashion sense and locs?" I ask.

Hayden laughs, grabs his phone, and writes another message.

Paz. And NEVER call him short, he will hurt you.

I tick each name off on my fingers, "Hayden, Paz, César, Lela, and Dino?"

"Right. Okay, well, I'll probably see you later. Cool?" He jumps to his feet, an expression I can't read on his face.

"Sure?" I frown as he disappears into one of the classrooms. What the hell was that conversation?

CHAPTER 4
HAYDEN

SOME PEOPLE ARE BORN LEADERS. THEY STEP INTO A POSITION OF POWER like it's their birthright.

Then there are people like me, who dawdle on their way to the locker room after school, take forever to change into their gym clothes, kill as much time as they can lacing up their cleats, and silently pray all the while that a sinkhole will open up and swallow the fútbol pitch so they don't have to play the role of captain.

"Hayden!"

I'm ripped from my visions of sinkhole salvation by César, who punches my shoulder a little too hard to be considered playful.

"Hurry up. Practice is starting." César motions toward my idle hands, which hold untied shoelaces, before giving a grunt of disapproval and jogging outside.

I double-knot my cleats, then step into the sweltering heat, flapping my hands at my side to dispel the wave of trepidation that's washing over me.

It's already the fifth day of school, but I haven't acclimated to my new role as captain yet. And it doesn't help that every time I remember my **duties**, my **responsibility**, this shaky, insecure feeling creeps in.

I take a long, slow breath and shove the feelings deep inside. Sure, it's like swallowing glass shards and washing them down with a boiling cup of gasoline, but captains don't panic. Captains don't mess up.

Henry never messed up.

The familiar nerves start to dissipate as I catch sight of Lela in her usual spot and walk her way.

"Do you have notes for…" My question trails off as I notice that Lela isn't alone.

"Hi, Hayden." Casey half-heartedly waves at me. Her demeanor is disinterested, but her ocean blue eyes analyze me like I'm a test subject.

Suddenly those shards of glass are clawing their way up my throat and the gasoline is burning a hole in my esophagus. My whole body goes rigid. I look between Casey and Lela. "Why…why are you at fútbol practice?" I struggle for each word, my voice strangled and shaky.

"My mom's meeting is running late, so I'm waiting for her to pick me up," she replies, her tone indifferent. "And your cousin kidnapped me."

"Lies!" Lela exclaims. "If anything, I coerced you."

"I fail to see the difference," she grumbles.

I wring my hands, fighting the urge to run away and never look back. I start replaying our chance hallway encounter from a few hours ago, when Casey discovered my secret. It didn't seem like that big of a deal at the time, and she doesn't strike me as the kind of girl who enjoys blackmail. But it dawns on me that she holds my most private information in the palm of her hand, a grenade she could set off at any moment.

Playing fútbol is a family tradition. But music? That's something special. Learning dances from low-quality Broadway bootlegs, teaching myself guitar when nobody else is home, memorizing song lyrics instead of doing homework—those things are sacred to me.

Casey watches me for a beat, eyes fixed on my fidgety hands. "So, Lela told me you're captain of the soccer team, huh?"

"That's…not important," I breathe.

Lela's brows shoot into her hairline. "'Not important?' Jesus, Hay. Don't let my mom hear you say that," she warns.

I look over and see Coach glaring at me. She beckons me over with a curled finger.

My heart roars in my chest like a car backfiring as I leave Casey and Lela and join Coach. I force my hands to stop flapping and try to display a calm expression for the rest of the team.

She wouldn't tell Lela what happened in the hallway, would she? I told her I wouldn't say anything about her hearing loss, so why would she say something about my dancing? Unless…oh no. What if she doesn't even realize it's a secret? What if she assumes everyone knows about it already and spills?

I should have clarified I didn't want anyone knowing…why didn't I think of that at the time?

I'm screwed. Absolutely **screwed**.

"You're leading practice today," Coach tells me.

My muscles constrict again, leaving me frozen as I stare at my teammates.

Coach blows her whistle. The shrill sound pierces through the haze of my panic.

"What's wrong with you?" Coach asks. "Be a leader." She shoves my shoulder and I stumble toward the team.

I suck in a breath and exhale shakily.

"Should we start with circle passing?" I stammer, looking to Coach for confirmation.

"I don't know, **should** we?" She bears a startling resemblance to César as her nostrils flare and one thick brow hikes above the other.

"Circle passing," I decide. "Two-touch circle passing."

Throughout the first drills, my attention keeps drifting toward the sidelines. Lela chatters to a seemingly uninterested Casey as I pass the ball back and forth with Jacob. Lela nudges Casey and laughs while I jog up and down the pitch with Nathan.

During our first water break, I lurk as close to the girls as I can without raising suspicion.

"It's okay, you can tell me. I won't say anything. Girl code," Lela murmurs, unaware Casey can't hear her very well.

She blinks at Lela for a second, then answers. Interesting. She must lipread. "I guess—" Casey pauses when she spots me eavesdropping and quirks a brow. Lela follows her line of sight, and I choke on my water and stifle a coughing fit.

Crap, crap, **crap**.

I should have…what, written out a contract on my Notes app and made her sign it? Sliced our palms and made a blood oath? Okay, maybe not that.

But I should have done something.

All-consuming, overwhelming panic erupts within me. Nausea roils my stomach. A bolt of lightning cracks through my chest. My lungs constrict.

"Hay? What's wrong?" Paz gently touches my arm. "Talk to me," he says, lowering his voice.

I would talk to Paz if I could. But the storm of emotions swirling inside me can't be summed up into words. I open and close my mouth several times. The explanation is on the tip of my tongue, but every time I get close to finding the words, they evaporate.

Some things defy explanation.

Coach blows her whistle again to signal the end of water break, and everyone darts back onto the pitch, save Paz and me.

"I'm f-fine," I squeak out, the lie catching in my throat.

Paz clearly isn't convinced but doesn't have time to press the issue with Coach yelling our names. "Okaaay. Whatever you say."

We run one drill after another. I watch out of the corner of my eye as Casey waves goodbye to Lela and dashes toward the parking lot, where she's whisked away by a blue Mom Van.

Lela buries her nose in her smutty book, and all is well again. (Not counting the violent and persistent fear that my world will come crashing down in a matter of hours, that is.)

The team works on penalty kicks for our last few minutes of practice. I've always been the go-to for penalty shootouts, even when Henry was on the team. It seems counterintuitive, because it's all about being levelheaded in a high-pressure situation, but I'm inexplicably good at scoring PKs.

I line up a shot, then try to fake out our keeper by sending the ball in a different direction than my body is pointed.

Except something is different today.

I miss penalty after penalty. Each shot I take is caught by Gabriel or goes completely askew and misses the goal.

Every missed shot starts to feel like a personal attack. I have to bite down on the inside of my cheek to keep from yelling whenever the ball flies past the goalpost or lands short.

Not enough power. Too much power. Nothing in between. That's how things have been today.

"Hayden." Coach appears out of thin air, her jaw locked. "What kind of example are you here to set?" she snaps. "A captain we can all be proud of, or a softie who brings shame to his family?"

My throat tightens as I hear my teammates snickering.

Coach checks her watch, fury burning in her eyes. "Practice is over. Go home," she announces to the team. "And Hayden"—Coach snags my arm, holding me back—"get your head in the game. Man up."

The other boys head for the locker rooms, but Paz, César, and I veer toward the bleachers, where Lela is waiting.

Paz walks backward, an impish grin on his face. He begins humming "Get'cha Head in the Game" from HIGH SCHOOL MUSICAL.

"Can you not?" I mutter.

"C'mon, Hay"—he holds his hands up in faux defense—"don't be afraid to shoot an outside J." He cackles and leaps away when I reach out to swat him.

"Isn't that basketball?" César muses from beside me. "Outside J?"

Paz heaves an overly dramatic sigh. "You caveman! The sport itself is irrelevant. HIGH SCHOOL MUSICAL was a turning point for Gen Z culture, and it's basically a requirement that we reference it whenever applicable."

"Paz! Would you please just shut up?!" I shout as we come to a stop in front of Lela.

Paz's playful smile is replaced with shock. Lela and César look at each other, then me. To be fair, the outburst is out of character. I'm supposed to be the Mom Friend. The unruffled, put-together, even-keeled one. Hah! If they only knew…

I scrub my hands over my face and plop onto the Astroturf near Lela.

Those icky, horrible feelings linger as I force air into my lungs, taking strained breaths. But slowly, I pull myself together.

"Lo siento, amigo mio," I say on an exhale, looking at Paz.

Paz and César join us on the ground. Paz scoots close to me. "Is this about the new girl?" he asks.

"No." I grit my teeth.

"You're a terrible liar." Paz tsks. A major downside of being friends for so long is that Paz and I can practically read each other's minds. It's honestly freaky.

"He's right," César butts in. "You tuck your thumbs in whenever you lie."

I glance down at my hands and find my thumbs hidden in my palms. I make a show of untucking them, but the damage is done.

I want to change the subject to something besides Casey, in case Lela brings up whatever they were discussing (and that "whatever" turns out to be the tap dance routine I performed in the hallway during fifth period), but Paz is insistent.

He focuses on Lela. "What were you guys talking about?"

"Nothing. I couldn't even get her to admit who on the team she thinks has the best butt even though I promised not to tell anyone, so I thought maybe she's a lesbian. But later she mentioned an ex-boyfriend. Which doesn't mean she's **not** a lesbian, but, you know, without wanting to make assumptions, she's definitely giving off bi vibes." She nonchalantly combs her fingers through her curtain bangs.

"Okay, but about the butts? Jacob could crush a watermelon with his glutes." Paz waggles his brows. "Whoa, wait, we've confirmed she's bi!? Or possibly a lesbian?! True fact?!" he screeches. "Not just like 'I'm an ally so I'm wearing a pride flag shirt'?"

Lela laughs. "Jacob? Nice butt. Terrible kisser. And whatever she is, I'd definitely not peg her as straight." She shrugs.

"The queers just keep winning!" Paz wipes an invisible tear and sniffles loudly, then launches into a discussion with Lela about bubble butts.

The only thing I get out of the conversation is that my secret—my music, my safe place, my refuge—is still that. A secret.

I send a silent thank-you to Casey, but embers of panic continue to glow in me. She didn't tell anyone today...but that doesn't mean she won't tell someone tomorrow.

CHAPTER 5
CASEY

"ONCE YOU HAVE A PARTNER, COME DRAW——OUT OF——HISTORY HAT!"

Mr. Gibson's announcement snaps me out of my daze. It's not auditory fatigue this time; it's just that his lectures are so mind-numbing that I can't help zoning out in his class (I swear he googles "Top 10 Historical Events to Bore Teenagers to Death" when creating lesson plans).

He's standing at the front of the classroom, shaking a novelty Uncle Sam-style hat—the History Hat, I presume. I look around as students partner up and approach Mr. Gibson, drawing slips of paper from the hat. I wish I hadn't missed what we're partnering up **for**.

I think of asking Lela to be my partner—group projects are one of the most hellish things about high school, but working with Lela might be bearable. By the time I locate her, though, she and the Barracudas' goalkeeper, Gabriel, are already in line together. I'm not surprised; she couldn't stop drooling over him when we were hanging out during soccer practice the other day. Good for her for shooting her shot.

"Caaasey!" a familiar voice singsongs from behind me. Paz stops in front of my desk, dragging Hayden along by the wrist. "Let's be partners!" Paz flashes a toothy grin.

Confused, I look from one of them to the other. "Aren't you guys already partners?"

"Now, I'm not known for mathematical prowess, but there are twenty-nine students in this class, which means"—he pauses to poorly mimic the sound of a drumroll—"one group will be a trio!"

"Or one person will work alone," I counter, raising a brow.

Paz rolls his eyes. "Would you rather work with us, or some randos?" He leans closer to me and says conspiratorially, in a voice just loud enough for me to hear, "Rando *straight* people?"

I fight an amused smile. "What is the project anyway?" I ask, hoping they were paying more attention than I was.

"We have to——presentation——American Revolution——due in a month——October tenth——" Paz is apparently trying to set the world record for fastest school project explanation.

"Paz." Hayden places his hand on Paz's shoulder. He eyes me almost apologetically, then says, "We can talk about it later."

What he doesn't say is: "Later, when it'll be quieter, and you'll be able to hear it better." The unspoken words are somehow more meaningful than anything he could have said.

I mirror his small, nervous smile. "Okay. Sure."

"Yay!" Paz squeals. "This'll be fun! We'll be the three musketeers!"

"Oh, uh, I wasn't agreeing to—" My objection is interrupted when Mr. Gibson squats next to my desk.

"I'm glad to see you've made friends!" He talks to me very slowly, the way you'd talk to a toddler whose language center hasn't fully developed. I try to not let that bother me. "Everyone else already chose their project, so you kids get this one." Mr. Gibson turns the History Hat upside down and a single slip of paper floats onto my desk.

Still addressing me like I'm an alien species, he adds, "If you need help, please reach out, but I'm sure you're in great hands with Mr. González-Rossi and Mr. Cabello-Tesfaye." He gestures to Hayden and Paz.

"Uh, thanks, but I work best alone. Can I do the project by myself?" I ask.

"I think it'll be good for you to work with the others! I bet it's tricky to make friends with your heari—"

"Okay, alright! Got it! Thank you!" I rush, masking Mr. Gibson's words. Hayden already knows about my hearing loss, but Paz doesn't. And I really don't want him treating me differently. Talking like I don't understand English, observing me like a zoo animal when I walk down the halls, thinking of me as a burden.

I just want to get through this year and get back to Portland.

Paz pumps a triumphant fist in the air. "Three musketeers! Three musketeers!" he chants, earning a stare from our classmates.

Hayden grabs the paper from my desk as the bell rings. I sling my backpack over one shoulder and quickly slip into the hall. Unfortunately, my escape attempt is foiled; Paz, Hayden, and Lela are following me. Lela links our arms and grins.

"You teamed up with Paz and Hayden? You're practically one of us now!" she says.

I pry my arm away from hers and sigh. "Mr. Gibson forced me to."

"Oh, come on, Casey. Just because my brother is an ass, it doesn't mean **we** can't all be friends!" She gestures between herself, Hayden, and Paz.

"Why are you so insistent on befriending me?" I stop and turn to face them, clogging up the foot traffic in the hall. "I'm not some stray animal in need of a home!"

Paz eyes me. "Now that you mention it, you do kind of have feral-street-cat vibes…"

"Shut up, Paz," Hayden hisses, jabbing him in the ribs and face-palming.

I roll my eyes and turn on my heel, done with the conversation. "Don't follow me," I call over my shoulder. But—to absolutely nobody's surprise—Paz catches up to me and throws his arm around my shoulders.

"Hay and I have fútbol practice after school, but we can meet up after that to work on the presentation!" he suggests.

"Can't," I say, sliding out from underneath his arm. "I'm busy this afternoon."

It's not just an excuse. My first vocal lesson at the Rossi Music Studio is today.

"Tomorrow?"

"Busy," I deadpan. That, however, *is* an excuse.

He stares into my soul. "Okay, this weekend. We'll meet at the library on Saturday morning."

I sigh, sensing he's not going to stop badgering me until I commit to a study date. "Sure. Fine. Saturday."

"Three musketeers!" he mouths, acting out a sword fight while walking backward toward his next class.

When the final bell rings that afternoon, a headache is thumping against my skull in steady beats, like there's a metronome inside my brain.

Between the angry wave of auditory fatigue and the sea of chattering students clogging up the corridors, it's no surprise I get lost trying to navigate the labyrinth that is Palmera High's hallways.

I scan the names of classrooms as I pass them, trying to retrace my steps, but come to a halt when I realize I've wandered into the performing arts area of the school.

I've been actively avoiding this part of campus. In fact, it might sound weird, but another reason Palmera appealed to me was the lackluster reputation of their performing arts department. I remember Dad telling me the music classes were much better at Oceanview Prep, and me rebutting that it didn't matter how good their music program was if I couldn't participate in it. At Palmera, there would be no painful reminder of the music classes I've lost.

But, because this is just my effin' luck, I've ended up in the hall where Palmera's few music classrooms are—the one place at school I swore I wouldn't go.

I should turn around and leave immediately. But a small hint of curiosity takes root, and I can't help wondering what these rooms actually have to offer. What kind of instruments does the school have? How qualified are the teachers?

I crane my neck to peer into one of the rooms and don't see anyone inside. It doesn't seem like anyone is in this whole section of Palmera right now. The irresistible urge to poke around overtakes me and I continue down the hallway.

There are two dingy classrooms in this hall, called Mozart and McCartney: Mozart houses a small piano, a shelf with books of sheet music, and a very dusty violin, cello, and harp. McCartney has regular and bass guitars, a microphone, and a small drum kit. A third, smaller door is unmarked, and I assume it must lead to some sort of custodian's closet.

I'm about to leave when I hear faint piano music. I glance toward Mozart, but the room is empty.

My hearing is notoriously unreliable, but I tilt my head toward the janitor's closet and swear I hear another note. Following the sound, I walk to the door and peer through the small glass window.

Inside, there's a boy with an ugly orange sports jersey and a mess of curls using an upside-down mop bucket as a makeshift bench for a tiny spinet piano. His fingers float across the keys, head gently swaying to music.

It's Hayden.

What. The. Hell?

What in the world is he doing playing piano in a dinky storage closet?

I knock on the door, but he doesn't stop playing, so I push it open. His fingers seem to ghost over the keys, like he's barely touching them, but the tune is fierce. Frantic and desperate.

My brain cells are currently about as useful as the letter 'P' in the word "raspberry," so it takes me longer than it should to recognize it as "No Good Deed" from WICKED.

Mesmerized, I lean against the open doorway and watch. The song explodes through the room and its fiery, pleading emotions cascade down on me. When the final notes have faded, I slow-clap, like I did a few days ago after his NEWSIES performance.

"Bravo, bravo," I cheer.

Hayden whips around so quickly he tips his mop bucket-slash-piano bench over and goes tumbling onto the floor.

He clambers to his feet, a wild look painted across his features. "C-Casey…" he stammers. His fists are wound tight in the orange fabric of his shirt, but I can tell they're trembling.

"You could go professional with that," I joke, trying to lighten the mood. "Tap routines, soccer tricks, Broadway songs. You're a one-man variety show."

"What is that s-supposed to mean?" he demands, voice breaking. "Why are you here? You shouldn't be here! Please leave!"

"It was a joke," I explain. Then I realize his eyes are wet and his chest is rising and falling with heavy breaths. I frown at him.

"It's just…you're…I mean…you can't tell anyone! And you can't be here! Don't ever come here again, do you understand me? Never!"

I freeze, startled by his sudden personality switch. Where's the Hayden who rescued me from César on my first day of school, or the Hayden who offered to accommodate me after learning about my hearing loss?

I really don't understand this kid. One minute, he's attentive and caring. The next, he's losing his cool or blowing me off. I saw him dance around and play the piano a little bit—so what?! That's literally not even one of the top ten most embarrassing things you can be caught doing at school.

We continue to stare at each other. Gradually, his eyes soften, and he blinks away tears and flaps his hands.

I finally break the silence. "What's going on, dude?"

He starts to say something but stops himself. Instead, he snatches his backpack from beside the spinet and pushes past me, disappearing down the hall.

When I finally manage to exit the building, the muggy heat swirling around Palmera's front courtyard suctions my corgi butt-print button-up to my skin. The hot air makes my lungs feel sticky, which I didn't know was a way lungs could feel until now. When I get back to Portland, I will never complain about the cold again.

Forcing the weird-ass interaction with Hayden to the back of my mind, I check the time on my phone: 3:51 p.m. My vocal lesson is rapidly approaching, and I still haven't decided how to feel about it.

On one hand, I want to get my music back, to be some semblance of the girl I once was. On the other hand, I'm keeping my guard up. I've had too many bridges burned recently to be hopeful, so I'm preparing for the worst-case scenario.

As I speed-walk through the courtyard, I spot César chatting with a fellow soccer player. My sworn enemy narrows his dark eyes, scowling like he's challenging me.

I'm so sick of this guy. He has no reason to be pissed at me. I get that he's indignant about my dad's job—trust me, I'm more embarrassed about it than anyone—but how is that my fault?

Now, me being pissed at him is entirely justifiable. Because on top of blaming me for my dad's job, he's had the audacity to start showing up to algebra class earlier every day to re-claim his desk. He even wrote his name on **every corner**! Seriously, who gets that worked up over arbitrary desk ownership? (We're not going to talk about how I've also been engaging in desk warfare by crossing his name out and carving my own name. He started it!)

I adopt a don't-mess-with-me expression and straighten my posture, shooting an equally nasty look his way. The only good thing about having dated Victor is that I now know how to deal with egotistical jocks.

César better not underestimate me. Pettiness is a war I **will** win.

Halfway to the parking lot, I hear someone shout my name. I turn to see Lela jogging toward me, sleek black hair flowing behind her like a slow-mo movie sequence.

She skids to a stop. "Do you want to hang out while the boys are at fútbol practice?" I glance at the athletic field filling with soccer players but I don't see Hayden anywhere. Part of me wonders if he's okay, but I shake it off.

"I can't," I say, scanning the parking lot for Mom's van. Without thinking, I add, "Maybe tomorrow?"

Lela's lips (which are glossy and plum purple today) curl into a bright smile. "Okay, see you tomorrow." My body tenses as she pulls me into a hug.

Damn it. Why did I say that!?

I break out of the embrace and try to keep my face neutral. I shouldn't have agreed to hang out. I'll need to brainstorm a convincing excuse before she can corner me tomorrow, because Lela is hard to lie to. She's like a human polygraph.

I see Mom's van in the pickup spot and walk over, wondering what kind of spell Lela cast on me to get me to say yes.

I had one rule. One. No Friends. Yet somehow, in just over a week, I've acquired at least three. (Plus, an archnemesis!) And something tells me they aren't going to be easy to get rid of.

Though, at this point, Hayden's semi-friendship is up in the air. I haven't quite figured him out yet. He's like a puzzle I don't have all the pieces to. And I hate to admit it, but that bothers me. I wish I could stop caring or wondering about him, but for some reason, I want to know what's going on in his weird head.

"Who's your friend?" Mom asks with a smirk as I climb into the passenger's seat.

"*L-E-L-A,*" I use SimCom as I fingerspell, knowing Mom's receptive fingerspelling is subpar on a good day.

"She's cute! Oh, how do you sign cute?"

I tuck my ring and pinky fingers, then brush my index and middle fingers down my chin and into my palm. "*Cute.*"

"Lela is"—Mom repeats the sign—"*cute.*"

I buckle up, connect my phone to the van's Bluetooth, and launch Spotify. One Direction blares as we drive away from Palmera.

"Story of My Life" ends right as Mom parks in front of a sky-blue, two-story house. A sign posted on the front door confirms this is the right place: THE ROSSI MUSIC STUDIO.

"Do you want me to walk you to the door?" Mom asks.

"I'm okay. Thanks."

"*O-K* ... well, I'll be back in *one hour,*" she half-speaks, half-signs.

I slam the car door shut and approach the house. As I knock, I find myself praying this teacher won't be like Laurel. My heart thunders while I wait. After a few seconds, the door swings open and I'm greeted by a white woman about my mom's age with kind blue eyes.

"Hello," the woman says with a smile, "it's nice to finally meet you! I'm Taylor."

"Nice to meet you," I parrot, and step inside.

The house is quaint and cozy. A small table by the door holds a bowl of keys, a shoe rack is overflowing with varying sizes of sneakers and sandals, and a mat welcomes guests in multiple languages.

Taylor leads me into a brightly colored music room. An opera degree from Vanderbilt University and an assortment of signed Broadway Playbills hang on the yellow walls. A white baby grand piano sits in the center of the room; its lid decorated with hand-painted palm trees in colors ranging from neon green to rich purple.

"I read your mom's notes." Taylor sets up a folding chair for me, then sits on the piano bench. Her warm smile starts to put me at ease—it feels like I've seen this smile before, but I don't know why, since this is the first time we've met. "I did a bit of research before our lesson," Taylor continues, "and I've found that some deaf people can 'hear' music through vibrations." She takes out a notebook and pen. "I was wondering if you'd be comfortable feeling my throat as I guide you through warm-ups, so you can copy the vocal eases?"

I know that if I put my hands on my Bluetooth speaker, I can feel the music, "hearing" notes through touch that I can't hear through my ears. That's another thing three hearing specialists accused me of faking. If it's not within the realm of their universe, it must be fake, right?

But how can you explain your way of interpreting sound to someone who's never experienced sound that way?

I never considered applying the touch technique to singing, though.

Surprised by her idea, I take a beat before replying. "Um, sure? It might work?"

"Let's give it a shot!" She turns toward the piano, fingers hovering above the keys. "Place your hand here," she taps her throat.

I stand next to the piano, facing her while my fingers gingerly rest on her throat. I'm relieved that we seem to be alone in the house. I wouldn't want someone walking in and thinking I'm strangling my vocal coach.

"We're going to start with sliding fifths." Taylor's fingers float across the piano, pressing on five different keys, her voice matching the notes.

The sound prickles my fingers and I gasp. I can feel her vocal cords vibrating—the buzz of a thousand bees underneath my fingertips. I've felt heavy bass on my speaker, and if the volume is high enough, I can feel piano or acoustic guitar. But feeling live singing in this way transports me to a new plane of existence.

Taylor watches as I bring my other hand to my own throat, taking a deep breath before copying the vocal ease, matching the frequency of my vibrations to hers.

We continue to go higher and higher, the vibration of her vocal cords softening as we climb, and we finally reach a pitch I can't hear. C above middle C. I'm left with guesswork as I feel her sing, attempting to match the pitches above that note by instinct.

Taylor claps after we finish. "That was perfect! Let's try descending five-note scales."

The lesson passes in no time. Taylor easily adapts her teaching style, becoming tactile and showing rather than telling. She incorporates her own hand gestures to tell me when I need to be conscious of breath support or watch the nasality of my tone. Her version of sign language. **Sing** language, if you will.

By the time the lesson is over, the apprehension I was feeling has been replaced by a sense of fulfillment. "Thank you so much," I say to Taylor. A genuine smile tugs on my lips. "You're an amazing teacher."

"And you're an amazing student. I look forward to working with you." Taylor leads me to the front door. "For our next lesson, how about you pick out a song we can start working on?"

"Sure. See you next week!" I grin as I exit, floating on cloud nine.

Miami will never feel like home, but maybe it won't be as bad as I thought.

CHAPTER 6
HAYDEN

I'M CONVINCED CASEY'S STRINGS OF FATE HAVE GOTTEN TANGLED UP IN my own. Either that, or she's a stalker. That's the only way to explain how she's caught me in the middle of a secret Broadway performance twice in the span of two days. Twice!

Ever since she intruded on my storage closet sanctuary this past Wednesday—the one spot in school I can go to calm down, a spot none of my friends know about—I've done everything in my power to avoid her.

But now, thanks to Mr. Gibson's assignment, I **have** to be around her. For a whole month.

It's Saturday morning, and Paz, Casey, and I are meeting in the library at ten to strategize about our history project, a deep dive into France's role in the American Revolution.

The air-conditioning in the library is on full blast, but I'm sweating bullets, my nerves going haywire. My eyes are fixed on the wall clock across the room. 10:03 a.m. I'm too far away for this to be plausible, but I swear I can hear it **tick, tick, tick,** reminding me that Casey's going to arrive any second.

My fingernails dig into my palms, leaving crescent-shaped imprints behind. 10:06 a.m. The clock continues counting down, and with

each passing second it feels like I'm sinking further underwater. ***Tick.***
Tick. Tic—

"Hi."

I peel my eyes away from the clock and they land on Casey. She stands a few feet away, studying me with a mix of curiosity and…caution?

Not that I can blame her for feeling wary around me. I did kinda explode at her on Wednesday. But in my defense, I felt cornered. Exposed. Vulnerable.

Except she didn't know that.

I've really made a mess of this whole situation, haven't I? Maybe I'm the one in the wrong here. She had no way of knowing what that room means to me. Or how overwhelmed and nervous I get before fútbol practice. Or how desperately I need to focus on something other than my racing heart and restless thoughts.

"Hayden?" Her voice interrupts my spiraling. She's sitting across from me now, brows settled in a frown. "You good?"

"Y-yeah. Good. Great. Perfect," I choke out a thesaurus' worth of adjectives, all of them lies. I'm a lot of things, but "good" is definitely not one of them.

She stares at me, unconvinced, but doesn't have time to respond before Paz plops into the seat next to me. For the first time in his life, he stays silent, his focus shifting between Casey and me.

"This is an interesting energy we've created," he loudly comments after assessing the situation.

He's quickly shushed by Mrs. Weaver, the strict, ancient librarian.

"What's up with you two? What happened?" he pries at a more acceptable volume.

"Nothing's up!" I rush.

"Nothing happened," Casey says at the same time, her eyes trained on his lips.

He clacks his tongue and clasps a hand over his heart. "Fine. Be that way. Exclude me. I'm not deeply hurt, really. Fake friends are just a part of life," he laments.

I sneak a glance at Casey and catch her trying not to smile. Then her eyes meet mine and her amused expression disappears.

Paz has the attention span of a goldfish, so he immediately changes the subject. "Oh my God, wait! Did you guys see that Gabriel and Lela paired up?" He waggles his brows. "Do you think they're a thing now? I heard—"

"Can we please focus on the project?" Casey interrupts his gossiping. Paz shuts up but doesn't seem happy about it.

"Thank you," she continues, sliding a laptop out of her backpack. "So, how are we doing this? Written report? PowerPoint?"

"No, no, no, we can't do a plain ol' report!" Paz exclaims. He yanks a thick binder out of his knockoff Gucci messenger bag. "We should present our project in"—he pauses for suspense and flips to the first page in the binder—"play form!"

A Pinterest-style collage of eighteenth-century French fashion and extravagant palaces is glued to the first page. On the second there's a handwritten script starring the Marquis de Lafayette, Benjamin Franklin, and King Louis XVI.

"We can do costumes and everything! Casey, because you're new, I'll let you be King Louis. You're welcome," Paz chirps.

Silence ensues. I can't tell if she missed what Paz was saying or if she's ignoring him, but after a long beat, she closes the binder and turns back to her laptop. "PowerPoint it is."

"What!? No! I spent so much time on this! I pulled an all-nighter to storyboard! And I take my beauty sleep very seriously," Paz protests.

"Mr. Cabello-Tesfaye!" Mrs. Weaver whisper-yells from the front desk, finger pointed at Paz. "Lower your voice, young man!"

"Sorry, Mrs. Weaver," he murmurs, and flashes the librarian a fake smile. As soon as she looks away, he rolls his eyes. "Why is everyone trying to stifle my creativity? This is homophobic."

She ignores him again. "Hayden, you and I will do the written sections. Paz, you pull together pictures. We'll meet at ten on Saturday mornings to put our materials together. The presentation is on October tenth, right? That gives us three more meetings to get everything done."

I gingerly raise my hand. "Casey? Uh, do you think you'd be able to assemble the actual slideshow?" I ask. Paz doesn't have a laptop and mine is Henry's hand-me-down that stopped updating after Windows 7.

She stares at me, focusing on my lips, then nods and mumbles an "mm-hmm."

"Great!" Paz claps. "Let's get started. The sooner we start, the sooner we finish and I can leave this stuffy-ass library."

Forty minutes into our study session, Casey is clacking away on her keyboard, I'm reading about the early childhood of the Comte de Rochambeau, and Paz is scrolling through pictures of eighteenth-century Paris-inspired makeup looks on Pinterest.

"Oh my God, you guys, I just had the best idea!" Paz squeals, tearing Casey and me away from our research. "We should add a soundtrack to our presentation! Think of the drama, the romance, the intrigue."

Casey considers Paz. "Actually…that's not a bad idea. It would have to fit the historical context, of course. But I bet we can find some good French harpsichord music."

"Harpsi-what?" Paz's face screws up in confusion.

Mrs. Weaver presses a finger to her lips and shoots Paz the dirtiest look an eighty-year-old woman is capable of. "Final warning, Mr. Cabello-Tesfaye!" she hisses.

"Or," Casey continues, unable to hear Mrs. Weaver's threat, "piano would work too. And if we do piano music…"

Her focus shifts to me. Oh no. Oh crap.

Don't bring it up, don't bring it up, don't bring it up—

"…I have a keyboard I could bring from home and Hayden can play live. Live music might help people, like, stay awake."

My heart goes into arrythmia, skipping several beats. "No, no, no. No way!"

"He told you he plays piano?" Paz asks her. "You two seem pretty friendly these days, hmm?" He eyes me, a smirk teasing the corner of his lips.

The fact that I play piano isn't a secret. My mom was insistent that each of her kids learn an instrument; even his majesty Hat-Trick Henry played flute when he was younger. But it's also not something I broadcast widely. And even though my family and friends know I play piano, no one knows about my secret rendezvous with the piano at school, and they definitely don't know I play showtunes.

No one except Casey.

"Actually," she replies to Paz, "he—"

"Told her! Yeah, I told her!" I blurt before immediately mouthing "I'm sorry" to Mrs. Weaver.

Casey studies me with an expression similar to the one she had when she arrived at the library. But this time it's less cautious and more curious. I shoot her a look I hope conveys my desperation to keep everything she's witnessed between us.

"I've learned a lot about Hayden," she says to Paz. "He's a very… interesting person. In fact—"

My leg moves of its own accord, and before the action has time to register, my foot hits Casey's shin.

"What the hell is your problem?!" she roars, scooting her chair back and rubbing the spot I kicked.

"C-Casey, I'm so sorry, I didn't mean to—"

"You kicked me!" Her eyes are wide, jaw dropped.

I don't have a chance to explain how my leg was momentarily possessed by a shin-phobic ghost before Mrs. Weaver is hobbling over to our table, her wrinkled face twisted into a scowl. "That's it! You three, get out!"

Casey doesn't need to be told twice. She shoves her laptop into her bag and storms toward the exit.

How do I always manage to make crappy situations ten times worse than they already are? I want to fling myself off a cliff!

I launch out of my chair and run after her. Direct confrontation is my least favorite thing in the world, but that's the only way I can fix this. No dancing around it. No excuses. Just honesty. (And maybe a little pleading.)

Casey's halfway down the block by the time I catch up to her. She's faster than she looks.

"Wait!" I reach out and snag her backpack strap. She whips around. "I'm so sorry."

"You kicked me. What are you, five?"

"I didn't mean to! I p-panicked!" I can barely hear my own voice. It's drowned out by the thundering heartbeat echoing in my ears. My shaky hands wrap themselves in my shirt.

Her eyes flicker down as she notices my anxious tic. Then she sighs, shoulders relaxing on the exhale. "Is that what happened on Wednesday? You panicked?"

The memory is hazy, blurred by the tension seizing my body. When I'm in a bad headspace, it's hard to focus on anything. But I guess "panic" is the best way to describe it—my already heightened emotions intensified when I realized she was there, in my safe space, watching me.

So I lost my cool. I bit her head off. I probably scared off the only new person I've been interested in befriending since meeting Paz in second grade.

I shrug, unable to reply.

She sighs again. "Why is it a big deal? You like Broadway. So what?"

I pause, the words caught in my throat.

Maybe it's a "big deal" because my whole life I've been compared to my brother. Everyone expects me to be Henry 2.0, and Henry would never be a musical theater nerd. So how could I ever come clean about my love for showtunes? I'd become the poster child for "family misfit"!

Or maybe it's because my career path was decided for me the day I was born, and Broadway star was never on the table. González boys become fútbol players. Period. What if my family finds out I have other ambitions? What if they tell me it's not allowed? I'm not sure I can handle their disappointment.

Or maybe it's because, hello, horrible stage fright, anybody? I'm basically a ball of anxious energy disguised as a teenage boy. Even if I wasn't disowned by my family…if they knew I'm playing and singing and dancing, they might want to watch me perform. And that's about as terrifying as the thought of free-falling out of a plane.

And maybe it's a big deal because I've never, ever shown my true self to the people I love. Because what if they only love the Hayden they **think** I am? I couldn't take that. I'd rather have them keep the fake me around than leave the real me behind.

But I don't say any of that. I can't say any of that.

Instead, I stammer defensively, "I-I don't like Broadway!"

"Mm-hmm. Right. Because teen boys who aren't Broadway fans are notorious for performing NEWSIES tap routines and pounding out renditions of WICKED songs."

"Er, um…" I wring my hands, nervous thoughts swirling in my head. "Can we please just keep…**that**…between us? I kinda have a reputation to uphold."

"Right," she nods, eyes narrowed, "because a big-shot soccer star couldn't possibly enjoy showtunes."

"Please, Casey," I beg. "Please. I'm sorry about kicking you," I add.

She considers me for the longest minute of my life. "I forgive you."

Then she turns and walks away.

"But what about—"

"See you next week." She waves without turning back.

…I'm screwed.

CHAPTER 7
CASEY

It's been four days since the Great Library Kicking Incident, and I haven't interacted with Hayden once—it's obvious he's going out of his way to steer clear of me.

For some reason, his silent treatment and skittishness have been bugging me. But today I have my second vocal lesson, and I'm hoping that working with Taylor again will push this Hayden problem right out of my mind.

"Did you pick a song to work on?" Taylor asks after I finish my warm-ups.

I reach into my backpack and retrieve sheet music for Elton John's "I'm Still Standing." Taylor scans the material with a smile.

"Great choice. Why'd you pick this song?" She arranges the sheet music in front of her.

"It's sort of, well, for lack of a better term…it's a screw-you anthem."

"I like that! A screw-you anthem." She laughs. "You're right, though. The lyrics evoke——feeling——resilience." Her words cut out, but I understand her intention.

Taylor's smile doesn't waver as we begin to work. We dissect the song piece by piece. A crescendo here, note extension there.

Before I know it, an hour has passed, and our lesson is over. Taylor leads me to the front door. "See you next week," she says.

"See you—" I'm interrupted by my phone buzzing in my pocket. I pause halfway out the door and check it.

Wed, Sept 21, 5:07 PM

Running a few mins late. Crisis at work.

I tsk when I see Mom's message. "A few minutes" in Mom Speak could be five minutes or thirty, especially if it involves a work crisis (which probably means she's calming down some spoiled corporate man-child who doesn't like the length of the grass at their company retreat).

"Everything okay?" Taylor asks, placing a gentle hand on my shoulder.

"My mom's going to be late to pick me up," I explain.

"It's eighty-nine degrees outside," she says, her tone concerned and motherly. "You should wait in here." She ushers me back into the main house and leads me to the kitchen. I sit on a barstool as she pours me some lemonade.

"Thanks, Taylor." I smile and take a swig. "You don't have another lesson now?" I ask as she pours herself a glass and relaxes against the counter.

"No. The student I teach after you canceled."

A question pops into my head. "Sorry to change the subject, but do you know anything about eighteenth-century French composers? It's for a school project," I ask. Since Hayden was diametrically opposed to playing live, we'll have to put together a playlist.

Her eyes light up at the mention of classical music. We get swept into a conversation about Jean-Jacques Rousseau, Jean-Philippe Rameau, and Jean-Féry Rebel (apparently eighteenth-century French people weren't very creative with names), and I'm only torn out of it when my phone buzzes again.

A new text from Mom: **Almost there.**

I thank Taylor for the lemonade and expert advice on composers, then head for the door.

Outside, I stride toward the driveway, a grin on my face. Today was a good day—something that had become rarer and rarer. It feels like I'm starting to find my footing with Taylor and rekindle my relationship with music—something I wasn't sure I could do.

Before my happiness has a chance to sink in, I slam into a figure running toward the front door and tumble onto the concrete.

The figure squats, checking on me. "Oh my gosh, I'm so sor—" His apology stops short when he sees who I am. "Casey?"

Warm hazel eyes blink at me. Hayden's eyes. "W-what are you doing here?" He raises his voice, presumably so I can hear him better.

Dino stands behind him. "Why are you shouting at her? Damn!"

He turns to Dino. "Go inside, Mamma is——" He lowers his voice to a range I can't hear. Dino rolls his eyes and jogs into the house, leaving me sitting on the driveway while Hayden looks down at me.

"Why are you here?" He repeats his question, his expression a mix of confusion and alarm.

"I just finished a vocal lesson. What are **you** doing here?" I turn the question back on him. Surely, he and Dino don't take singing lessons? After catching him tap dancing and playing piano, I wouldn't be surprised, but Dino doesn't strike me as particularly musically inclined.

Hayden's eyes widen. "Wait, you're taking vocal lessons from my mom!?"

I adopt a similar expression, jaw dropped. "Your **mom**?! Are you saying Taylor is your mom?"

Now I know why Taylor's smile and aura seemed so familiar.

"So you're saying this is just some big coincidence?" He eyes me suspiciously.

"Dude, what else would it be? Do you think I'm stalking you or something?"

He shrugs, his cheeks turning red. "I dunno. Maybe."

"Don't flatter yourself, buddy. Geez."

His eyes squeeze shut and his shoulders rise as he takes a deep breath. He repeats this a few times, then sits down and starts pulling at the grass in the front yard. Eventually, he asks, "Does it hurt?"

I frown at him. Is this one of those bizarre questions Hearing people ask D/deaf people?

Noting my confusion, he motions to the huge purply-green bruise on my shin. "Duh, it hurts. You're a **soccer player**," I enunciate. "You've been professionally trained in the art of kicking things."

This draws a laugh out of him. His freckled nose crinkles, braces peeking out as his lips tip upward. I can't help but smile back—he's sort of adorable. "I really am sorry."

"I'm fine." I use SimCom, instinctively touching my thumb to my sternum, other fingers extended.

Hayden's eyes light up, intrigued, and for a moment he seems able to set aside his anxiety. "That means fine?" he asks.

I nod. *"Fine."*

"Fine." He repeats the sign. *"Fine. Fine. Fine. Fine."*

I chuckle. "You know," I start, "I think I owe you an apology too. I might've teased you a little too much about the Broadway thing."

"Might've?"

"Dude, don't nitpick my apology."

He mimics zipping his lips and tossing the key into the yard.

"But now I really don't get why you act like music is such a big secret," I continue. "I mean, your mom is a singer."

His Adam's apple bobs as he swallows, blinking rapidly. "It's…complicated. There's a lot of…expectations for me. But I really don't want to talk about it right now. Can you please just keep this between us? It's important to me."

I squint at him. He squirms uncomfortably, waiting for my answer.

I'm one hundred times more curious about him than I was before, but I get the impression that Hayden isn't someone you can demand answers from. And I don't need to understand, or even know, why something is important to someone else in order to respect it.

In hindsight, I definitely took the teasing too far. I hope I can make up for it now.

I poke his knee. "I won't tell anyone. Promise. Besides, you also know my secret, so what would be the point?"

"So you're only keeping my secret because I know yours too?"

"Not entirely. Having leverage is never a bad thing, though." I wink. "Kidding! Actually, it's been sort of nice to have someone I don't have to social bluff about my hearing loss around."

A wave of relief washes over his features. We smile at each other.

"Hey, I followed you on Instagram a few weeks ago." He changes the subject.

"Seriously? Now *that's* stalkery."

"I couldn't help it. You have a beautiful voice." He blushes.

Thank you, I say using SimCom, bringing a flattened palm down from my chin in his direction. For someone so secretive, Hayden is also extremely honest. I don't think he could be disingenuous if he tried.

"Thank you?" he asks, then copies the sign. *"Thank you. Thank you. Thank you."*

Over his shoulder, I see Mom pulling to a stop in front of the driveway.

"My mom's here." I stand up.

Hayden smiles at me and hops to his feet.

"Quick," I say, "tell me your favorite musical. DEAR EVAN HANSEN? THE BOOK OF MORMON? HADESTOWN?"

"I'll see you at school tomorrow." He dismisses me with a shake of his head.

I get into the van and plug my phone into the charging cable, then roll down the window. Making a last-ditch effort, I call out, "LES MIS? WAITRESS?"

He turns and walks inside, ignoring me.

Halfway home, my music is interrupted by a notification.

I pluck my phone off the center console and find an Instagram message:

@HeyitsHayden West Side Story :P

CHAPTER 8
HAYDEN

WHENEVER I GET THE CHANCE AFTER SCHOOL AND FÚTBOL PRACTICE, I lurk outside Mamma's music room, spying on her vocal lessons.

My favorite student of hers is Hakim Williams. Hakim is a baritenor, which is my self-assessed range. This makes him the perfect candidate for spying, but since his lessons are on Fridays, when I'm usually working at El Pollo Cubano, I haven't listened in on them in a long time.

Today, though, the restaurant is closed. The gas main is being repaired by the city, and our stoves are currently useless. So, this afternoon I'm pulling an Ursula from THE LITTLE MERMAID, attempting to siphon off Hakim's vocal magic and apply it to myself.

Mamma guides him through warm-ups while I scribble the occasional note, my interest piqued when she starts playing a piano rendition of "Anti-Hero" by Taylor Swift in a pitch that matches Hakim's range.

"You're straining during the second verse. Remember to lift your soft palate," Mamma instructs after Hakim sings the song once.

Hakim sings the verse a cappella; his voice sounds brighter and well-rounded.

My notetaking ceases as I'm swept into the rhythm of the song. I close my eyes and rest my head against the door, getting lost in Taylor

Swift's genius songwriting, Mamma's expert piano accompaniment, and Hakim's smooth vocals.

"Great job, Hakim!" Mamma's voice snaps me out of the musical trance. "I'll see you next week."

Crap! I've been tuned out for almost thirty minutes!

I scramble to my feet and hurtle down the short hallway to avoid detection. Dino watches me come barreling out of the hall, his brow cocked.

"¿Qué estás haciendo?" He reaches over and mutes the fútbol match he's watching.

"I'm not doing anything!" I rush, a bit too defensive. I tuck the notepad to my chest and head for the staircase.

"Yeah, on second thought, don't tell me what you're up to. Plausible deniability or whatever," he mumbles. I start to head upstairs but he calls out, "Wait! Hay? Can you help me with my 'hocus pocus' later?"

I poke my head out from the stairwell. "I thought Tía said your 'hocus pocus' is as good as Henry's?"

Dino messes with the stray threads on his ripped jeans. "I might've exaggerated," he mumbles. My brother, the embellisher. Last time he attempted a 'hocus pocus'—one of the hardest fútbol moves—he nearly broke his nose face-planting onto the ground.

"Why don't you ask Papá to help?" I glance to where our dad is working in the backyard.

Dino grimaces. "You're such a jerk. You won't even help your little brother? Wow, man."

I suck in a breath. "Fine. I'll help you. Tomorrow, though."

"Thanks, ugly." He flicks the sound back on the TV.

And there's the little brother I know and love.

My feet pound against the stairs as I make a beeline for my bedroom, the desire to experiment with new vocal techniques eating away at me.

"Hey, bro." I greet my pet iguana, Buñuelo, who's basking under the heat lamp in his terrarium. In seventh grade, some classmate asked if I wanted him. Being a twelve-year-old boy who didn't have much of a prefrontal cortex, I obviously took him home. He's been my buddy ever since. (Much to Mamma's dismay. She thinks lizards are gross. But I'm pretty sure Buñuelo thinks **she's** gross, so they're even.)

I lift up the edge of my mattress and hide my notepad, then grab the cheap speaker I bought for my phone. I head into the bathroom and lock the door.

After turning the water to the hottest setting, I plug in the speaker and queue up "Anti-Hero." I'll get more accurate results if I follow the same song Hakim was using, even if the key is different. And I'd never turn down an excuse to listen to Taylor Swift.

I strip out of my cargo shorts, Houston Dynamo jersey, and underwear, leaving them crumpled in the corner. The water burns my skin as I step into the shower. I push my hand past the curtain and press play.

I do all my singing in the shower. The sounds of the water, the fan, and the music block out most of my voice. The shower is my refuge from prying ears—as long as I don't belt. Unless you're in a soundproof booth, not much blocks out a high belt.

The water and song wash over me. My core relaxes on the extended notes, and I sail through them with ample breath support. Mamma drills her students on deep, stable diaphragmatic breathing. It's been permanently etched into my brain by now.

I shampoo my hair as the song ends, rinse as Spotify plays "Defying Gravity," and step out of the shower to the tune of "People Watching."

Three, six, maybe ten songs later, I dry myself off and head to my bedroom to plug in my phone, then change into flannel pajama pants and a loose-fitting V-neck, hand-me-downs from Henry.

I head downstairs and find my family gathered at the dinner table. Papá shoots me a pointed look, nonverbally commanding me to sit down.

"Thank you for gracing us with your presence." Papá eyes me, forking a bite of Mamma's homemade lasagna into his mouth.

"On that note: I think Hay should pay the water bill." Dino piggybacks off Papá's shade. "He takes hour-long showers. Seriously, Hay. Jack off in your room."

"Dino Alonso González-Rossi! Not at the dinner table, please!" Mamma's expression is so scandalized I have to laugh, but after I've recovered, I shoot my brother a look.

"Scusami, Mamma," Dino breaks out an apology in Italian, an obvious attempt to butter her up so he'll be quickly forgiven. But as soon as she looks away, he smirks in my direction. I stick my tongue out at him. Not my most mature moment, but he deserves it.

We stop talking to eat, our silverware clinking in the quiet.

"Mamma?" I break the silence. "Is Casey Kowalski going to be continuing vocal lessons?"

"I didn't realize you know Casey," she says.

"She's Hayden's new friend," Dino jumps in.

Papá raises a brow at me. "It's not like you to make friends!"

"Wow, thanks, Papá," I scoff. "I guess you're right, though. We're not exactly friends. We're just working on a history project together."

"Ah, I didn't mean it like that. You're just a bit awkward, mijo." Papá tries to make his comment sound better but doesn't succeed.

"She's a wonderful student. We're scheduled for every Wednesday at four p.m." Mamma steers the conversation back to my original question. "Why do you ask?"

"No reason! Just wondering." I don't want to let them know how curious I am about Casey. The teasing would never end.

"Anyway," Dino interrupts, "did I tell you Tía said my passes are gold-standard now? Like, youth-academy level."

He receives praise from both our parents. I duck my head and eat, hoping they won't start asking me questions about practice or my captaincy now that we're on the subject of fútbol yet again. I swear, the only thing they seem to care about is the legacy of the Floridian Broldans.

I help Papá clear the dishes after dinner, then head back upstairs. Casey is still on my mind as I ignore my homework and rewatch HAMIL-TON, which definitely counts as research for the group project. I pause after "The Story of Tonight (Reprise)."

Aside from a quick hello in history class yesterday, Casey and I haven't really talked since we cleared the air after her voice lesson two days ago. Even so, my instinct tells me she could use someone in her corner. Keeping secrets because you don't know how others might react, feeling like you don't really belong are things I can relate to. But I also know there are things she's dealing with that I'll never understand. High school is hard enough as is...but trying to navigate it after losing your hearing?

An idea pops into my head. I click out of my current tab and type "free ASL lessons" into the search bar. After scrolling through a few different websites, I find one that features short lessons from a Deaf teacher and has an ASL sign dictionary where you can search for specific words.

I go through the contents of an entire lesson in one sitting. I repeat phrases like "nice to meet you," "my name is," and "I'm learning ASL" over and over until they stick. The lesson threw in some fun signs too. My personal favorite is "turtle," which involves closing your four right fingers into a fist while your left hand curves over the right like a shell, and wiggling the right thumb like a head peeking out.

After I finish the lesson, I grab my phone and open Instagram. Since Casey doesn't want to reveal she's Deaf-Hard of Hearing at school yet, I can't exactly walk up to her and start using ASL in the middle of the hallway, but I want to find some way to share my newfound ASL knowledge with her.

And, though I would still prefer it if she didn't know about my Broadway obsession, I can't change the fact that she does know. And since she does…maybe it'll be nice to have someone I don't have to pretend around.

Sept 23 at 7:22 PM

@HeyitsHayden Would you like to hang out tomorrow morning after we work on the project?

As soon as I've sent the message, a wave of anxiety crashes over me. Does this border on creepy? Will she think it's strange that some random guy is asking her to hang out after only a few weeks of knowing each other? A guy who kicked her in a library?

Or what if she thinks I'm asking her out? Oh Lord. Oh no. What if she **wants** me to ask her out and I end up trapped in a one-sided relationship where I can never reciprocate romantic feelings but I don't end things because it would be too awkward and we're both miserable for the rest of our liv—

My spiraling is interrupted by a reply.

Sept 23 at 7:26 PM

@Casey.K.Sings why do u DM like an old man?? i feel like my grandpa ghostwrote that lmao

@HeyitsHayden Oh…sorry? Anyway, how do you feel about hanging out?

@Casey.K.Sings can't. busy.

@HeyitsHayden Doing what?

@Casey.K.Sings i fail to see how that's any of ur business? but since we're talking about the project…tell paz to send me his material!! it's been a week and idek if he's started!! ☹

@HeyitsHayden Okay, I can tell him! What about a week from Saturday? Can you hang out then?

@Casey.K.Sings can't. i have stuff to do before my 1st ASL lesson

@HeyitsHayden You aren't taking Palmera's ASL classes?

@Casey.K.Sings nope. palmera's classes are taught by Hearing teachers. english ASL & Deaf ASL have differences. i wouldn't wanna take a Hearing teachers ASL class y'know?

@HeyitsHayden Lol you mean like non-native Spanish speakers teaching Spanish?

@Casey.K.Sings yeah…like that. i recognize the unfortunate double standard but i can't control my dads job y'know?

@Casey.K.Sings (unlike ur cousin seems to think ☹)

@HeyitsHayden Haha César is a little intense but he's a good guy. Don't take it personally

@Casey.K.Sings ☺ he started it. i'm just defending my honor!!

@**HeyitsHayden** Anyways, how about we hang out TWO weeks from now? :D

@**Casey.K.Sings** mmm nope. i'm busy

@**HeyitsHayden** ...I didn't say which day.

Seen 7:30 PM

@**HeyitsHayden** Casey? Hello?

Seen 7:32 PM

@**Casey.K.Sings** ughhh i'll consider it. on one condition! u have to tell me ur fav musical theater song 👀

@**HeyitsHayden** This is extortion :(But fine. Probably Gee, Officer Krupke. But only the original—not the 2021 remake. What's yours?

@**Casey.K.Sings** a man of taste. mine is Words Fail

@**HeyitsHayden** Oof. That song is so depressing, though. And I feel like Dear Evan Hansen is a red flag musical.

@**Casey.K.Sings** oh yeah major red flag energy. but its not my fault the music is so good 👻

@**Casey.K.Sings** ok i have to go do hot girl shit (chemistry homework) pls leave me alone now

@**HeyitsHayden** Haha okay. Just let me know what you decide about hanging out in two weeks! :)

CHAPTER 9
CASEY

AFTER A SLOW AND BORING WEEK OF SCHOOL FOLLOWED BY A SATURDAY morning spent researching the history project in an underfunded public library, walking into a University of Miami classroom on Saturday afternoon and being greeted in sign language is a breath of fresh air.

The ASL instructor, a woman with blonde hair, gives us a cheery smile. *"My name is B-R-I-A-N-A,"* she signs, the middle and index fingers of her hands tapping together at a ninety-degree angle, then fingerspells her name. *"I'm the teacher."*

"Nice to meet you. My name is C-A-S-E-Y. I'm excited to take your class!"

Briana seems surprised by how smoothly I introduce myself. She raises her brows, indicating a yes or no question. *"You're aware this is a beginner class?"*

I motion toward my parents, who watch our conversation in bewilderment. *"My parents are beginners. My ASL is…"* I blank on the sign for "intermediate."

Briana catches my drift. *"Oh, I see,"* she taps a 'Y' handshape toward the floor. *"Welcome. I'm glad you're here!"*

I've been here two minutes, and this class is already leagues better than Palmera's ASL activities. Taught by a Deaf teacher, with students who (I hope) legitimately care about studying the ins and outs of the expressive, beautiful language and learning about Deaf culture—not a bunch of Hearing kids looking to beef up their college applications.

I have a feeling ASL and vocal lessons are going to be the highlights of my week.

Briana introduces herself in sign after the classroom fills with students. She plugs a projector into her laptop and pulls up a fingerspelling chart that shows each letter in the ASL alphabet next to the corresponding English letter. Mom's eyes widen when Briana asks us to introduce ourselves.

She calls on each person by pointing at them. When my turn comes, I pivot to face the class, point to myself, and tap both sets of index and middle fingers together twice. Without having to check the chart, I fingerspell my name slowly. Many of the students take notes.

"My sign name is"—I form a 'C' with my right hand and drag it down into a 'Y.'

Receiving a sign name is a rite of passage for Deaf folks. It can be something recognizable about your appearance, a reference to your career or hobby, or a play on the letters of your name.

But you aren't allowed to give yourself a sign name—it must be chosen for you by a Deaf person. My Deaf ASL tutor back in Portland gave me my sign name during our lessons.

Mom is up next. She stands up and glances nervously at the alphabet chart. She's always struggled with fingerspelling. *"My name is…"* She peers over her glasses at the letters. I give her a supportive smile when her eyes flit to me. *"C-X-I-S-T-I-M-E."* With each letter, her hand bounces up and down aggressively instead of staying steady like it should. Mom grins, not realizing she mixed up two letters.

Briana chuckles to herself, also noticing Mom's mistake.

Mom's attempt is pretty good, aside from the few wrong letters and the hand bouncing. But Dad, the man fluent in **four** spoken languages, has never been able to wrap his head around ASL. When it's his turn, he messes up every part of his introduction. Briana lets him try again. Ever the overachiever, he fails even more spectacularly on his second try.

She flaps her hand at Dad to get his attention. *"Your name is S-T-A-N, right?"*

Dad signs, *"No."*

Briana looks at me for the answer. *"Yes, his name is Stan. He's just confused,"* I clarify.

She laughs. Near her temple, she flicks her index finger upward and nods. *"I understand."*

After that, the hour-long class passes in a blur. I don't mind going over fingerspelling, numbers one through ten, and basic phrases. Being immersed in a friendly, understanding learning environment is worth the repetition.

"Sign language is so——" Dad mumbles once class is over and we're back in the car.

Relegated to the back seat, I look to Mom to fill in the blanks. She draws her bottom lip between her teeth as she thinks through her translation.

"Anyway," he continues, "who is hungry?" He starts the car and pulls out of the parking lot. "There is a restaurant——five stars on Yelp——could be——sound good?"

Mom frowns from the passenger seat, body twisted to face me. She searches her limited ASL vocabulary for the right signs.

Moments like these make me wish I could disappear. I inherited Dad's fast talking and goofy humor, but I'm not able to keep up with his banter like I used to. I know he isn't trying to exclude me, but we always circle back around to Mom poorly interpreting what he says, and it not being relevant by the time I understand.

It's part of why I'm a serial social bluffer.

I shake my head as Mom begins to sign, signaling she doesn't need to repeat what Dad said. I answer the part of Dad's dialogue I did hear. "I could eat."

My parents chat as we drive. I tune them out, knowing I'd get frustrated trying to untangle their quiet conversation. Following conversations when you're Deaf-Hard of Hearing is like being fed an endless stream of encrypted messages that you have to translate *immediately* or else the bad guys win.

I'm given bits of dialogue or the general outline of a sentence, and I have to piece together the possibilities, sort through a lexicon of lip shapes, and decode the message before the conversation has moved on.

More often than not, my mission fails. It's a great source of aggravation for all parties.

I hope it'll get better with time, but after only four months of practice, my decoding technique is highly unreliable and incredibly exhausting.

Dad turns a corner, and the scenery changes in the blink of an eye. Colorful buildings line a busy sidewalk, palm trees sway in the late September breeze, and the sun is still high, casting ample light on the lively atmosphere.

We pass several chicken statues painted in an array of bright colors. Next to one of the huge birds is a sign that reads: WELCOME TO CALLE OCHO.

Dad snags a rare street parking spot and beams as we exit the car.

"Isn't it wonderful?" He claps his hands together and soaks in Calle Ocho with wide eyes like a child on Christmas morning.

"It's cool," I agree. Miami has its charm.

We walk down a stretch of red brick sidewalk with plaques built into the walkway, Miami's very own walk of fame. Unfamiliar names are printed on the stars in the center of the plaques: OLGA GUILLOT, LEOPOLDO FERNANDEZ "TRES" PATINES, BETTY PINO.

Dad stops in front of a bright yellow clay building nestled between a clothing store and a café. The weathered, chipped blue sign on the front of the restaurant reads EL POLLO CUBANO.

My senses are inundated as we enter the restaurant. Sweet and savory spices prickle my nose, and the cold air creates instant goosebumps. The restaurant is empty apart from an older couple in the corner.

"It looks like we can seat ourselves," Dad says, pointing to a sign near the register. "You pick."

I scan the restaurant, trying to calculate the quietest spot. My eyes land on a table near the front window, away from the bustle of the kitchen.

Once we're seated, my eyes nearly bug out of my head when I spot Hayden hurrying over to our table, decked out in an apron with a tray of water precariously balanced on one arm. "¡Buenas tardes!" His lips are curled in a fake, customer-service smile.

He sets my water in front of me, then does a double take. His hazel eyes flicker between my parents and me, a panicked expression on his face. "W-what are you doing here?"

"What are **you** doing here?" I match his surprised expression.

He places three menus on the table, swallowing his nerves with a timid smile. *"Dad,"* he signs, then motions toward the whole of the restaurant.

"Your dad owns the restaurant?"

"Yeah. Er...*yes*," he bobs an enthusiastic fist.

I look at his hand, the action finally registering. Hayden just signed to me. Twice.

"You know ASL?" I sign. He stares at me blankly. Okay, maybe not. "How did you know those signs?" I ask out loud.

"I researched it. I know turtle too!" He demonstrates his knowledge.

My No Friends refrain flies out of my head at the sight of his nose-crinkling, braces-revealing smile. His eyes sparkle with pride in his new ASL knowledge. My heart flutters, and I return his smile.

"How do you sign restaurant?" he asks, not giving me time to dwell on the interaction.

I swipe the letter 'R' on one side of my chin, then the other. *"Restaurant."* I use SimCom.

"Restaurant. Restaurant. Restaurant," he signs. I chuckle. After a few more repetitions he asks, "And...these are?" He gestures toward my parents.

"Oh! Mom, Dad, this is my..." I point to Hayden, then pause. I don't think we've officially become friends yet. We're more like...friend adjacent.

But what am I supposed to say? "This is the weird kid I'm doing a school project with and also keeping a secret for even though I don't understand why, oh, and remember when I told you I tripped and bruised my leg? Actually, he kicked me! Ha. Ha."

"…my Hayden." I cringe as soon as the phrase leaves my mouth. I should have just said friend. 'My Hayden' is ten times worse than 'friend.'

Dad offers him a firm handshake. "Stanisław Kowalski." He narrows his eyes at Hayden—his don't-mess-with-my-daughter-or-else Dad Face—but his smile gives him away.

Mom waves at him. "Cristine."

"Nice to date you." He beams as he signs to my parents, proud of his accomplishment.

His expression falters when I start to snicker. "Hayden, this is *meet.*" Except for the index, all my fingers are tucked to my palm. I bring my hands together. "You signed *date.*"

'Date' is similar, but with 'D'-shaped hands instead of tucked fingers.

The blush that erupts on Hayden's face makes me feel bad for correcting him. He shrinks into himself and cringes. "Sorry."

I tap my thumb to my chest, fingers spread. *"You're fine,"* I assure him.

"Let me know when you're ready to order." He distances himself from the conversation and leaves me chuckling while Mom observes suspiciously.

An interrogation about my "cute new friend" ensues. I bury my face in my hands and refuse to re-emerge until Hayden returns to take our orders. Mom taps my shoulder when he arrives.

Dad orders in Spanish. Hayden and I exchange a knowing glance. Mom takes one last look at the menu and points to the arroz con pollo.

He jots down their orders and turns to me with an expectant look. *"What…you…want?"* he asks in broken sign.

"Surprise me." I was so busy hiding from Mom's incessant questions that I didn't get a chance to peruse the menu, but judging solely from the smells wafting from the kitchen, everything here is delicious.

He makes another note, then returns to the kitchen.

"He's nice. And cute! Very cute." Mom's eyes are alight with mischief. She thinks she's onto something.

When Hayden returns, he hands my dad a plate of juicy pork with a side of what looks like flattened and fried banana. Mom gets rice and chicken in a neat little bowl. My plate holds a sandwich that seems to contain pickles, ham, and cheese.

"This is a cubano," Hayden explains. "It doesn't look like much, but it's the best thing on the menu."

I take an uncertain bite and I'm blown away by the combination of flavors. Spices, sweetness, tang. "Alright. You win."

He winks at me and returns to the front of the restaurant with extra pep in his step.

After dinner, I head to the front counter. Hayden wiggles his fingers in a wave.

"Did you like it?" he asks as I grab a wad of napkins and start wiping my hands.

I nod. "I've never had Cuban food before."

He feigns a look of horror, his hands pressed against his heart, jaw dropped.

"Look, dude. Cuban food isn't huge in Portland. It's mostly sushi burritos and kale." I hold up my hands in faux defense.

His nose rises in disgust. "I've never had kale."

"Pro tip: don't."

A man with a bushy mustache, a friendly smile, and a slight limp exits the kitchen. He hands Hayden a paper bag and mutters something.

"On the house." Hayden passes me the bag. "They're buñ——" His voice cuts off as a pan loudly clangs in the kitchen.

I flick my index finger near my temple and shake my head. *"I don't understand."*

He takes a pen out of the cup on the counter and grabs the bag, writing on the paper. His tongue peeks out from between his lips in concentration. When he's done, he hands the bag back. I read his loopy, pretty cursive handwriting, then peek inside at the pile of sugary fried dough.

Buñuelos.

He starts to say something, then looks over his shoulder and whips dramatically back around to face me. "I have to go. See you at school. Cool?"

"Sure?"

Without further explanation, he darts into the kitchen and disappears into what I assume to be the walk-in freezer.

Hayden González-Rossi: king of New York, subject changes, and dramatic exits.

CHAPTER 10
HAYDEN

"Sooo... you and Casey seem to have gotten close," Paz says as he queues up FIFA. "Do you like her?"

We're sitting cross-legged on the floor of his postage stamp-sized bedroom, surrounded by chip bags and soda cans as we prepare to start one of our weekly Sunday-night gaming sessions. Paz's vintage eighties poster of a shirtless Rob Lowe watches over us from its spot above the staticky, archaic TV that's barely able to connect to his PS4.

"Yeah. She's cool," I answer.

"C'mon. You know what I mean. Do you *like* like her?" He waggles his brows and smirks.

I sigh heavily as I grab a gaming controller. "Why would you even ask me that? I've told you I'm not interested in dating anyone. Ever."

"Alright, alright. Damn. It was just a question!" Paz tsks. "Ready to get your ass handed to you?" He motions toward the PS4.

Ignoring him, I scroll through the team options and select Houston Dynamo to face off against Paz's Inter Miami. The in-game whistle blows, and my poorly rendered Dynamo player runs downfield, stealing the ball from Paz's player.

After a few minutes of silent gaming, I ask, "Do you think we would've stayed best friends this long if you hadn't started playing fútbol with me in fourth grade?"

Paz shoots me a look. Understandable, considering my question was totally out of the blue. "Of course we'd be friends."

"But is fútbol the only thing we have in common?"

I hope the answer is no. If the sole basis of our friendship is a mutual love for the sport, it'll crumble if I ever work up the nerve to admit my true feelings about playing.

"If you join the track team in the spring, we'll have that in common too!" he jokes—he's been trying to get me to join the team for a year now, while César's been lobbying for me to make béisbol my new spring activity. Hah. I can barely handle fútbol; the last thing I need on my plate is a second sport—different season or not.

When I don't reply, Paz sighs. "Why does it matter? We did start playing fútbol together. Also, we both think Camila Cabello's CINDERELLA dress was the ugliest thing ever, but that her 2021 VMAs look was iconic and extremely underappreciated. And—why are you looking at me like that?" Paz cuts himself off when he notices me staring.

"Just wondering how long you're going to rant about Camila Cabello's dress choices." I sigh. My player sends the ball sailing into Paz's goal, and he lets out a string of colorful curses.

We play two more rounds in silence, not counting the in-game sounds and smack talk. I switch my team both times, first to the Seattle Sounders, then to Atlanta United, but Paz remains committed to Inter Miami.

The silent spell is broken when Paz scores his third goal using number nine, also known as a computer-generated Hat-Trick Henry. The game finishes 4–0.

"Yes!" he exclaims. "What a stud." Wildly button-mashing, Paz has Henry run around the pitch doing the chicken dance as his celebration.

"Please don't call him a stud," I grumble, shoving a handful of chips in my mouth and sulking.

Paz sticks with Inter Miami yet again as he queues up the next game.

"Can you pick a different team?" I ask, scrolling through the options.

"Why? I'm on a winning streak."

"B-because I asked you to." My voice cracks like I'm thirteen, and I cough.

Paz cocks a brow. "Why are you being so weird?" He sets his controller down and finishes his third soda, then crushes the empty can.

"I'm not being weird," I scoff. "I'm asking you to change teams."

"Hayden. You are. True fact."

He's right. But I can't exactly tell him that I want him to switch teams so I don't have to see Henry, even in video game form. Because that sounds childish and petty.

Paz's hands grab mine, which makes me realize I've been absent-mindedly wringing them. "Okay, talk to me. What's wrong?" He turns to face me.

I pull my hands out of his grip, and everything comes pouring out before I can stop it. "I hate Henry."

Paz's jaw unhinges.

"No, no," I correct myself. "I don't hate him. I love him. But I don't even know who he is anymore, you know?"

His mouth snaps shut again.

"He was my best friend—I mean, besides you. But Henry is…Henry. We spent every second of our lives together until one day he just left. Like it was nothing. Like I was nothing."

A memory of the day Henry left flashes in my mind:

"Mamma, don't cry," Henry says, chuckling. He gives Mamma a hug and wipes her tears. "Fort Lauderdale is only forty minutes away! I'll see you guys all the time," he reassures us.

All of us—Tía and Tío, my cousins, Dino, Mamma and Papá—are gathered in our front yard to see him off. He works his way down the line, doling out hugs and joking lightheartedly about how things will be a little different, but he'll always be the same ol' Henry.

When he gets to me, he spouts some funny story about growing up that I barely register through my tears. Finally, he flashes his signature pearly grin and yanks me into a tight hug.

"I'm ... nervous," I whisper into his chest, voice quavering. It's not that I'm not happy for him—I am—but my whole family has already been going on about how I'll be filling Henry's shoes. How I'm expected to just magically be everything Henry was once he's gone. How proud Abuelo would be if he were here ...

"Nothing will change, Hay! Except, now, I can score you guys the best seats in the stadium," he jokes. "I'll text you all the time, okay? You'll probably get sick of me!" He glances toward the car Inter Miami sent to drive him to Fort Lauderdale. "I have to go. I'll call you guys as soon as I'm settled."

He gives Mamma another quick hug before jogging down the driveway. I raise my hand to wave goodbye, forcing myself to smile supportively, but he never looks back.

Just like that, my older brother, my best friend, leaves. And he can't even spare his family a second look.

Henry lied that day. Everything changed. I can't even remember the last time he texted me. Once he achieved his goal of becoming an MLS player, he became too good for his dorky, awkward, not-nearly-as-talented little brother.

I shake off the memory and turn my attention back to Paz. He's wide-eyed and frozen, digesting what I said. Eventually, he replies, "You're not nothing."

I laugh bitterly. "I'm nothing without Henry's name attached to mine."

"That's not true. Don't say that." Paz shakes his head.

"Really? Then who am I?"

His brows furrow and he chews his bottom lip. "You're Hayden. Why do you need to be anyone else?"

I laugh again, but this time it's a teary one. Loneliness engulfs me as I look at Paz and realize that he's not looking back at **me**. He's looking at the carefully crafted version of Hayden González-Rossi that I put on for the world. The responsible middle child, the Mom Friend, the team captain.

I've buried the real me so deep inside myself that even my best friend can't see.

"You have n-no idea who I am," I whisper, tears clouding my vision. My chest rises and falls heavily. "You've never seen the real me."

Paz tries to hide the hurt that crosses his face. "What are you talking about? I know you better than anyone."

I don't reply. I can't. Not when it feels like all of the pressure of earth's atmosphere is pressing against my chest. Leaving me breathless. Forcing me to hold more than I can take.

He squeezes my hand. "Show me, then. Show me the real you—whoever that is."

I stare at him, blinking away the wetness in my eyes.

"What are you waiting for? Show me. C'mon," he urges, almost goading me.

"I have a confession," I mumble.

"Awesome, I love those."

"You can't tell anyone."

He sticks his pinky finger in the air. "I swear on my father's life."

"But you hate your dad," I remind him.

"Oh my Go—do confessions usually take this long?!" he groans.

I shoot him a look.

"Okay, fine, I swear on Camila Cabello's life."

I steady my shaking hand enough to interlock our pinky fingers. A huge wave of vulnerability washes over me as Paz's finger curls around mine.

I've been keeping my musical aspirations a secret for years. It's not a simple dream to say out loud, or to try to explain to people. So, I've kept it locked away behind a wall of fútbol practice and family expectations. But at what cost? My happiness? My sanity?

Because here's the thing: when Casey saw the real me—even though I didn't intend it, even though it terrified me—I got a glimpse of what it might feel like on the other side of this secret. To be able to sing and dance, and be myself.

Although she probably doesn't realize it, she took some weight off my shoulders. But there's still too much to carry on my own. Secrets are heavy.

"I don't want to play fútbol," I blurt inelegantly.

Paz's face falls, but he withholds judgement. "¿Qué?"

"I want to be on Broadway."

Silence fills the room again. Paz blinks at me for a minute—an entire sixty seconds.

"Are you being serious?" he finally asks.

I nod. "I've been eavesdropping on Mamma's lessons for three years and applying the techniques to my own voice."

He scoots closer, listening intently as the rest of the story spills out.

"I haven't told anyone because there's all this pressure to be like Henry. To be the Floridian Broldans. Carry on the dynasty. But I'm not Cristian Roldan, Paz." I gulp.

He nods as I explain, listening to every word. After I finish, Paz wipes my tears away. "Lo siento. I didn't know you felt this way."

"My family would be so disappointed if I told them. I mean, my abuelo left his home country to pursue fútbol. My dad was the captain of the Barracudas and would've gone pro if he hadn't gotten injured during senior year. Henry is on his way to becoming a superstar, Dino will probably make varsity as a freshman, and not to mention, my tía would wring my neck!" I rant. "In what universe would they not be disappointed in me?"

Paz pulls me into a bone-crushing side hug. "You said you don't know who you are? You're Troy Bolton in HIGH SCHOOL MUSICAL. You have to break free." He says this with a completely straight face.

I laugh at the comparison. Leave it to Paz to bring up HIGH SCHOOL MUSICAL in a completely serious manner during a heart-to-heart.

I lean my head against his shoulder and smile to myself. That wasn't as scary as I'd thought. The world didn't burst into flames, and Paz didn't denounce our friendship. Progress.

"Thank you," I breathe.

"I'm always here for you. It doesn't matter if you like fútbol or Broadway. You're still my best friend. You're still my family." He squeezes my shoulder. "But I will warn you," he adds, "I am **not** a Chad."

"You're a total Sharpay."

Paz flips his locs with one hand. "Damn straight."

CHAPTER 11
CASEY

"CASEY! THERE YOU ARE!" MY MUSCLES TENSE UP WHEN A FAMILIAR VOICE chirps behind me as I stuff books into my locker during lunch break.

I take a deep breath before closing my locker and turning around, mentally preparing myself.

Sure enough, Audrey is standing nearby, flashing me an unnerving Cheshire cat grin. "I haven't seen you——why'd you stop——ASL club misses you!"

I don't believe her for a second. I bet she only misses having some-one around to feel superior to, by signing too fast for me to understand. But instead of saying that, I just stare at her, tightening my grip on my backpack straps.

My silence doesn't deter her (most unfortunately), and she continues, "The ASL Club wants to organize——ASL practice night——we'd love your participation!" Her speech gets lost in the background noise, but I don't care enough to ask her to repeat herself. "Can you join us for lunch?"

"No," I deadpan. I try to squeeze past her, but she blocks me.

She pats my shoulder patronizingly. "Ohhh, I think I get it now. You're embarrassed by how little ASL you know, right? It's okay. We love helping beginners, really!"

I scoff in her face and push her hand away. "Are you kidding me? You—"

"Hey, Casey," someone interrupts. I turn and see Lela approaching. She's smiling, but when she notices Audrey, her expression morphs into a frown.

"You can go, Audrey." Lela scowls, and for a split second she resembles César. "She's going to eat with us."

Audrey clenches her jaw and looks between us, apparently debating whether to reply. "Fine," she says eventually. "See you around, Casey." She leaves without another word.

Once Audrey is gone, Lela rolls her eyes. "God, she's such a busybody. You good?"

I swallow. "Uh. Sure. How do you know Audrey?"

"She's always——recruit transfer students and freshmen to her little club. I think——presidential sway over a group makes her feel important or something. Anyway"—Lela brushes it off with a flick of her wrist—"let's go." She loops her arm through mine and leads me toward the cafeteria.

"I don't like eating in the cafeteria," I mutter. "Thanks for your help with Audrey, though."

Before she has a chance to protest, I free myself from her grasp and push through Palmera's front doors. I groan as the direct sun hits me, instantly warming my skin. In early October back in Oregon, I'd be wearing sweaters, not crop tops.

I settle at the one table in the front courtyard that gets shade and unpack my homemade lunch. It's quiet out here, and I'm looking forward to a peaceful thirty-minute break.

I guess I don't necessarily mind hanging out with Hayden, Lela, or Paz (I might even, in a weird way, maybe, sort of like them), but whenever

I spend time with them my No Friends rule becomes harder to commit to, and I have to remind myself Hayden is just an anomaly.

Sure, he's accommodated me. But that doesn't mean the others will. Nobody has in the past. If I operate under the assumption that everyone else will be like him, I'll get hurt again. No Friends means no being treated like a circus attraction when they discover my hearing loss.

No Friends means I'm keeping myself safe.

I peel a banana and open the history book I checked out of the library last Saturday. Just as I'm about to go cross-eyed from all the outrageously fancy and unpronounceable French names, someone slams their lunch tray down on the other side of the table.

"Can you sit somewhere el—" The words die in my mouth when I look up from my book and find Paz settling onto the opposite bench. He's followed by Lela, then Hayden, and finally an obviously disgruntled César.

I scan the courtyard for an empty table I can relocate to, but by now they're all occupied. Damn it. I'm trapped.

I sigh and swallow my bite of banana, turning to Lela. "I told you I can't eat with you."

She shakes her head. "No, you said you don't like eating in the cafeteria. So, I brought everyone to you!"

"Yeah, and it's humid as hell out here," César mumbles. "Did we really have to——" his complaining fades to an indecipherable murmur and I glare at him.

Lela rolls her eyes. "You run around in eighty- and ninety-degree weather to play fútbol in October and béisbol in April, but you're going to complain about *sitting* at a table in the *shade*?"

"If it bothers him that much, he's free to go back inside," I add before turning to him and saying, "It wouldn't cause me any grief to not spend my lunch break with you."

In response, he raises the eyebrow that has a scar cutting through it and passive-aggressively shovels a bite of mushy cafeteria spaghetti into his mouth.

"Um, so…" Hayden starts, attempting to defuse the tension per usual. "Our last study session for the project is this weekend!"

"Correct."

"Er…are you excited? To be done?"

"Mm-hmm."

He blinks his hazel eyes at me, his smile awkward. I can tell he's trying his best to strike up a conversation, and it feels a little mean to watch him flail, but I'd be lying if I said it's not slightly entertaining. I fight a smile as he runs fingers through his unruly curls.

Eventually, I let him off the hook. "Speaking of which, Paz, you need to send me the pictures for the last few slides before we meet on Saturday. The Wi-Fi at the library is shit, so I can't download high-res files there."

Paz heaves a dramatic sigh and slumps forward. "It's always 'send this,' 'send that,' but never 'thank you for all of your hard work, Paz. We really appreciate you, Paz!'" When I simply stare at him, he continues, "Fine. I'll send——tonight. But can I have those?" He points to the Oreos I brought and juts his lower lip.

I roll my eyes and toss him the Ziploc bag. He blows me a kiss. "Do you play baseball too?" I ask Hayden and Paz, figuring if César plays it in the spring, they probably do too. They seem to be a trio.

"Nope. I run track and Hayden does absolutely nothing," Paz chirps, popping a whole cookie into his mouth.

"I don't do 'absolutely nothing'!" Hayden refutes. "I just don't play any other sports. And, well, this is probably sacrilege for me to say, but béisbol is kinda boring."

Paz snort-laughs and César heaves a disappointed sigh, but the topic is forgotten when Paz starts interrogating Lela about Gabriel.

It's easier to follow a conversation outside, but I still don't catch everything. I find myself tuning them out to preserve whatever dredges of auditory energy I have left, especially since I have a vocal lesson after school. I can't be completely exhausted.

As I'm polishing off my homemade PB&J, my phone buzzes on the table. I wipe jelly off my hands and pick it up. Onscreen, there's a message from @HeyitsHayden. I peer at him from over the top of my phone but he pointedly avoids eye contact.

Intrigued, I check the message.

Oct 5 at 1:23 PM

@HeyitsHayden You look tired. Do you have a headache because of the talking?

@Casey.K.Sings yeah but its not too bad. Paz is a blabbermouth tho

I look up from my screen again. Hayden's eyes are pointed toward his lap, secretly reading my reply under the table. There's something endearing about him discreetly checking on me while his friends chatter around him.

@HeyitsHayden Haha yeah, he is. So, I was thinking... since this Sat is our last study session...maybe we can hang out after? :D And please don't dodge my question again! It's been almost two weeks since I first asked!

@Casey.K.Sings i've spent years perfecting the art of evading questions. it adds to the whole sexy enigma thing i have going on

Seen 1:25 PM

At the dreaded 'seen' notification, I hazard another glance up. This time he's looking right at me with a frown, unamused by my antics. I guess I can see why he's annoyed. He's making a genuine effort, and I keep shooting him down. Yet, for God knows what reason, he hasn't given up. If anything, he's just doubling down, trying harder to befriend me.

The longer he stares at me, the softer his expression becomes, as if silently telling me he's okay with whatever I decide, but he **hopes** I'll say yes. And…well, maybe one hangout wouldn't be the end of the world.

After everything he's done for me…I can set my No Friends rule aside for one weekend. One.

Hoping I won't regret this, I type a response.

@Casey.K.Sings fiiine. 😊 let's study at my house and then u can stay for a bit after. only like 30 mins tho! i have to rest before ASL

@HeyitsHayden Deal!! Send me your address and I'll send it to Paz! See you on Saturday morning!! :D

CHAPTER 12
HAYDEN

ON SATURDAY MORNING, I HOP ON THE WEATHERED SKATEBOARD I bought at a yard sale last summer and sail down the residential streets of Miami.

According to my phone, Casey only lives ten minutes away. But the differences in our neighborhoods become starkly apparent when I turn the corner onto her street and find uniform rows of newly constructed houses, many with FOR SALE signs posted in lush front yards. Children speed by on their fancy, definitely-not-bought-at-a-yard-sale bikes, while yoga-pant-clad suburban moms chat in driveways.

I pass a sign that causes a laugh to buck in my chest: WELCOME TO CORAL GROTTO!

Lord, have mercy. Casey lives in a neighborhood with a ***name.***

I skid to a stop in front of a lackluster white house. I double-check the address she provided, then knock on the door.

Casey's dad answers. "¡Hola! ¿Cómo estás?" he greets me.

I take a step back, startled by the enthusiastic welcome. "Bien. ¿Qué bolá?"

"¡Estoy bien!" Mr. Kowalski claps his hands. "Come in, come in!"

Inside the color scheme is all-white. White floor, white furniture, white kitchen appliances. It kinda reminds me of Kim Kardashian's creepy mausoleum house, aside from a few things: family portraits on the living room walls, a blue rug under the coffee table, a vase of yellow tulips on the kitchen island.

By far the most unique thing about the house is the hairless cat that comes running up to me, its pink skin jiggling. I feel indecent looking at such a creature.

"That's Jell-O," Casey says from the staircase. "She's ugly, but she's sweet."

I smile and reach down to greet Jell-O. She sniffs my hand and flicks her tail in disdain before trotting off, mrrping. "I see why she's called Jell-O."

Mr. Kowalski laughs, but Casey must not hear my comment because she shoots her dad a confused look. *"J-E-L-L-O,"* I methodically finger-spell, then point to the cat. *"She's…"* I never thought I'd require the sign for 'jiggly.'

I flail my arms in a generally fluid way then fingerspell, *"J-I-G-G-L-Y."*

She laughs. *"Yes,"* she signs, then says, "Let's go to my room." She turns on the stairs, but her mom flaps her hand from the kitchen.

"What's up?" Casey asks.

Mrs. Kowalski requests she keeps the door open. Casey's eyes widen. She points to me, jams the fingertips of two curved hands to her chest, then touches her knuckles together by her heart, and moves her thumbs up and down like she's texting. Mrs. Kowalski's gaze settles on me, one brow raised.

I fidget with my Houston Dynamo jersey and try not to stare. I have no idea what she just signed to her mom. This must be how Casey feels around Hearing people—sometimes unable to understand more than a word or two. I catch her mom signing *"O-K,"* but that's all I recognize.

She leads me up the twisty staircase and into a much homier room. A white rug with sunflowers covers the hardwood floor. Her walls are decorated with an eclectic assortment of music-themed posters ranging from musicals (DEAR EVAN HANSEN, SHREK THE MUSICAL) to boy bands (DAYDREAM, One Direction) and even a few artists I don't recognize (Florence and the Machine, Stray Kids). A sleek electric keyboard is stationed near her desk, a shirtless firefighter calendar hanging above it. I decide not to question that.

"Nice," I smooth my right palm over my left, then, not knowing the sign, I say, "room."

"Room." She supplies the sign, then plops onto the sunflower rug and opens her laptop.

"Room." I repeat. I put both signs together. *"Nice room."*

Right as I sit across from her, Paz comes barreling in. Casey shoots him a disapproving look.

"You were supposed to be here twelve minutes ago," she chides.

"Well, damn, sorry I'm not perfect, Casey." He clasps a hand over his heart before sprawling out on the rug. "Your house is nice, by the way. Very gentrification-chic."

"Let's get started," Casey says, launching PowerPoint. "Paz, thanks for sending those photos. Hayden, do you have the notes on the…which treaty was it?" She looks up from her screen with a frown.

"Ugh, why does France have so many damn treaties, anyway?" Paz cries. "The Treaty of Paris, the Treaty of Versailles, Élysée Treaty. France is like the Oprah of treaties. 'You get a treaty, you get a treaty, everyone gets a treaty!'"

This earns a chuckle from Casey, but she quickly refocuses. "Hayden?"

"Oh, sorry. It's the Treaty of Alliance." I grab my handwritten notes about the terms and conditions of the treaty and start reading them to her. Until this project, my only knowledge of the Treaty of Alliance came from listening to "Guns and Ships" from HAMILTON.

At last, after thirty minutes of work, we all squish together with our backs pressed against Casey's bed to watch the final product and make sure we're all happy with it.

"It's okay," Paz hums after the slideshow ends. "But it'd be better with a slide about Timothée Chalamet."

I laugh. "Wasn't he born in America, though?"

"More importantly, he had no involvement in the Revolutionary War," Casey grumbles, then continues, "If you guys are okay with it, I'll add the music Hayden chose and put the slideshow on a flash drive for our presentation on Monday."

"Yeah, that sounds good!" I say.

Paz shrugs. "I guess. I'm just glad it'll be over before fútbol practice starts."

"Wait, what? Haven't you guys been in practice for weeks?" Casey asks, confused.

"No. That was Coach's boot camp. According to her, we're 'a bunch of losers who need extra practice to win the championship.' Official practice and varsity tryouts are next week," he explains.

Thank God tryouts are next week. Maybe then Dino will stop bouncing off the walls in anticipation.

"Um. Okay. Well, we're set here. You're free to go," she says jokingly, nudging Paz.

"Hurrah! The three musketeers part ways!" he exclaims, heading for her bedroom door. "Hay, you coming?"

I gulp and wrack my brain for an excuse. "No. Uhh…I want to double check the playlist."

Thankfully, he takes my lie at face value and leaves. Once he's gone, Casey and I sit awkwardly side by side, her shoulder pressing into mine. Neither of us says anything. My hands get clammy as I replay an ASL video in my head, anxiety swelling as I mentally run through repeating the signs to her.

Finally, I turn to face her. I point to myself, touch the fingertips of two bent hands to my chest, and end by hooking my pointer finger into a question mark.

She nods and waits for me to ask my question. After a long beat of me not saying or signing anything, she chuckles and pokes my knee. "What's up?"

"Can…you teach…me…sign?" I sign, saying a silent prayer that I remember the grammar.

Casey's eyes narrow. "Where'd you learn that?"

"Online."

"Damn." She releases a low whistle. "You're getting good."

A blush spreads across my cheeks. "Will you? Teach me?"

"I'm still learning ASL. I'm not qualified."

"We can learn together!" I suggest.

"I don't know." She stands up and looks out her window, face twisted into an unreadable, tense expression.

I pushed her too far, didn't I? After everything that happened between us, she was already hesitant to hang out with me. Why did I think it would be a good idea to bring up ASL lessons so soon? What if she thinks I pity her, or have some hidden, nefarious motivation? She probably hates me now! I've ruined our fledgling friendship before it had the chance to begin—

"Earth to Hayden?"

Casey's words draw me out of my thoughts. Her eyes flicker to my trembling hands. She looks concerned.

I force my hands to stop shaking and paste on what I hope is a relaxed smile. That's me. Relaxed. Go with the flow. A cool guy. Oh yeah. Totally.

"What'd you say?" I ask after the lump in my throat dissolves.

"Are you sure?" she repeats in ASL, pointer finger dropping from her chin.

I knock my fist twice. *"Yes."* I might not be sure of much, but I'm committed to this.

"Well…I can't **teach** you," she emphasizes, "but…I guess we could practice on Wednesdays, after my singing lessons." She offers a hesitant smile.

"Yes!" The timing is perfect. I get home from fútbol practice right as Casey's vocal lesson is ending, and my cousins work the Wednesday shift at El Pollo Cubano. "I want to be able to talk with you in ASL. I know you get headaches from too much verbal input."

Her brows knit, eyes glued to my lips. "I get red eggs?"

I press my pointer, middle finger, and thumb together. *"No."* I grab my phone and type a message.

I want to learn ASL because you get bad headaches from people talking.

"Oh, headaches!" She laughs, returning my phone. "Damn. I really have to hone my lipreading skills."

My lips curl into a smile. I don't think I've heard her really laugh before now. It's bright and airy, like a soft violin that ties a whole orchestra together. Subtle but important.

I like it when she laughs. I'd like to make her laugh again.

She notices Jell-O standing on her keyboard and whisks the cat off it. I type a new message. I'm nervous I'll offend her or make it seem like I'm challenging her identity, but curiosity outweighs my trepidation.

How does being deaf/hoh work exactly? I know what deaf means and I know what hoh means, but how can you be both?

My hand trembles as I turn the screen toward her. Her eyes scan the message. A blink-and-you'll-miss-it frown crosses her face.

She sits back down and dumps the purring, cat-shaped lump of flesh into my lap. Jell-O kneads my khaki shorts and headbutts me. I suppose we've completed our incredibly brief enemies-to-friends arc.

"In general, my ears function at about fifty-percent volume. I can't hear whispers, or the letter 'H,'"—Casey nudges me and chuckles softly—"and there are whole pockets of sound I can't hear at all. Like…" She stands and moves toward her keyboard, turns it on, and plays a C above middle C. "I can't hear anything above this, or anything below this." The next note is a D below middle C.

Not wanting to startle her, I tap her shoulder as I come to stand behind her. "You're deaf when it comes to certain pitches?"

She nods and her messy bun comes undone, brown waves cascading down her pale face. She scoops her hair back up.

I take the opportunity to run my fingers against the smooth plastic keys. I smile at the small stickers on each key that label the notes. They bring back a childhood memory: five-year-old me squished next to Mamma on the piano bench, scanning the notes while my tiny fingers plunked "Mary Had a Little Lamb," falling in love with music.

My heart starts beating quicker and the air in the room thickens. I take a deep breath and push the memory out of my mind. "D-do you play?" I ask her, gesturing toward the keyboard.

"Not really. I can't read sheet music, but I try my best." She notices my hand position, fingers lined up. They naturally fall into place whenever there's a piano nearby. "Play me something." Casey nudges me. "I need to hear your musical genius again."

"I'm not a musical genius."

"Ugh, protégé. Maestro. Whatever you prefer. Now play." She slaps my upper arm.

My fingers hover over the keys as I mentally run through my repertoire. She already heard "No Good Deed," and Beethoven is too old-school for my taste, but unfortunately that's the majority of what I have memorized. Except for the entire HIGH SCHOOL MUSICAL soundtrack, which Paz made me learn to fulfill one of his deranged fantasies.

Based on Casey's affinity for Broadway, I have a feeling HIGH SCHOOL MUSICAL is the way to go.

I give into my inner Troy Bolton and begin playing "Breaking Free."

She rests her hand on the keyboard's speaker and examines my fingers as they drift from key to key. Her eyes shut and she brings her other hand to her throat as she hums along, perfectly in tune.

I close my own eyes and let memory guide me through the song. During the second part of the chorus, I start to sing softly while I play. I keep my voice quiet on purpose, hoping she won't hear, but my eyes flutter open when she gasps. Not quiet enough, I guess.

"Wow, you sing too? Is there anything you can't do?"

Hah. Function like a normal human being, maybe?

"I'm nowhere as talented as you," I admit.

"Mm, well, my talent has gone down the drain."

"What?" I recoil. "You have a beautiful voice."

"I didn't sing properly for months. My vocal cords went stagnant." She sighs heavily.

Casey and I are more alike than I realized. I hide my love for music away, and she's lost her confidence. We both have musical trust issues.

Anxiety flirts with my psyche as an idea comes to me. "Sing a duet with me right now," I challenge her.

I'm surprised by my boldness. My usual audience is shampoo bottles and a loofah, not another human. But for some reason, my heartbeat doesn't speed up and my palms don't go sweaty at the thought of singing with her. She's already seen my other two performances, and I don't want to sound cocky, but my vocals are miles ahead of my tap dancing.

Casey huffs a laugh. "Yeah, no."

"Oh. Okay." I gulp. And just like that, my self-assurance disappears.

We stand by her keyboard avoiding eye contact, the epitome of awkward.

Finally, she exhales sharply. "Fine. One song."

"Seriously?"

"Start playing before I change my mind, Mozart."

My fingers automatically find the perfect placement and start playing. Her bedroom is filled with the opening notes to "Breaking Free."

She interrupts my flow. "Wait, wait."

"What's wrong?" I chew my lip, expecting her to back out of the impromptu duet.

"I have an odd request…" She shuffles uncomfortably. "Can I feel your throat? The vibrations of your vocal cords will help me harmonize better."

I send her a reassuring smile. "Of course."

I take her hand and place it on my Adam's apple, then start the song over from the beginning. The tone is off, the sound gritty, but I give the keyboard some leeway. It'll never measure up to a baby grand.

Casey reads my lips as I sing and keeps her fingers on my throat. When she joins in, her voice is soft and tentative at first, but she grows in confidence when we reach the main chorus and a breathtaking high belt pours out of her. Her high notes combine with my low, a seamless ebb and flow.

We start improvising, riffing on the original piece, turning an old song into something new. A smile spreads across her face and I smile right back.

My fingers still and the song concludes. Unexpectedly, she laughs and pulls me into a hurried hug as I come down from my musical high.

"Casey, your voice isn't stagnant. It's incredible," I say after we separate.

She looks up at me through her eyelashes, scanning me for insincerity, but she won't find any. I'm telling the truth.

Her voice is remarkable—her effortless high belt, graceful mixed voice, and striking tone in the lower register; the way she intuitively knows what notes are being played and how to match them even without the ability to hear them.

"Maybe…" She stops to think through her next sentence. "Maybe we can sing together again. Like, regularly."

My hand nervously scrunches the fabric of my jersey. I've been taking small steps with music—opening up to Casey, confessing my aspirations to Paz, singing in front of someone else—but this seems an awful lot like jumping into the deep end.

As if reading my mind, she takes my hand, her expression softening. "You're the first person who's tried with me since I lost my hearing. I realize I've been…well, a little bit of a dick, and we've had a lot of ups and downs in the month we've known each other…but I really do appreciate the effort. It would be a shame if your voice went to waste."

I slow my breathing and give her hand a squeeze. This feels like a breakthrough. I think I'm slowly chipping away at her layers and revealing what's underneath. I'm starting to trust her, and it looks like the feeling might be mutual.

"You want to sing again? For real?" I ask.

"*Yes*," she signs. "Your voice is beautiful; you should be showing it off more. But we don't have to."

I let go of her hand and grab my phone. She waits patiently while I type. Jell-O makes her own music as she walks across the powered-up keyboard.

If you practice ASL with me, I'll sing with you.

Casey chuckles as she reads my note. Her smile is radiant and genuine, filling me with warmth. *"D-E-A-L."*

CHAPTER 13
CASEY

IT'S NICE TO HAVE A SATURDAY MORNING TO MYSELF AGAIN SINCE HAYDEN, Paz, and I presented our slideshow on Monday. But I'm glad Hayden and I still get to hang out on Wednesdays for ASL practice.

I'm done pushing him away. I was convinced he'd would give up wanting to become friends, but he proved me wrong and stuck around. And somehow, we've reached a new level of friendship.

When we sang together, it felt right. I wasn't worrying about how I sounded or stumbling over notes I can't hear anymore.

So, being the mastermind I am, I've come up with a plan that will (I hope) help Hayden feel more relaxed when we sing together.

I send him a DM as I'm leaving ASL class.

Oct 15 at 2:17 PM

@Casey.K.Sings u at home?

@HeyitsHayden No. El Pollo Cubano.

@Casey.K.Sings ur shift almost over?

@HeyitsHayden Yeah, I worked the early shift so I'm off in 15 mins. Why?

@Casey.K.Sings do u have plans after?

@HeyitsHayden No…why?

@Casey.K.Sings yay! meet me outside when ur off duty
@HeyitsHayden WHY??

I put my phone back in my pocket as I sign goodbye to Briana and walk out of the classroom with Mom and Dad in tow.

Dad tucks me under his arm as we walk to the parking lot. "You are getting fast at signing. You will be fluent before too long."

"Briana is a wonderful teacher!" Mom jumps in. "I wonder if she'd be open to doing online lessons after we move back to Portland."

For some weird reason, the mention of returning home makes me frown, but I shake off the feeling.

"Hey," I say to Dad when we're in the car, "can we stop by El Pollo Cubano? I might've told Hayden we'd pick him up…"

In hindsight, I should've asked for permission before telling him to meet me.

Dad frowns. "We were going to make kluski śląskie this afternoon. Mom already bought the ingredients."

"I forgot about that when I invited him over," I say. "Can we make it another time?"

"Mój Boże, there is no loyalty in this family," Dad sighs.

Mom leans over and whispers something to Dad. I don't hear what she says, but afterward he agrees to pick Hayden up, saying I better not flake on our upcoming family STAR TREK marathon.

Dad turns on the radio, and his annoying Polish accordion music drifts into the back seat. I roll my window down, the warm wind messing up my hair as we fly down the street.

Outside the restaurant, Hayden sits on the curb, chatting with César. When Hayden sees our car, he hops up and waves goodbye to his cousin. César spots me and his lips curl into a grimace. I match the expression and we have a staredown, like we're in an old Wild West movie.

Hayden gets into the car and César stalks back into the restaurant.

Before buckling up, he hands Mom a paper bag. "I brought these for you guys."

"Thank you!" She brings a hand down from her chin and looks inside the bag. "What are these called again?"

"Buñuelos," Dad, Hayden, and I answer in unison.

Hayden and I start snickering, and Mom peeks into the back. Her eyes flit between him and me. She gives a knowing smile.

"He has a boyfriend," I tell her in sign.

She chuckles before turning back toward the windshield.

At home, I drag him to my room, not wanting him to be cajoled into joining Dad's Polish dumpling cooking party.

"Thank you for the ride!" he calls out, waving at my parents as we run upstairs.

I slam my door and yank my hair into a low bun as he walks over to my bed and takes a seat next to Jell-O, awkwardly stroking her wrinkly skin. "Uh…what am I doing here?"

I open the drawer on my bedside table, retrieve a noise-canceling Bluetooth headset, and connect it to my phone. He watches, trying to figure out what I'm doing.

"At our last lesson, your mom said my hearing loss is actually sort of a strength for me, singing-wise," I explain. "You know how most singers tend to feel anxious about hitting extreme notes? High or low?" He nods like an effin' bobblehead while I explain. "Well, your mom and I sort of figured out that those notes don't intimidate me anymore. Because I can't hear them now, I don't have that mental block."

I hold the headset out to an apprehensive Hayden. He must realize where I'm going with this. "If I take away your auditory cues, it may make you more comfortable with singing. You won't judge yourself because you can't hear yourself."

He shakes his head, curls dancing. "No, no, no! I can't!"

"Why not?"

He wrings his freckle-kissed hands. "I just can't, okay?"

I walk to him and smile reassuringly. "You're safe with me."

He stares for a long moment, hands nervously bunching his shirt. Finally, he exhales slowly, nods, and puts the headset on.

I hold my left arm horizontally and swing my right hand in a wide 'U' shape over it, then, brows downturned, I form two thumbs up in front of my chest and alternate raising and lowering them. *"Which song?"*

He chews his lip, nervously teetering in front of my bed. "'Anti-Hero'?" He shrugs.

I launch Spotify and play the song.

His chest rises as he takes a deep inhale, screwing his eyes shut. His lips start moving but I don't pick up on any sound.

I recognize the signs of anxiety taking hold of him. Wringing hands, shaky breathing, heavy swallowing. I take one of his hands. He opens his eyes and looks into mine. I squeeze, wordlessly telling him I know how terrifying it is to put yourself out there.

Hayden cranks the volume on his voice, and sound waves tickle my ears. His body begins to relax, shoulders dropping from their defensive position. He taps his throat and offers a small, nearly imperceptible nod, inviting me to place my hand over his vocal cords. When I do, I feel them vibrate as he produces rich, beautiful tone. The pulsations become stronger as he slips into low chest voice.

His cords move more and more slowly as he delivers the final note. The sound echoes through my fingertips long after he's stopped singing.

He refuses to look at me as he removes the headset.

"Hayden…your voice is like taking a walk in autumn."

A smile creeps onto his face. *"What?"*

"The trees rich with color, vibrant and powerful. But also the calming sensation of crisp leaves crunching in just the right way."

He laughs, his braces showing. "The way you see things is so beautiful. You live in another dimension. You came up with that description when you only heard, what, half of the actual singing?"

"I'm learning that sound can be overrated when you can feel music in your bones. It's electric…" I trail off, a familiar light bulb switching on above my head as I say the words 'it's electric.' My songwriting light bulb.

I spin on my heels and grab the yellow notebook off my desk, flipping to an empty page and scribbling down the words. They may turn into a song someday.

"What's that?" Hayden asks.

I peer at him over the top of the notebook. "My songwriting journal."

"Wait…you write songs? Why didn't you tell me that?"

"Because songwriting is terrifying. I've written my soul into the pages of this book. And someday, when people hear my songs, they'll know my innermost thoughts and say anything they want about them."

He takes a seat at the edge of my bed. "I get that. Being yourself, being honest, is hard."

I sit next to him. "Plus, I can't ever put instrumental to my songs. I'm no Mozart," I jab him playfully.

"Maybe I can help with that," he suggests. "If you're comfortable showing me the lyrics, I can come up with an accompaniment to some of your songs. We can have an Elton John and Bernie Taupin moment," he jokes.

The idea makes me wary. But he's already shared so much of himself. Revealed the hidden corners of his personality to me. Maybe I can trust him with my hidden parts, too.

I hand him the book.

He runs his fingers along the smooth leather cover, then gingerly flips through pages jam-packed with things I've never said out loud—things I can only confront by writing them into a song.

He stops at my most recently completed song, "Lionhearted Girl." His face screws in concentration as he reads some of the words.

FEARLESS BUT ALONE, SHE HAS NOWHERE LEFT TO GO.

THAT LIONHEARTED GIRL, SHE IS BRAVE, SHE IS STRONG.

BUT SHE IS LOST NOW HER WORLD IS A WHISPER.

"Send me a video of you singing this," Hayden says. "I have an idea."

CHAPTER 14
CASEY

WHEN MY VOCAL LESSON ENDS ON WEDNESDAY, I'M FILLED WITH A SENSE of satisfaction. Taylor and I started working on "She Used to Be Mine" from WAITRESS—a notoriously difficult song, full of notes I can't hear. It went remarkably smoothly, and we made a lot of progress.

As soon as I leave the music room, I'm snapped out of my musical daze when I smack into Hayden. The boy has an unparalleled talent for lurking.

"Oh gosh, sorry!"

Taylor places her hands on my shoulders and steadies me. "Are you alright?" Her tone is concerned, but there's an amused smile on her face.

"I'm fine." I reply. "Someday you're going to give me a concussion," I grumble at him.

As we start to leave, Taylor asks, "Hayden, have you written Henry a birthday card yet?"

"Yeah, uh, I'll totally write one soon. Anyway, Casey and I have to go now." He clumsily tries to exit the conversation.

"Wait, who's Henry?" I ask.

Taylor frowns at her son. "You've never mentioned Henry?"

He instantly tenses up. "I dunno." He stares at the floor.

"Henry is Hayden and Dino's older brother." Taylor beams, visibly proud of this Henry character. "He plays for Inter Miami."

Hayden doesn't look up, too focused on picking at his nailbeds and chewing his lip.

"Inter Miami…is that a soccer team?" I ask Taylor.

"Inter Miami is David Beckham's team," she clarifies.

"Oh! He's the guy married to Posh Spice, right?"

Suddenly, Hayden starts laughing. Then his laughter turns into coughing. Or maybe his coughing turns into laughter? It's hard to tell.

"What?" I ask using SimCom. "What did I say?"

"Nothing." He wipes tears from his eyes. "I'll write a card tomorrow, Mamma."

Before Taylor can reply or I can ask why Hayden never told me about the existence of a third González-Rossi brother, he takes my hand and leads me upstairs to his room.

This is my first time in here. I do a slow turn and take it all in: shelves filled with soccer trophies, twin bed pushed into one corner, and a huge terrarium in the other corner that takes up half the space in the cramped bedroom.

I walk over to the tank and I'm greeted by a lizard sprawled out under a heat lamp.

He kicks random piles of clothes under his bed and throws a towel around his neck. He introduces his roommate. "That's Buñuelo, my emotional support iguana."

I lean down and look into the lizard's beady reptile eyes. "Can I hold him?"

He nods, takes the lid off of the tank, and scoops Buñuelo up by his chubby belly. "Be careful, he likes to lick people."

"Well, hello, Buñuelo." I cradle the lizard in my arms, taking a seat on Hayden's bed. "I'm Casey. But your father informed me you may view me as a human-flavored lollipop, hm?"

Buñuelo flicks his tongue across my cheek.

"I'm going to take a quick shower, be right back." He motions to his sweaty, fresh-out-of-soccer-practice self and heads into the hallway. Buñuelo settles into my lap, nuzzling me like Jell-O would. He's a very cat-like lizard.

I take the opportunity to snoop around Hayden's room. Holding Buñuelo in one arm, I poke around his shelves, smiling at family photos and judging his taste in literature. His closet door is open, so I take a quick peek inside, and my interest is caught by an old acoustic guitar covered in stickers, some clearly older and faded: The Who, Jimmy Carter 1976, the Stonewall Riot. But there are newer, brighter ones too: a holographic iguana, a heart with the asexual pride colors, and a palm tree.

Wow. So, Hayden is a powerhouse. He plays guitar, piano, soccer, and has a stunning voice. But he undersells himself. He doesn't believe in himself.

I can't blame him for that. I'm the same way.

Buñuelo and I are engaged in an interesting dialogue about the constitutional rights of iguanas when Hayden returns, a mess of damp hair falling in his eyes.

"Ready?" I sign, shaking the letter 'R.'

He nods, places Buñuelo back in his tank, and sits next to me on the bed. "Before we get started, I wanted to show you something." He pulls up a video on his phone and presses play.

130

The video starts with him sitting on the mop bucket in front of the spinet piano. The closet is dark since there aren't working lights inside, but I can see his tongue poking out in concentration. Then my song starts to flow through the phone speakers.

Tears well in my eyes as Video Hayden begins singing. My words—my deepest, rawest emotions—combine with his accompaniment to create a tenacious, defiant piece with somber undertones. He's captured the meaning behind the lyrics perfectly.

"That lionhearted girl, she's been brave for far too long." Video Hayden delivers the final verse, and the recording stops.

Real Hayden turns to me and gauges my reaction. "I can change it if—"

"No!" I interrupt, startling him. "Sorry. Please don't change it. It's perfect." I take his phone and send myself the video.

"I'm glad you like it. I can do more if you want." He smiles brightly.

Putting myself out there was a risk, but it paid off. My songs aren't going to stay trapped in my notebook any longer.

"I'd love that," I laugh in disbelief, blinking tears away. "Thank you. You don't know what this means to me."

"Send me more songs when you get the chance, I'll play around with them. But now, you owe me some ASL practice."

I pause for a beat to recover from hearing my song for the first time, then spread an array of papers between us. He watches, curious.

"Do you know how to 'sing' the ABCs?" I gesture toward the chart with the ASL alphabet on it.

He shrugs, right hand twisting side to side. *"Kind of?"*

"Let's start with that. *A-B-C-D...*" I sing as I form each letter. Not my best work, vocally. But good enough.

"E-F-G." He copies my handshapes, messing up here and there, but correcting himself on the fly. *"X-Y-Z."* He smiles, looking accomplished, then realizes I'm still going.

I'm still using SimCom—or SingCom, I guess. 'Y' shaped hands move downward from my shoulders, I tap the fingertips of a bent hand to my temple, place a flat palm to my chest, and spell ABC. *"Now I know my ABCs."* I press my flat right hand to the backs of the fingers on my left hand and bump the right hand forward; then I bounce my right index finger off the back of my left wrist, point to Hayden, and wave my right hand in a U-shaped arc over my horizontal left arm; then I press my fists together, thumbs up; I point to myself; and finally rub a flat palm over my chest. *"Next time won't you sing with me?"*

He watches in awe. After I'm done, he claps. "Now that was musical genius."

"It's only the alphabet." I shrug. "Do it with me now!"

He follows my instructions, gaining traction as we progress. After several repetitions, we get through the entire song. He struggles to remember "sing," so I tell him to imagine he's conducting an orchestra. He doesn't mess up after that.

We run through basic conversations. I play the part of a stranger introducing myself and ask Hayden's name. He replies by slowly finger-spelling, his wrist dipping with each letter. Like how Mom spells.

"No bouncing," I correct him. "If you bounce your wrist"—I demonstrate by jerking my hand up and down—"it's really hard to see what you're spelling."

His second attempt is devoid of obnoxious bouncing. He thrusts a flat palm toward me, taps an 'H' over another 'H,' then shakes an upturned palm back and forth. *"What's your name?"*

"My name is C-A-S-E-Y. My sign name is"—I show him my sign name.

"Whoa, whoa, hold on." His features twist in confusion. "What is a 'sign name?' How do I get one? I don't want to spell my name constantly!"

I do my best to explain what sign names are. Hearing people often underestimate the sacredness, so I make sure to reiterate it.

"Only Deaf people can give sign names?" Hayden asks.

"Right."

"So…can you give me a sign name?"

"You can't ask a Deaf person for a sign name. It has to be freely given." His face falls and he starts to apologize, but I cut him off. "Okay, look, I think I might be breaking the rules but…since you asked so nicely…"

He smiles. "Thanks."

I never thought giving someone a sign name would be so much pressure. I find myself struggling to come up with a good one. Something that conveys Hayden's indescribable spirit.

I study him. He's sort of like the human embodiment of an anxious golden retriever—jittery, but pure-hearted with a contagious smile.

After serious consideration, I form an 'H,' then make two upward strokes near the corner of my mouth. *"Hayden."* I use SimCom.

"Wow, I love it!" he gasps. *"Hayden. Hayden. Hayden. Hayden."*

I laugh at the repetition. "This means *smile*," I make the same movement, this time with both my right and left index fingers. "And obviously this is '*H*,' for Hayden."

"It's…*beautiful.*" He waves a hand over his face and closes his fingertips by his chin. Then he forms a new sign. His index finger, pinky, and thumb stick upward, and his middle and ring fingers are tucked into his palm. The sign means "I love you," but using SimCom, he says, *"I love it."*

I kiss my closed fist. *"Love it. KissFist,"* I correct, using SimCom. "You said you love me."

A deep, rosy blush spreads across his cheeks, but before he has a chance to dwell on the embarrassment, Dino barges in.

"Mamma told me to tell you dinner's ready. Casey, would you like to join us?" Disinterested, he recites this like it's a script he's memorized.

"No thanks, I have to go." I stand up and give Hayden a hug, lingering for as long as I can. Breaking my No Friends rule might be paying off. Just a smidge.

"See you tomorrow, *Hayden*." I wink, using his sign name for the very first time.

CHAPTER 15
HAYDEN

IT'S BEEN A WEEK SINCE OUR FIRST SIGNING PRACTICE, AND I'VE BEEN reciting the ASL ABCs nonstop to prep for my meet-up with Casey after her voice lesson tonight. But there's something else on my mind as I head to school: today, results from the several rounds of varsity tryouts will finally be posted. Dino's been bouncing around all morning, incessantly chattering about the tryout process and the other candidates.

When we finally get to school, he races toward the bulletin board in the front office. I have a feeling he's made the team. His 'hocus pocus' is iffy, but in general, Dino's technique rivals Henry's.

When I step into the office, César is lifting Dino into the air, grinning, and hugging him. "The legacy is complete!" he cheers. "Welcome to the team, 'Alex.'"

"Ha. Ha." I force a laugh at the inevitable comparison to Alex Roldan, the youngest Broldan. "Congrats, Dino," I add unenthusiastically as I read the other names on the list. There are going to be a lot of new faces at our first official practice of the season this afternoon—a lot of people who expect me to be the perfect captain…

"Now"—César claps Dino's shoulder and leans in conspiratorially—"if you ever want to join a spring sport, I could teach you some béisbol tricks."

While César continues promoting his béisbol-is-the-second-best-sport agenda, Paz pulls me into a bear hug. "You okay?" he whispers, standing on tiptoes to reach my ear. I wrap my arms around him and bury my face in his locs.

When I don't reply, Paz pulls away, concerned. We relocate to a corner of the front office as the other fútbol hopefuls crowd around the results. "Why haven't you quit already?" he asks, still whispering.

It's a valid question. Paz has been waiting for me to quit the team since I confided in him. And I've tried! I've lingered outside Coach's office every day. I just can't bring myself to knock on the door.

I mess with one of his long locs. "I dunno."

"Coach will find a replacement. You don't have to worry about that."

"I feel like you're pressuring me," I say a bit too loudly, pushing Paz away.

All eyes land on us. Even the mean office lady squints at us. César's eyebrow jumps—the one with the silly line cutting through it that he wants everyone to think is a cool scar (he actually shaves it). "You guys good?" he asks.

I tuck Paz's loc behind his ear. "Lo siento, amigo mio."

"It's okay." He smiles, his hurt expression fading.

Through the office window I see Casey enter the school. She cranes her neck in search of our group—we usually hang out on the main staircase before classes start. I raise my hand to wave at her, but Hurricane Audrey swoops in before she can see me.

She shoves a paper toward Casey. Casey jolts, startled by Audrey's sudden appearance, and her eyes double in size.

Audrey Simons is a jump scare incarnate. You never see her coming, but when she shows up, you run away.

Casey frowns as Audrey signs at warp speed.

Feeling like the guy who saves baby ducks from greasy ponds in Dawn soap commercials, I make a beeline for them, waving to catch Casey's attention. A look of relief crosses her frazzled features. I throw my arm around her shoulders and smile. I twist my free thumb upward, then point at Casey. *"How are you?"*

She lowers her flat right hand from her chin, resting it palm-up in her left hand. *"Good!"*

"I wanted to ask—"

My perfect excuse is interrupted by Audrey's annoyed huff. *"Since when have you known sign language?"* she speaks as she signs, her blue eyes scanning me.

"A while. Casey's helping me."

Her eyes narrow and it immediately makes me uneasy. *"Well, I guess you can come too,"* she signs and speaks, clearly irritated by my presence.

"Come to *what*?" I sign what I can remember and say the rest at a volume Casey can hear.

Audrey thrusts one of her flyers toward me. *"The ASL Club's doing a chat night every Thursday. It's open to all levels. Even people who are in the verrrry early stages, like yourself,"* she speaks and signs.

Nice subtle burn, Audrey.

She turns to Casey and continues signing and speaking. *"I'm sorry the ASL Club made a bad first impression. I hope you'll give us another chance. It'd be awesome to have you!"* Her fake smile disappears as César lumbers over, nostrils flared and arms crossed.

"I hope you're not bothering anyone. Again." César sizes her up. He glances at Casey, then at me.

Audrey scoffs. "I'm not bothering anyo—"

Casey rolls her eyes at César. "Dude. Mind your business. This seriously doesn't involve you."

Audrey jerks her head up and down. "Right! We're fine. We're friends."

"Yeaah, okay, I definitely wouldn't go that far." Casey takes a step back, shooting Audrey a disapproving look. "Audrey was just leaving," she says, shooing her away.

Audrey doesn't need to be told twice. She scurries down the hall and disappears into a swarm of ASL Club minions.

"You really think you own this school, and that you can just butt into other people's conversations, hm?" Casey grumbles at César.

He takes a sharp inhale. "I wasn't butting in for your benefit." He glances at me, then back to Casey. "You're awful presumptuous."

"Oh my God, what is your problem?" she groans.

"Well, one of my problems"—César inches closer but Casey crosses her arms defiantly instead of backing up—"is people who show up to a new school, disrupt a routine, intrude on a friend group, and don't follow house rules."

She scoffs. "Oh, I'm sooo sorry I forgot to follow your arbitrary edicts, Your Majesty." She mimics a curtsey, tone dripping with sarcasm. "Maybe one of your fangirls can do that instead." She gestures toward the gaggle of girls hovering nearby. Those same girls used to obsess over Henry, but I guess now that Henry has graduated, César is their new fixation.

Apparently, being elected captain doesn't automatically increase your crush appeal, though, since the "fangirls" (as Casey dubbed them) glommed onto my cousin instead of me. But since I have zero interest in romantic or physical relationships, I'm relieved things worked out this way.

César cracks a small, satisfied smile. "Well, at least you finally apologized."

She grits her teeth. "You're a real sweetheart, aren't you?"

"The sweetest." He winks before turning on his heels and leaving. Lela and Paz fall into step behind him. Casey shoots daggers at his back as he walks away. Halfway to the staircase, César stops and calls over his shoulder, "Hay. Let's go."

"*Sorry,*" I sign to Casey, rubbing an apologetic fist over my chest. "Are you okay? Do you want me to walk you to class?"

"No, go ahead. His Majesty has beckoned you." She gives a final eyeroll before heading to her locker.

I jog to catch up to César as he climbs the stairs. "You really don't have to be so rude to her," I mumble.

He cocks a brow. "Without knowing anything about me, she accused me of being an entitled jerk. How is **she** not the rude one?"

"To play devil's advocate"—Lela loops an arm through her older brother's—"you **are** a jerk and you're also being a bit entitled over your desk. It's a piece of wood. Why is it worth all this drama?"

"It's the principle of the matter," he tsks. "She can't just waltz in and expect everything to go her way—especially since her dad is taking job opportunities away from locals."

"You're such a bonehead," Paz chimes in as we reach Palmera's second floor. "Did you decide that your dad should be a chef? Or your mom should be a fútbol coach? No. It's not like Casey can control what her parents do, so I don't see how her dad's job is a valid reason to dislike her."

"Shut up, Paz." César sucks his teeth. "I can dislike whoever I want."

"Okay, but consider this…" Lela pulls César to a halt. "**We** all like her. You're the only one who doesn't. Wouldn't that seem to indicate this is a **you** problem? Hmm? You should just clear the air. This is painful for all of us."

"No! It's a **her** problem," he insists. "I didn't start this, so if she wants to clear the air, she's free to do that."

I sigh and exchange exasperated looks with Lela and Paz.

What makes this situation even more frustrating is that César and Casey have a lot more in common than they think, though that's probably why they can't stand each other. Is it some unspoken rule, like opposites attract, that similar people automatically despise each other?

"You'll figure it out," I mutter, trying to be supportive without taking sides. I am Switzerland in this feud—completely neutral. I have to be, since they're two of my closest friends. "If you and Casey just spent more time together, I think you'd actually like each other."

César shoots me the most incredulous look I've ever seen. "Yeah. That's going to happen."

CHAPTER 16
CASEY

PALM TREES SWAY IN THE WARM OCTOBER BREEZE AND A FLOCK OF cranes flies overhead as I sink onto the warm Astroturf of the soccer field during lunch period.

"Hey." Paz pokes Lela's thigh as she pulls food out of her backpack. "Can I have your brownie?"

"Absolutely not." She clutches the dessert protectively.

He slumps against Hayden and retrieves his own food from his messenger bag. Hayden's arm hangs lazily around Paz's shoulder. "My mom never packs me dessert," Paz complains. "She thinks sugar gives you cancer or something."

"Wha di——rey——wan?" Dino interrupts through a mouthful of chips. He looks directly at me and I try to play it cool, but have absolutely no idea what he said. I look from Dino to Hayden, trying to subtly ask for context.

From where he's sitting next to Hayden and Paz, César squints at me, following the conversation closely. Why is he so nosy? Don't boys usually stay out of drama?

Hayden stares at me, confused, and I widen my eyes toward Dino. When it clicks, he swallows his food and asks, "Yeah, what did Audrey want?" His voice is louder and clearer than Dino's, which is helpful, but he's also way more conspicuous than I was hoping for.

"Oh," I force a chuckle and turn to Dino. "She was inviting me to an ASL Club thing. She's the president or something, right?" I act clueless, pulling the crumpled-up flyer out of my pocket.

I go to pass it to Dino, but César snatches it out of my hand with a scowl. He needs to go back to kindergarten and relearn basic manners.

César scans the information. "ASL Coffee Night?"

"Wow, you have basic reading comprehension. Congratulations."

César watches me like a hawk, but I refuse to falter under his scrutiny. Finally, after a few beats, he points to me, touches fingertips to his temple, and fingerspells. *"You know ASL?"*

My eyes bug out of my head. What the fuck?!

Usually, I match César's indifferent expressions or fight fire with fire, but this rattles me. (Hey, you'd be rattled too, if your sworn enemy randomly started using a language there was no indication he knew!)

I look around the circle we're sitting in and see everyone's focus flicker between César and me. Okay, so, it wasn't my imagination or some annoyance-fueled hallucination. He signed!

When I don't reply, César drags a slow, deliberate 'D' from his ear to his chin. He points at me, then hooks his finger into an ASL question mark.

"César!" Lela reaches over and lightly smacks her brother's cheek. "¿Qué tipo de—" Her rapid-fire Spanish goes right over my head.

Panic rises in me. Shit! I know it's impossible, but I swear I can hear my heart **thump, thump, thump** against my rib cage. Tears form in my eyes, and I try to stave them off.

I will not cry over this. I signed up for more heartbreak when I kept hanging out with them, even though I knew, after what happened in the past, that there could only be three possible outcomes once they found out about my hearing loss.

1. Laugh and think I'm joking, then, as soon as I start having trouble communicating, never talk to me again.

2. Halfheartedly ask what accommodations I need but ignore everything I tell them, say it's too frustrating to be around someone so "high-maintenance," and never talk to me again.

3. Go slack-jawed, stare at me like I'm a Martian who just exited a spaceship…and never talk to me again.

However it plays out, I lose my whole group of friends. I'm crushed and alone for the second time.

But there's no use lying. I'd only be delaying the inevitable.

I take a deep breath and clear my throat to interrupt their bickering. All eyes are pinned on me. "I, uh, well…yeah." After a long pause, I finally bob my hand. *"Yes."*

"Whaaat?!" Paz screeches. "What is happening!"

Hayden gives his hair a sharp tug. "Shut up, Paz!"

I laugh so that I won't cry. "I'm Deaf, Paz," I explain. "Well, Deaf-Hard of Hearing."

Paz gapes at me, gears turning. After thirty seconds of thinking, the best he can come up with is: "But…you can talk."

"Seriously, Paz! I love you, but please shut up," Hayden begs, and flashes me an apologetic smile.

"I lost my hearing six months ago," I clarify. "I can talk, sure. But lots of Deaf people can. Even those who were born deaf."

I feel my emotions slowly drain from my body until it's like I'm standing across the field, watching someone else explain her hearing loss. Maybe it'll hurt less to see "that girl over there" get dropped by her new friends. She can pick herself back up so that I don't have to, because I'm not sure I even could.

The girl across the field launches into an explanation so well oiled, it's clear she's given it hundreds of times. She could write a book: HEARING LOSS FOR DUMMIES or maybe LOSING YOUR BEST FRIENDS IN UNDER TWO MINUTES FOR DUMMIES.

I zone back in as my speech concludes, and the circle is silent. I'm used to silence by now…but this one is jarring.

César meets my eye and I tense up, but his expression is gentler than usual. As in, he isn't frowning, but he's not **not** frowning. *"I'm…sorry,"* he mumbles, using SimCom. "I've…maybe…been hard on you." Each word is strained, like it's hard to cough up.

I frown at him and shake my head. "I don't want you to apologize to me just because you found out I'm Disabled and feel bad for me. If you're going to apologize, it should be because you recognize you've been an asswipe and you genuinely feel bad about it."

His mouth scrunches to one side and he squints at me but doesn't say anything else.

Desperate to avoid more crushing silence, I turn my attention to Lela. She smiles, and maybe I'm fooling myself, but it doesn't strike me as a pity smile.

"Do you know sign too?" I ask her. Earlier, when César signed, she seemed to understand what it meant.

"Yes. Our uncle is Deaf," she signs. "We FaceTime him a lot."

Hayden's jaw drops. "Oh my gosh, how did I forget that? Your Tío William——the one——lives in——right? It's been like——and——but still."

I frown, getting lost in the speech. Hayden notes my confusion and gets out his phone.

Their uncle in California is deaf. He's from their dad's side. TBH I forgot about him because the last time they visited was, like, five years ago.

I bounce a 'Y' toward the ground. *"Oh, I see."*

"Hey." Lela gently touches my shoulder. "Why didn't you tell us?"

My mouth presses into a line. Pouring my heart out, round two. Here goes nothing.

"When it happened, my friends in Portland didn't even care. And my boyfriend—my ex-boyfriend," I clarify, glancing at César since he gave me such Victor vibes when I first met him, "broke up with me because 'it's too much work' to date me."

My bottom lip wobbles. "None of them made any effort to accommodate me, and they'd known me my entire life. So if they wouldn't, why would you? You guys don't really know me, and I'm only going to be here for a year, anyway." I wipe my eyes.

Hayden flashes a soothing smile, his braces peeking out. "You're not too much work," he says.

With those five little words, the tears start spilling and I fall apart. Lela scoots closer and envelops me in a tight hug, stroking my loose curls. After a minute, Paz and Hayden join us. César and Dino keep their distance, but César awkwardly pats my head like I'm a stray cat.

Out of all the possible scenarios I had painted in my mind, ***this*** was never on the table. I was convinced that they'd want nothing to do with me. That they'd move on with their able-bodied lives and never spare me a second thought. That I'd cry because I felt devastated and abandoned—not because, for the first time in six months, I'd feel like I'm being seen as whole.

Not half-Deaf, half-Hearing. Not half-accepted, half-shunned. Just me. Just Casey.

CHAPTER 17
CASEY

AT OUR ASL PRACTICE SESSION YESTERDAY, HAYDEN ASSURED ME THAT everyone truly meant it when they said they'd be there for me at lunch, but I still fully expect things to be weird when I show my face in school this morning. I mean, I Kim-Kardashian-after-losing-her-earring ugly-sobbed. That's **mortifying**.

But in a plot twist that seems out of character for the Netflix writers scripting my life, my friends just greet me like nothing happened. My little breakdown is washed away with the start of the new school day.

Well, that's not entirely accurate: some things have changed.

Throughout the day, Hayden and Lela sign as much as possible, and Paz keeps his Notes app open during lunch so I can be included in conversations. César doesn't give me attitude, though he's not exactly friendly, either. He's tricky to read.

I guess there are people who will reject you for your differences and people who will take you as you come. You just have to wait until the right people come along.

The way my new friends immediately accepted me restores my faith in humanity a smidge, and after some reflection, I decide to take

Audrey's apology at face value and give Palmera's ASL Coffee Night a try. What's the worst that could happen?

I send Lela a message as I'm leaving school: **i'm going to the ASL club event. wish me luck lmao**

"I swear, you're addicted to that thing," Mom says as she drives.

"Yeah, yeah." I tuck my phone into my pocket. "At least my generation can communicate without sending telegrams."

She shakes her head, chuckling. "You're so disrespectful."

"Carrier pigeons?"

"Casey Marie Kowalski!" Mom reaches over and flicks my leg. "I am not ***that*** old!"

We continue swapping generational insults while Mom runs a few errands, and then it's time for ASL Night. She drops me off in the café parking lot, and I smooth the button-up that she bought me—the navy fabric adorned with pink and purple ASL letters as a nod to my sexuality and disability. #Ally.

I give myself a pep talk as I approach the building. It's going to be fine. I've been letting past experiences dictate too much of the present. The ASL Club deserves a second chance. Tonight, they'll pleasantly surprise me, and everything that happened will be water under the bridge.

Right?

The bitter aroma of coffee surrounds me as I step into the café. I spot Audrey and a few other familiar faces sitting around a large table in an area near the back that's been sectioned off. I make my way toward them, and a woman with curly blonde hair stands to greet me. *"C-A-S-E-Y, right?"*

"Yes." I force a smile. *"I'm Casey"*—I show her my sign name.

"My name is—" The woman moves her fingers too fast as she fin-gerspells. *"My sign name is,"* she forms a 'K' and taps it above her heart like a name tag. *"I'm the ASL teacher."*

"Nice to meet you." I repeat her sign name and pretend like I caught the spelling.

She points to the front counter and encourages me to place an order, signing that the meet-up will start momentarily.

I smile at the cashier as I step up to the counter.

"What can——?" He mumbles with a bored sigh.

My brain plays a speed round of Mad Libs and fills in the blanks. "I'll have a guava iced tea, please."

The boy frowns and punches something into the iPad in front of him. His lips move but no sound registers. He looks up from the screen. "——fruit?"

"Uh. Guava?"

He blinks at me like I just said the most brainless thing ever. My heart races. His mouth moves again, but no words register. I consider fleeing.

"Are you out of guava?" I ask.

Yes or no questions are my best friend when something doesn't make sense. People almost always nod or shake their head when they answer.

The boy nods. "Yeah."

"Okay. Uh, do you have"—I glance at the menu—"passion fruit?"

"I literally just told you we did." His tone turns condescending.

"Sor—" I stop myself from apologizing. I shouldn't have to apologize for my disability, even if some able-bodied person finds it inconvenient.

"I'll have a medium passion fruit iced tea, then," I say, swallowing my frustration.

The cashier types my order into the iPad, rolling his eyes at me. I clench my jaw and internally talk myself down.

Either ordering an iced tea took longer than I thought or Palmera's ASL Club has a teleportation machine, because by the time I turn around, there are dozens of students crammed around the table, all conversing in sign.

I pull out a chair and sit next to a white boy with fidgety hands and the beginnings of facial hair. *"Hello."* I salute him, a formal ASL greeting. He returns the gesture. *"My name is C-A-S-E-Y."*

He purses his lips, timidly touching his right fingers to his left palm. *"Again."*

I slow my fingerspelling. *"C-A-S-E-Y."*

He fakes a smile and nods. I know it's fake because I use the same smile constantly. The one you give when you definitely don't understand something, but don't want to ask someone to repeat themselves a third or fourth time.

He points to himself, studying his fingers as he carefully spells his name. *"L-I-A-M."*

"How long have you been learning ASL?"

Liam flicks a finger by his temple. *"I don't understand."*

Maybe I'm confusing him because I'm not technically using proper ASL word order. ASL sentence structure can be perplexing when you're a native English speaker.

I repeat my question more slowly this time. Liam holds up three fingers.

"Three weeks?" I slide the back of my right hand, which displays the number three, across my left palm.

His fist bobs twice.

"Cool!" My thumb rests on my sternum, fingers wiggling.

Liam repeats the sign for cool, squinting confusedly. *"That sign… means… what?"*

I fingerspell as clearly as I can. *"C-O-O-L."*

His eyes light up, and he excitedly flicks his index finger near his temple. *"I understand! But… I know… cool."* He twists his pinched index finger and thumb near the corner of his mouth.

"That means the same thing!" I shake a 'Y' between us. *"Cool"*—I use my version—*"and cool"*—his version—*"both mean C-O-O-L."*

Liam seems astonished there can be multiple signs for one word. (He's going to malfunction when he learns there are over thirty different signs for strawberry.) A lot of Hearing people don't realize that ASL has synonyms and regional accents, just like English. It's like how some English speakers say soda while others say pop. Even Briana uses some different signs than my Portland ASL teacher did—West vs. East Coast.

I'm trying to figure out how to explain this to Liam without causing his head to explode when the teacher who greeted me flaps a hand. *"Please use 'cool' here."* She uses Liam's version. *"It'll confuse my students otherwise."*

"Your students can sign it that way," I argue. *"But I use a different sign."*

"You've joined our group, so please use our signs. Thank you, Casey." Her patronizing smile fades as she turns back to Audrey and resumes their conversation.

Now I'm irritated. Who is she to tell me not to use my signs? I wouldn't tell a Southern person to stop saying "y'all," simply because I don't say it.

Eventually, 'K' announces that we'll be going around the table and introducing ourselves. She calls on Audrey first. *"My name is A-U-…"* She

151

fingerspells her name at the speed of light, not taking the beginners into account. *"My sign name is"*—Audrey curves an 'A' down her face, starting at her eyebrow and ending at her chin. *" 'K' chose it for me!"*

Jessica goes next, then Asshole-Marco; they both sign far too quickly for the beginners and introduce themselves using the "sign names" a Hearing teacher gave them.

My attention is pulled from the group by a slight commotion at the entrance, and I see Hayden, Lela, César, and Paz stroll into the café, laughing and joking. The boys are still sweaty—they must've come straight from soccer practice.

Hayden takes a chair from an unoccupied table and squeezes in between Liam and me. *"Hey! What are we doing?"*

"Introductions."

A few more people introduce themselves, and then it's my turn. I salute the group, place a flat palm on my chest, tap two 'H's together, then fingerspell my name slowly. I end by providing my sign name.

The group signs hello.

Hayden's leg nervously bounces underneath the table. I give him a reassuring nod and he introduces himself. *"My name is H-A-Y-D-E-N. My sign name is"*—He pulls an 'H' up from the corner of his lips, smiling. Seeing him use his sign name for the first time helps combat some of the frustration this group is causing me.

'K' points behind us, asking for someone's name. I look over my shoulder and see that César, Lela, and Paz have pulled up chairs to sit behind Hayden and me. César meets my eyes and nods, an indifferent acknowledgment that's somehow still friendlier than his signature frown. I narrow my eyes at him, suspicious. He's been acting nonchalant around me—as opposed to pissed off by my mere existence—since he learned about my hearing loss, but I'm not sure I trust it. I do want him to stop being an asshole, but not because he feels sorry for me.

Just because I'm Deaf-Hard of Hearing doesn't mean I can't beef with someone.

"I'm C-E-S-A-R." He introduces himself in ASL, looking bored.

Lela greets the group next, then looks at Paz, who suddenly clues in to the fact that he's supposed to introduce himself.

He curls a loc around his finger and waves at the group.

I flap my hand to get everyone's attention, then introduce him. Paz shoots me a grateful smile and relaxes into his seat.

Liam goes next, then a few new students. Once everyone has made their introductions, we break off into smaller groups to practice conversing in sign. Audrey and her gang of lightning-speed signers sit together, ignoring the rest of us. 'K' plays an ASL game with Liam and the other newcomers, her back turned to me.

Wow. I really thought the ASL Club had turned over a new leaf, but it seems like they intend to keep excluding me. Great job with your "outreach program," Palmera.

I lean into Hayden, point to him, then arc an index finger toward myself until it points toward the floor. I lower a flattened hand from my chin. *"You came. Thank you."* I repeat the sentence for those behind me.

Lela smiles and César gives a terse nod. Paz sees the others reacting and bobs his head. I guess D/deaf people aren't the only ones who social bluff.

Our group of misfit toys claims a table where we can sip our drinks and casually sign in peace.

"Hey, what's the sign for soccer?" Paz asks.

I tap my flattened right hand under my left. *"Soccer."*

Hayden frowns. *"Why do you sign soccer like that?"* he signs, then speaks the words he doesn't know signs for, "That's a weird sign for it. Wait, how do you sign weird?"

I form a 'C' handshape in front of my mouth and pivot it down at the wrist.

"Weird. Weird. Weird," Hayden repeats.

'K' flaps her hand to get my attention, interrupting the conversation. She shakes her head, moving a 'W' in front of her face, the fingers that form the 'W' bending as she moves her hand right to left. *"Weird,"* she corrects.

Why can't this lady stick to hosting her ASL-for-Hearing-people party and leave me alone?

"They mean the same thing," I reply.

'K' purses her lips. I'm no mind reader, but she looks seconds away from making another condescending—and quite possibly ableist—comment.

"The 'W' is English." My fingers move faster than I thought possible. My sentences are mostly in the wrong order, but I'm not letting it stop me from giving her a piece of my mind. *"My sign isn't wrong. Your sign isn't wrong. But one is Deaf and one is English."*

"Who taught you that?"

"My teacher. My Deaf teacher."

'K' scoffs. I can't hear it, but I can see it. *"Who's your teacher? What's their name?"*

My jaw locks into place and I stare at her, astonished by how far she's pushing this. Hot anger propels me out of my chair, and I push it into the table with a slam. The students who weren't paying attention jolt. All eyes on me.

"You know what?" I address the whole group, blood boiling. "You all run around with 'sign names' that your Hearing teacher gave to you, you correct my Deaf signs, and you do absolutely nothing to accommodate me.

"Why are you even learning ASL if you're going to exclude Deaf people? ASL wasn't invented so you can gossip without people understanding or get 'easy' foreign language credits. It was invented for people like me. People who **can't fucking hear you**!" I shout.

Someone grabs my hand—one of my friends—but I push them away, storming through the café and rushing outside. I slam the door behind me. Tears obscure my vision as I speed down the block before finally collapsing onto the curb and sobbing into my knees.

I'm tired of this bullshit.

The isolation, the loneliness, the never fitting in. Never being Hearing enough or Deaf enough to be fully accepted in either world.

I sit on the concrete, completely alone, and come to the realization that silence is the only thing I feel.

Silence has swallowed me whole. It's become an emotion. A hopelessness that's beyond words. I'm so empty, so tired, that I feel **nothing**.

It's the loudest silence imaginable.

CHAPTER 18
HAYDEN

THE NEXT MORNING, THE TENSION AT SCHOOL IS PALPABLE.

When Dino and I enter the building, I see Audrey and Marco standing in the middle of a big cluster of students, talking in hushed voices. Groups of kids crowd around phones, sharing earbuds and whispering to one another.

I fight the urge to march over to them and give them a piece of my mind about the crap they pulled on Casey last night. Marco sees me staring and waves tauntingly, daring me to make a scene.

"You'll just make things worse," Dino whispers, gripping my arm. "Go check on Casey."

My brother may not have many smart moments, but he's right. I'm not equipped for a schoolyard brawl. And all that matters right now is Casey.

I jog over to the staircase where my friends are gathered...except Casey isn't with them.

Lela immediately stands up when she sees me. "Have you heard from her since her mom picked her up last night?"

"No," I sigh. "She hasn't been answering texts or video calls."

César sits on the steps, shooting daggers in Marco and Audrey's direction.

"I don't blame her for laying low. Have you seen this shit?" Lela shoves her phone at me; onscreen are a series of posts from @ActuallyAudrey. My face twists into a horrified expression as I scroll.

The posts detail (with an astounding level of embellishment) how "someone" went completely off the rails at a school-sanctioned ASL event designed to raise awareness for the Deaf community.

"Look at the replies," she says grimly. "And Marco's account."

I click through and see that Marco shared Audrey's posts along with a video of Casey's impassioned coffee shop speech. The video is captioned: **When the "deaf" attack LMAOOO**

"This stuff is all over," she explains. She reaches over to click out of Marco's video, and dozens of other posts pop up. Posts calling Casey slurs, stories about the "fake deaf girl" at school, and shared TikTok remixes of her speech.

My jaw drops. What the hell is wrong with people!?

"What if we took it to Principal Vega?" Paz suggests from his spot next to César. "There has to be a rule against cyberbullying."

Lela scoffs. "Remember when half the school was fat-shaming me on Instagram last year and I went to Principal Vega for help? What did she do?"

Silence.

"Exactly. She doesn't give a crap about students." She folds her arms.

I speak up. "We have to do something, though." They all look at me. "We have to show solidarity. Show everyone we stand with Casey."

Anger swells inside me when I think of all the terrible posts about Casey's hearing loss. What kind of people would say those things about someone?

Lela shakes her head defeatedly. "I'm not sure there's much we can do except—" The bell rings, interrupting her. "We'll talk at lunch," she says, scooping up her backpack.

César gets up, still scowling at Audrey and Marco.

I take out my phone and type a message to Casey. I can only imagine how she must be feeling. She really didn't want anyone at school knowing she's Deaf-Hard of Hearing, and now everyone does—except for the people who think she's making it up. Plus, everyone's acting like she's the villain of the ASL Club altercation, when all she was trying to do was stand up for herself.

Oct 28 at 8:01 AM

@HeyitsHayden Casey, I'm so sorry. Is there anything I can do? I'm here for you. <3

No response. No typing bubbles. No 'seen' notification.

I grunt in frustration. It's taking every ounce of self-control I have to not march over to Marco and confront him.

Around me, the day is starting as if nothing happened. The kids who were spreading rumors and watching that video head to their classes. It's easy to move on from cyberbullying when you aren't the target.

Distraught, I send one more message to Casey:

Oct 28 at 8:04 AM

@HeyitsHayden Don't listen to any of that crap online, okay? You're amazing. Just remember I'm here. I've got you.

I hope she sees it, even if she doesn't reply.

The first thing I do when the lunch bell rings is check my phone. To my dismay, there's nothing new. Casey hasn't even read my messages. Her phone must be on Do Not Disturb.

Paz props himself against my desk while I cram my stuff into my backpack. "No word?"

"Radio silence." I gulp, a sour feeling rising in my throat.

"Douchebags, all of 'em," Lela comments quietly so Mr. Gibson won't scold her for cussing in the classroom. She throws an arm around Paz's shoulders.

"We need to show everyone that—" I'm cut off by the sound of a commotion in the hallway. The last few lingering students quickly exit the classroom to see what's going on.

"Shut your goddamn mouth!" An extremely familiar voice shouts.

I rush toward the open classroom door. The hallway is packed with students, but there's one small area where people have formed a clearing to observe the heated exchange. I push my way to the front and find César pinning Marco against the lockers that line the upstairs hallway.

Marco glares at César. "Why do you care?"

"Because you're being an ableist dickbag." César stares right back. "I can snap you like a twig. Don't try me," he growls.

"I'm allowed to say and do what I want. Ever heard of freedom of speech?"

"Ever heard of a broken nose?" César snarls. Marco flinches as César raises a balled fist in the air. A gasp passes through the swarm of students.

"Hey!" Mr. Gibson rushes toward them. "Knock it off!"

César lowers his fist but keeps Marco pinned to the wall, sneering at him.

"Let him go, Mr. Ramirez!" Mr. Gibson commands. "Now!"

Big surprise: César doesn't let go.

I step forward and place a hand on César's shoulder. "César, don't do anything rash," I urge.

"You're seriously saying this dick doesn't deserve it?"

Mr. Gibson takes a step back, letting me lead the hostage negotiation.

"Oh no, he definitely does," I say. "But do you really want to be expelled your senior year? Pretty sure that's not going to look good on college applications."

César refuses to take his eyes off Marco, but I can tell he's thinking it through. Finally, after one last shove, he releases his grip and Marco tumbles to the ground.

Marco feigns grave injury, so Mr. Gibson bends down and helps him stand up. "Go to lunch, all of you," he instructs the crowd. "And you two"—he turns to César and Marco—"Principal Vega's office. Now."

"I'm being sent home for the day," César announces as he storms out of Principal Vega's office twenty minutes later. "Autocracy is bullshit."

"I'll never understand why being sent home from school is a punishment," Paz says as we all follow César to the exit. "Seems more like a reward. You're telling me I don't have to be in school all day? Um. Yes, please."

"Shut up, Paz! Don't encourage him." Lela glares at Paz before turning to her older brother. "Mom's going to kill you," she warns, stopping him near Palmera's front doors.

"Yeah, well, Mom's also going to have to drive you guys home after school now, unless you want to walk home," César tells Lela and me.

"Stay in school, kids." He salutes us with a sarcastic wink, then pushes through the doors.

Lela, Paz, and I head to the cafeteria in silence.

I can't stop replaying the events of last night. I should've said something. Right? I should've stood up for Casey. If I had spoken up—if I hadn't had been frozen by fear of confrontation, if I had been a better friend—she wouldn't be carrying this weight alone.

"Hey." I tap Paz. "Tell our teachers I felt sick and went home early. I have to take care of something."

Without stopping to explain, I race back toward the front doors, ignoring the stares from my schoolmates as I dash past them.

In the parking lot, I spot César's car right as he starts to pull out of his spot, and I run to catch up. He sees me coming and hits the brakes, then rolls down the passenger window.

"Can you take me to Casey's house?" I ask, catching my breath.

César unlocks the car and I climb into the passenger seat. "Are you skipping school?" he asks, looking at me like I've been body-snatched. Which is fair. I've never missed a day of school, much less played hooky.

"I need to see her."

He watches me with an unreadable expression. Then he nods. "Alright. Where's she live?"

I plug her address into César's phone. His GPS app starts giving directions as we pull out of Palmera's parking lot.

We drive in silence for the first few minutes. I glance his way occasionally, but his expression remains stoic.

"So…what did Marco do? Besides the obvious," I ask. César doesn't acknowledge me. "Did he say something?"

Nothing.

"You wouldn't have gotten that upset for no reason."

Crickets.

"You don't even like Casey. Why'd you risk expulsion for her?"

That gets his attention. We stop at a red light and he looks over at me. "I'd do the same for anyone."

"No, you wouldn't."

"Yes, I would."

"César. No. You literally would not."

His jaw tightens as we resume driving. "It's annoying that she won't accept my apology."

"Are you actually sorry, or do you feel sorry **for** her?" I think back to what Casey said the day César apologized. He had seemed resolute in his dislike for her before then, so I understand why the timing of his apology would make her suspicious.

He glances at me as we turn onto Casey's street. "I can see how my actions might've been misconstrued as rude. Or… entitled," he mutters.

I don't reply. That was a non-answer.

"Hay, you know me better than anyone," he continues. "Have I ever apologized when I didn't mean it? Would I pity-apologize to someone?"

"Well, if you really are sorry, you should try again. The last apology felt kinda half-hearted."

"Are you critiquing my apology?" César huffs. "She should also technically apologize to me, but I'm being the bigger person, so give me some leeway, okay?"

Our conversation ends as he parks in front of Casey's house. We walk up to her front door together. César stands a few feet behind me, hands shoved in his pockets, while I ring the bell.

A couple seconds later, the door swings open.

"Hayden." Mr. Kowalski smiles at me, but his greeting is devoid of the usual enthusiasm. "It is nice to see you."

"Hi, Mr. Kowalski." I smile back. "Is Casey home?"

He shakes his head. "I do not think she is up to visitors." The hurt in his eyes makes me want to push past him, run straight to her room, and wrap her in a hug.

"I r-really need to see her." I steady my voice as it wobbles. "Please, Mr. Kowalski."

Mr. Kowalski considers me and César for a moment. "You are a good friend, Hayden," he says eventually, reaching out to muss up my hair, "but she is not feeling well. I am sorry, boys."

That's the whole point, I want to argue. I'm here to comfort her and show her she isn't alone.

Instead of saying that, I don't say anything. Typical. Mr. Kowalski nods at César and me, wordlessly acknowledging our efforts, before closing the door.

CHAPTER 19
HAYDEN

I KNOW MR. KOWALSKI MEANS WELL, BUT I CAN'T JUST GIVE UP, SO I spend the rest of the afternoon and evening video calling and texting Casey. But she doesn't respond.

By the next morning, I still haven't heard from her, and I'm starting to feel desperate. After talking with Paz, we devise a plan. Of course, since it's Paz, the plan is ill-conceived and likely illegal. But sometimes, in dire circumstances, breaking the law is necessary…right?

"Okay, time out! I changed my mind! This is an awful idea!" I hiss as Paz and I creep through the shadows of an empty strip mall parking lot that night.

"We'll be fine. Calm down." He shushes me and zips his hoodie. We're both dressed head to toe in black, like the robbers from HOME ALONE.

"We're breaking into a **shooting range**!" I hiss.

He chuckles, twirling a set of keys on his finger. "It's not breaking in if you have a key."

The shooting range is the Pistolero Club—which is owned by Paz's dad. But still.

"Then why are we lurking in the shadows? And why are we dressed like this?"

He pointedly ignores me. He disables the security system, then sticks the key into the lock and turns it in faux slow-motion, humming the MISSION: IMPOSSIBLE theme song. He kicks the door, and it swings open with a loud squeal.

We tiptoe into the dark building. I grab Paz's hand and refuse to let go until he's turned the lights on.

He leads us through a series of locked doors and into a gear room filled with bulletproof vests, safety goggles, and rows upon rows of headphones. Paz unzips his backpack and stuffs four pairs of headphones inside. "Easy peasy."

We race away from the scene of our (probably?) illegal excursion, only stopping for Paz to lock the door and rearm the alarm system. Paz laughs and whoops all the way back to his house, then quiets down as we sneak into his backyard, where César and Lela are waiting for us, crouched under his bedroom window.

"Did you get the headphones?" Lela asks.

Paz unzips his bag and shows her the stolen goods. "Hell yes, we did." He pries his window open and hoists himself inside.

"Great," she says, following suit. "Though I still don't get why we couldn't just buy some at the hardware store for, like, ten bucks."

"Because, the intrigue," Paz quips with an eyeroll. "Plus…I'm on a budget."

Once we're all inside his room, I collapse onto the floor and try to catch my breath. "Holy crap, we just broke the law! We're thieves! We could get arrested! I would not do well in prison."

"It'd be juvie," César corrects.

"Hay, chill," Paz urges me. "We're just borrowing them. Without asking." He shoves his backpack under the bed, obscuring it from view. "Lela, you brought the shirts?"

"Of course." She dumps four shirts in various shades of bright orange on the floor.

Paz reaches into his closet and pulls out a bin of crafting and sewing supplies. I grab a jar of glitter, but Paz snatches it away from me.

"We are not using that! I don't need my dad coming into my room and seeing my floor covered in glitter." He shoves the jar back into the bin.

"I think glitter is the least of your worries," César chimes in, jerking his head toward the shirtless Rob Lowe poster.

Paz flips him off. "Leave Rob Lowe alone. Rob Lowe would never do me wrong. He's not like other guys." He tosses three bottles of black fabric paint to Lela, César, and me.

"Paz? Why do you have three bottles of black paint?" César studies his bottle while Lela and I spread shirts on the floor and place some lettering stencils.

"One is obsidian, one is ebony, and the other is jet black. They're different shades."

"They're…black."

"You troglodyte. Obsidian is vastly different than—"

"Boys, please." Lela shushes them. For the next few minutes, we craft in silence.

When Paz has a few letters painted on his shirt, he heaves a sigh. "I miss the days when we could dress up for Halloween. I wish Principal Vega didn't implement the 'no costumes' rule last year."

"But that means she would have to not be such a hard ass with no sense of joy," Lela tsks. "At least these are Halloween adjacent?" She motions to the black and orange shirts.

Paz shrugs. "I'll take what I can get, I guess."

After all the shirts are finished, Paz distributes the stolen-slash-borrowed headphones, and Lela, César, and I climb back out his window. César offers to drive me home.

"You're doing a good thing," Lela tells me as we pull into my driveway and I hop out of her brother's car.

I hope she's right.

CHAPTER 20
CASEY

WHEN THE MONDAY AFTER THE ASL NIGHT DISASTER ROLLS AROUND, I'm completely drained. Physically, emotionally, and mentally. My chest is heavy and there are dark bags under my eyes from a long weekend of exhausting emotional turmoil.

On top of all that, I don't even have the energy to do anything for Halloween today—a beloved holiday for queers and musical theater nerds alike. Definitely not the biggest problem I have right now, but still.

Nevertheless, I decide to suck everything up and go to school.

"Are you sure you don't want to talk?" Mom asks as she pulls to a stop in front of Palmera.

She and Dad still don't know exactly what happened, but they know something is going on. Dad stayed home from work to keep me company on Friday, and Mom won't stop trying to get me to talk to her. But I don't even know how I'd begin to explain what happened.

"Some kids are being assholes, but it's fine." I downplay everything, the lie burning a hole in my throat. I lean over and give Mom a hug, surprising her. She hugs me back and places a kiss in my hair before pulling away.

"I'm sorry, sweetie." She squeezes my shoulder. "But when I was in high school, everyone had the attention span of goldfish. I'm sure whatever is going on will blow over soon!" She's trying to comfort me, but the sentiment falls flat.

It'll all blow over.

The thing is, my disability won't blow over. Ableism and being called slurs won't blow over. People constantly challenging my identity won't blow over.

This isn't a one-time occurrence. Whether it's coming from assholes online, friends I thought I could trust, or complete strangers, I'm going to deal with this sort of thing for the rest of my life. There's nothing that can make *that* feel better.

As I grapple with that realization, the silence takes hold of me again.

Mom watches me, waiting for a response. "Case, I know I've been busy with work, but you can talk to me about anything," she adds.

My reluctance to rehash what happened outweighs my reluctance to go to school. If I keep my head down and pretend to be strong—even though my world is falling apart—I'll be fine.

"No worries." I force a smile and hop out of the van, slinging my backpack onto one shoulder.

Usually, I meet my friends by the main staircase before first period, but today I run into them as soon as I step inside. Palmera's front doors close behind me, and I take in the scene unfolding. Hayden, Paz, César, and Lela are engaged in a heated debate with Principal Vega, their backs to me. They all wear orange shirts and headsets around their necks.

What the hell?

I approach them and stand next to Hayden. He shoots me a quick grin before turning back to Principal Vega.

"You didn't get permission, Mr. González-Rossi," Vega says firmly.

"That's not a good reason, Principal Vega," Hayden argues.

"I can't allow you to——" Her words cut out, drowned out by the noise of students chattering around us. "——T-shirts——vulgar language——disrupt the school day." She sighs. "Palmera is a learning environment, not a social experiment."

"Principal Vega," César speaks up, "section twelve——student handbook says there's a zero-tolerance policy——bullying or harassment. And in section fourteen, it says all students——treated fairly, no matter their race, religion, sexual orientation, or disability."

I gape at César as he recites the school rules word for word. Did he seriously memorize the student handbook? I threw that thing away after my first day.

"By wearing these"—Hayden jumps in, holding up his headset—"and saying this"—he motions to his shirt, which has words I can't make out on the front—"we're showing that ableism matters to us, even if it doesn't matter to you."

My friends nod in agreement

Now I'm really confused. Is this some sort of niche Halloween costume I'm not cool enough to understand?

Principal Vega surveys us. "I admire the initiative you've shown, but—"

César doesn't wait for her to finish. He grabs the headset hanging from his neck and puts it on, directing a "screw you" facial expression toward Principal Vega.

170

Lela is next. She tucks her long hair behind her ears and slips on an identical headset. Paz follows suit.

Principal Vega considers them for a long time, then walks off without further commentary.

Hayden goes to put his headset on, but I stop him, grabbing his freckled wrist.

"What is all of…this?" I motion toward the orange shirt and headset. "Camp Half-Blood?"

He flashes an uncharacteristically proud grin, puts on his headset, and turns to me. Once we're face-to-face, I can read the words on his shirt: I CAN'T F*CKING HEAR YOU!

I recognize the phrase immediately. The video of me in the coffee shop has been playing on a loop in my head since Asshole-Marco posted it. Those are **my** words.

Tears threaten my eyes as I read everyone else's shirts. All of them say the same thing.

Wordlessly, Lela hands me her phone and shows me a post on her Instagram from ten minutes ago. In the picture, the four of them stand with their arms linked, wearing the headsets and gaudy neon shirts. The caption reads: **Solidarity. #ICantFuckingHearYou**

"We wanted to show everyone we stand by you," Hayden explains. He pulls an extra shirt out of his backpack and hands it to me.

I cry-laugh as he drags me into a hug. Baffled, I lower a flat hand from my chin in thanks, then pull the shirt on over my tank top. Principal Vega observes us from the front office, her expression disapproving.

When the bell rings, I wipe my eyes and turn toward César, Paz, and Lela, realizing that with their headsets on, they probably didn't hear it.

"Bell," I sign.

How the tables have turned.

For the first time since moving to Florida, I'm able to eat in the cafeteria without fear of getting overstimulated. My friends use sign or type notes instead of talking, which means I don't have to try to follow a verbal conversation in a noisy environment.

I type a message in my Notes app and pass the phone around the table.

i appreciate you guys doing this. you don't even know what it means to me

They all read the message, each cracking a smile.

I wave my hand to ensure they're paying attention. *"It's weird that I have the best hearing in the group right now. It's like F-R-E-A-K-Y F-R-I-D-A-Y."*

I smile my most genuine smile in months. In the six months since I lost my hearing, my life has been a hurricane of anger, sadness, and confusion. Weathering that storm of emotions, being Disabled in a society that looks down upon disabilities, learning a new language, losing my voice...all of that changed me.

I'll never be just Casey from Portland, Casey who can hear, again.

Someday, maybe that won't hurt so much. Maybe that Casey will fade into a distant memory, along with the sounds I can no longer hear, and I'll finally be free of this loud silence that holds me prisoner.

But now I realize that until that day—the day when it no longer hurts, when these feelings aren't so raw—I'll have people to lean on. People who love me unconditionally. People who came together to stand up for me.

I'm swallowing my last bite of food when I notice Jessica from ASL Club engaged in an argument with Audrey at their table across the room. Without warning, Jessica snatches her backpack from the ground and stands up. Several club members follow her and leave Audrey sitting alone with Asshole-Marco.

The ASL Club heads toward our table, Jessica leading the way. She stops in front of me, looking nervous. *"Hey, Casey…"* she says using SimCom.

From beside her, Liam offers a shy wave.

"Hi, Jessica." I paste on a neutral expression. "Liam."

"I wanted to tell you I'm sorry," she apologizes. *"I should've been more considerate of your hearing loss."*

Everyone else in the group nods and shakes 'Y's between themselves and her, barely making eye contact with me. *"Same,"* they unanimously agree.

"As Vice President of the ASL Club, I'm committed——mindful of how our actions affect others. I know——doesn't make up for——I promise we'll do better in the future," she speaks loudly while using SimCom to ensure I can hear most of her speech, but some of it still cuts out. And because I'm not fluent in sign yet, her signing doesn't fill in those blanks.

This unexpected uprising against Audrey by her precious club makes me happier than it should.

Hayden taps my shoulder. *"Why are you smiling?"*

"K-A-R-M-A," I fingerspell.

The ASL Club's public apology seems to trigger a chain reaction. Over the rest of the school day, I'm approached by a steady stream of students wanting to offer their support or say they're sorry. Some cite specific reasons, like a nasty comment they posted or a meme they shared; others just seem to want to jump on the solidarity bandwagon. I get the impression some people think it's ableist if they don't tell the Disabled girl they're sorry...for...something...

Cheers, man.

When the final bell rings, Lela takes off her headset and slings her arm around my shoulders. We head for the doors, intending to hang out while the boys have soccer practice. But before we can exit the school, a woman with a brown bob steps in front of us, blocking our path.

"Hi, Casey!" she chirps. "I'm sorry to interrupt, but I wanted to chat with you. Can we head to my office?"

I squint at her, trying to figure out why she looks familiar, then sigh when it clicks: she's the school counselor who greeted me with pamphlets on my first day. Colleen.

"I'm okay, thanks," I say, hoping to avoid being dragged into a meeting.

"I've heard you're having a tough time. I'd like to talk about it." Her cheery tone is firmer this time, indicating this is one of those "suggestions" adults make that aren't really suggestions at all.

I turn to Lela. "I'll meet you out there." She nods and I reluctantly follow Colleen down the fluorescent-lit hallway and into a cramped office. Inspirational quotes and racks of pamphlets hang on the walls.

Colleen sits behind her desk and motions to the chair opposite. I sit on the very edge, unable to get comfortable.

"How are you doing, Casey?" she asks. "Principal Vega told me you're having some trouble with your ASL Club friends?"

I fight an eyeroll. "First, the ASL Club members are **not** my friends. Second, if you consider ableist slurs all over social media to be 'some trouble,' then yeah. I guess I'm having 'some trouble.'"

I didn't mean the response to sound so indignant, but the whole situation is still fresh. It's hard to not be bitter about what happened—even after all the apologies and the show of solidarity from my friends.

Colleen frowns. "I apologize. I didn't mean to diminish your experience."

"Mm-hmm. Whatever. Can I just go? I don't need to be therapized."

She watches me for a moment before nodding. "Sure. But"—she walks to her pamphlet rack and picks a couple for me—"read these when you get a chance."

To be honest, I threw away the other pamphlets Colleen gave me as soon as I got home after my first day. I doubt I'll read these either, but to placate her, I take them. I glance at the first one. SO, YOU'RE BEING CYBERBULLIED: HOW TO DEAL WITH ONLINE HARASSMENT. I shove the other into my backpack without looking at it.

"I'm always here if you want to talk!" Colleen calls as I walk out the door.

On the soccer field, César is running laps with Dino close on his heels. He shoots me a lopsided smile as I walk past, and I reluctantly return it, still a bit distrustful of his personality change. Hayden trails behind them, looking like he'd rather be getting his wisdom teeth removed than be at practice. I find Lela on the sidelines and sit next to her.

"Hey, how'd it go?" she asks, looking up from the romance novel she's buried in.

"Fine, I guess." I shrug, turning my attention to the soccer players. Lela and César's mom gives each of them a ball, and they start running drills, dribbling between cones and bouncing the balls on their feet.

"Where'd you guys get these outfits by the way?" I ask her.

She chuckles. "I got the shirts at the thrift store, and we used Paz's fabric paint. Ah, yes, then Paz and Hay stole the headphones from Paz's dad."

"Stole, as in ***illegally took***?" I emphasize. "What is wrong with them?"

"They're teenage boys. It'd be easier to list things that aren't wrong with them." She rolls her eyes.

As practice continues, I pass the time by scrolling through the comments on Lela's post. As expected, a few people are being jerks, but most commenters are genuinely ashamed of their behavior.

I'm about to put my phone away when I receive a DM.

Oct 31 at 3:51 PM

@Just.Jess.24 Hiya Casey! It's Jessica. We just had an emergency ASL Club meeting & the majority voted to remove Audrey as president. I'll be taking her place & I promise u there will be BIG changes!

Damn. I did not see that coming.

I send a quick thank-you message to Jessica and chuckle to myself as I picture the look on Audrey's face the moment her ass got impeached. When practice is over, I grab my stuff and rush to intercept Hayden before he can disappear into the locker room.

"Hayden," I call out. He turns around and waits for me. "Can we talk?" I ask once I've caught up.

He nods nervously.

We walk back to the sidelines and sit.

"Thank you for today," I say.

He sighs. "I was worried I was overstepping. You don't need some Hearing boy to 'save' you, but I wanted to show up. To be there."

I smile at him. "I didn't see it that way. I know what you were trying to do. All of this," I motion toward the orange shirt I'm still wearing, "means the world to me. I've never had a friend like you."

The last of the walls I built to protect myself are crumbling away.

"Want to know something?" I lean closer to him. He nods. "These past six months, I've been secretly hoping my hearing would come back. I thought if it could disappear overnight, why couldn't it reappear?"

His lips curl into a sad smile.

"Don't do the pity smile, Hay. You're one of the only people who's never done a pity smile."

He quickly wipes his expression. *"Sorry."* He circles his chest with a fist.

"I was convinced I could never be happy without my hearing," I confess. "And even though I'm not ready to embrace being Deaf-Hard of Hearing with open arms, and there's probably a lifetime of internalized ableism I still have to work through, I think I'm inching closer to being happy."

He pulls me into a hug, and we stay there for a few long minutes. Then he pulls away.

"Thank you for confiding in me. I know it was a big deal for you to tell me that, and, well…I dunno. It makes me feel like maybe I can confide in you too?"

I smile again. "Of course. I'm here for you."

He sighs, then says, "Okay, here's my big confession: the first fútbol game of the season is on Friday and"—he sucks in a breath—"I don't know if I can do it."

"Do what?"

"Be who people expect me to be. The captain, the game changer, the decision maker. It…" He pauses, looking for the right words. "It feels like being a fútbol star isn't a **choice** for me, it's a **requirement**," he emphasizes. "There's no room for anything else. There's no room for the real me."

I place a hand on his knee. "Is that why you were so insistent on keeping music a secret?"

"Yeah." He nods. "I don't know what my family would think of me if I told them. Being part of the family fútbol dynasty is what's always been expected."

"Would it help if I came to cheer you on?" I suggest. What sort of friend would I be if I didn't show up to support Hayden, after all he's done?

He chews his lip. "Would you? Your support would mean a lot."

"Duh! I'm your biggest cheerleader." I grin at him and poke his knee. "You're going to kill it."

The sun hits Hayden's eyes just right, picking up the green undertones. He releases a tense breath and plants a clumsy kiss on my cheek.

"I love you," he signs. And this time it isn't an accident.

I repeat the sign and press it against his. "Te quiero."

CHAPTER 21
HAYDEN

Sports rivalries are a tale as old as time. Seattle Sounders and Portland Timbers. New York Jets and New York Giants. Yankees and Red Sox.

But those rivalries don't have quite the same level of hostility as the Palmera High Barracudas vs. the Oceanview Sharks.

For thirty-six years, the high school fútbol season has opened with a game between the Barracudas and the Sharks. And we have a six-year winning streak, one Henry dutifully upheld the last four years.

But tonight, all eyes are on me.

Literally.

My teammates are huddled around me, staring as I overturn mental couch cushions in an attempt to scrounge up motivating words for my pregame pep talk.

"Um…go team?" I squeak out when Jacob starts humming the JEOPARDY! theme song.

"Bro, he sucks at this," Nathan hisses to Gabriel. His voice is loud enough that I can tell he wanted me to overhear. Gabriel snickers.

César steps forward and looks to me for permission. I send him a small nod.

"We have to give one hundred ten percent tonight. We can't afford incomplete passes, red cards, fouls. None of that crap." He glares at the boys. "If we mess this up, there is no 'second chance.' There is no 'next time.' We lose tonight, and we throw six years of hard work out the window."

Everyone nods along to his speech.

"Play aggressively and play smart. Especially since there are scouts in the crowd tonight. ¿Entienden?" César roars.

The team shouts a jumble of enthusiastic yeses.

"Ah, and listen to your captain," he adds as an afterthought, slapping my shoulder.

Thoroughly pepped, we make our way outside in single file.

"César?" I whisper as we walk toward the pitch. "Are there really scouts here or did you just say that to motivate the team?"

"Mom's been sending my recruiting video to coaches at my dream colleges, and a few showed interest after I played well in that invitational showcase a few months ago, so they sent people to check me out," he says. "I bet some of the other boys can get on their radars too if things go well today. Plus…" He glances around, then leans down and whispers conspiratorially. "I heard Henry pulled some strings and got an Inter scout to come."

My body tingles with a familiar sense of panic, and a wave of nausea roils my stomach. Once we're on the pitch, I see hundreds of people crammed onto the bleachers. Most of the crowd is in red and white, in support of the Barracudas, but one small section wears green and gold: Oceanview colors.

I force the nerves down as each team's starting eleven is announced. When my name is called out, the onlookers start cheering wildly, and I wince.

"And tonight, we have a very special guest with us!" the announcer proclaims. "Our very own Hat-Trick Henry González-Rossi!"

The fervor escalates and my eyes snap toward the bleachers as I process this unexpected development. I scan the crowd for familiar faces and spot Casey in a red crop top and white shorts. She catches sight of me, smiles, and waves an "I love you" sign in the air.

Then I see him.

He's sitting next to Mamma, wearing his old Barracudas jersey. His blue eyes meet mine and he flashes his cover-of-SPORTS ILLUSTRATED grin, raising his hand in a wave.

I frown, picturing the headlines: HAT-TRICK HENRY GONZÁLEZ-ROSSI FINDS TIME IN HIS BUSY SUPERSTAR SCHEDULE TO ATTEND YOUNGER BROTHERS' FÚTBOL MATCH.

How charitable.

"Let's go, ladies." Coach's shrill voice cuts through the noise of the crowd. Her gaze settles on me, her expression unforgiving. Coach pushed me harder than ever in the week leading up to this game, trying to mold me into Henry González-Rossi 2.0.

"Hayden"—she death-grips my shoulder—"we can't lose this game. Do you understand me?"

I nod, but my search for a verbal reply comes up empty.

"Good. It's time for the coin flip. Go." She motions toward the center circle, where the Sharks' captain and the head ref are waiting.

My heart bounces around in my rib cage as I'm sucked into a whirl-pool of panic. I fight the urge to flap my hands, keeping them firmly clamped by my sides during the coin flip. The captain of the Sharks calls tails, and the Sharks win possession of the ball.

The game starts at a breakneck pace; a crafty Sharks midfielder weaves the ball between several members of our defense and passes it straight to one of their forwards. The striker takes off running, evading our fastest players without breaking a sweat. César slide-tackles the ball away.

Close call.

Around the thirty-minute mark, Gabriel misses a save, and the ball goes sailing into our goal. Nothing but net. The Sharks launch into a celebration, but César runs toward the ref, shouting, "That was offside!"

The referee is quickly circled by the rest of the Barracudas, but I watch from a distance. I should be with them. I should have been the one to call offside. I'm the captain! I should stick up for my team.

But I can't. My feet are frozen to the Astroturf just outside the tight huddle, anxiety digging its sharp claws into me, squeezing air from my lungs.

The ref consults with the linesman, then blows his whistle and throws one arm into the air. He declares the goal offside and has the point docked from the scoreboard.

Before I know it, the halftime whistle is blowing and the teams are trudging into their locker rooms. The score stands at 0–0.

Coach storms into the locker room while I frantically gulp water. The whole team goes still, waiting for her to unleash her fury.

"Are you trying to let them win?" Her shouting reverberates off the walls. "We're getting our asses handed to us!"

She whips her head toward me, and I shrink farther into the corner, trying to conceal myself behind Paz (which doesn't work at all because he's five-four and I'm five-seven).

"And you." Coach crosses the room, arms crossed and chin jutted. "What is wrong with you?" she barks. "You're embarrassing yourself—no, you're embarrassing Henry, who brought an Inter Miami scout here to see you play!"

"S-sorry, Coach." My voice wobbles. I hang my head to hide my watery eyes.

"Man up and act like a captain. You don't get to shirk your responsibilities and let someone else lead for you." She shoots César a withering glance.

After the thorough chewing-out, we head back onto the pitch. Coach makes some halftime substitutions, bringing Dino on for Nathan.

Dino wears a smug grin and steps into formation, pleased to be playing in his very first varsity fútbol game.

The second half kicks off, but I can't seem to focus on anything besides the sound of my heartbeat thundering in my ears. I'm plagued by thoughts of letting everyone down.

I push through the emotional turmoil and physical pain as the game progresses. I try to keep track of who has the ball and where the Sharks are, hoping I can sneak a shot past them and save the day by scoring the winning goal.

César nabs the ball from a greenshirt and sprints downfield. I keep pace beside him, watching his feet glide across the turf. César looks like he's floating when he dribbles.

His raw skill, the passion in his footwork, his unflappable focus—that's why César deserves to be captain. Not me.

Nimble as a gazelle, César lobs the ball toward Paz. It flies through the air and lands at Paz's feet. A perfect pass.

Suddenly surrounded by Sharks, Paz executes a gorgeous, highlight reel-worthy Maradona spin, nutmegs a Shark, and sends the ball toward me. I clamber to retrieve it, but stumble and wind up giving possession back to the Sharks.

In the final minute of the game, the Sharks get the ball dangerously close to our net. Scrambling, we position ourselves to block their shots.

Despite our efforts, a greenshirt kicks the ball with full force, sending it flying. I make the split-second decision to trust my technical abilities for once in my life and match his ballsy choice with one of my own, leaping into the air.

My head collides with the ball, and for a moment I think I've managed to head it away from the goal. Then I feel it: my head is angled slightly too far forward. The ball has actually bounced off the top of my skull and is flying backward. Toward Gabriel.

The world slows down in one game-changing moment. My teammates' eyes track the trajectory of the ball. Their faces twist into pained expressions.

Time speeds up again right as the Sharks start cheering and laughing riotously. They hug each other and run around like headless chickens. The small section of green-clad fans joins their celebration.

I turn around and see Gabriel sitting on the ground, face hidden in his goalie mitts. The ball is directly behind him, in the back of the goal.

I vaguely register the sound of the final whistle as the Oceanview Sharks are declared the winners, thanks to my own-goal.

I push past my discouraged teammates and rush toward the locker room.

My chest rises and falls violently, each breath a battle. I slam my fist into a row of lockers and let out a visceral scream.

My knees buckle and I collapse onto the cold floor. Tears cascade down my face as Coach's sentiments echo in my mind: "Be a leader." "Man up." "You're embarrassing Henry." "Make your family proud."

The words ricochet, reminding me of all the different ways I've disappointed people. Ruined every hope my family had of a fútbol dynasty.

I'm so caught up in my panic I barely notice the hand that comes to rest on my back, or the hug I'm pulled into. The way I'm helped up and led to the parking lot and eased into the passenger seat of a car.

Through my tears, I realize I recognize this car—the sleek red leather seats, the watermelon-scented car air freshener hanging from the rear-view mirror, the David Beckham dashboard bobblehead.

I turn toward the driver's seat as Henry—my perfect-in-every-way older brother—climbs in. "Let's get you out of here, kiddo," he says simply.

We drive for a while. The farther we go, the more my panic gives way to anger. I mean, what the heck? I haven't heard from him in months, and now he thinks he can just show up and "kiddo" me? Seriously?

I clench my fists and stare out the window as we drive in silence.

From the route he's taking, I can guess where we're heading: a small, hole-in-the-wall gelato shop an hour outside of Miami. Gelato is a family tradition from Mamma's Italian heritage. After the first game of every season, we make the trek to buy gelato from this specific shop. Provided the Barracudas win. (And we always win.)

I don't look at Henry until he's holding a cone of cioccolato all'azteca gelato in my face.

"This is going to melt if you don't get to work," he says with a small smile.

I ignore the cone.

"What, so, you suddenly have time for me?" I snap, my tone more aggressive than intended.

Henry's blue eyes widen. "Hay, I came to support you during your first game as captain."

"Pfft. I thought you were too busy being Messi and Beckham's protégé to care about me anymore."

He recoils, his expression stunned. "What?! Where is that coming from? I'm always here for you."

"No, you're not!" I grow more animated. "You said we'd still be the same, you'd just be in Fort Lauderdale. But you haven't texted me in months! It hasn't once occurred to you to ask how I'm doing or how I'm feeling about being forced to take over your captaincy! You're a liar, Henry. You don't care about anyone but yourself anymore!"

He draws a tense breath and frowns at me. "I'm sorry, okay? I'm sorry I didn't reach out more or ask how you were doing. But…you also haven't texted me. You haven't asked how *I'm* doing on Inter or how *I'm* settling into Fort Lauderdale. Yeah, okay, I've been doing a crappy job at staying in touch, but I've been under a lot of stress."

I eye him in disbelief. "What do you mean? Mamma says you're doing amazing and that all your teammates love you."

All I've heard for the past several months is what a crucial member of the team he is and how he's destined to become an MLS legend. What kind of stress could he be under? He's living his dream!

"Yeah, well. I lied. Sue me." He laughs defeatedly. "I was a stellar varsity player, but now I'm expected to be on Messi's level as an eighteen-year-old. Do you have any idea what that kind of pressure is like? And somehow I'm supposed to do this without my family or a support system nearby. But you've all been so excited for me and cheering me on, and it felt like if I told you the truth about how hard it's been… I'd be disappointing you guys."

This confession makes my head spin. Henry is supposed to be basking in his growing fame right now. He's supposed to have it all, not a care in the world. He's supposed to have let it get to his head, supposed to think he's better than all of us now.

But from what he's describing… it sounds like we're going through the exact same thing. Shouldering so many expectations that we're crumbling under the weight. Pasting on smiles and lying through our teeth that everything is fine. Worrying that if we come clean, we'll disappoint everyone.

I've been so focused on being mad at Henry for the intense pressure I'm under, resenting how he left me to fill his unfillable shoes, that I didn't ever stop to consider he might also be struggling.

My shoulders slump. "I didn't know you were going through that."

He shoots me a comforting smile. "And I didn't know you've been having a tough time, either. Apparently, we suck at communication," he jokes. "Are we okay now? Can we just try to, like, talk about stuff in the future?" He extends the gelato cone to me again. A peace offering of sorts.

"Yeah. We're okay."

I take a moment to get a good look at him. The first one I've gotten since he moved to Fort Lauderdale. Video calls don't do justice to his smattering of facial hair and cocky smirk.

In this moment, the last of my animosity toward him fades away. Right now, he's not Hat-Trick Henry. He's not Miami's Golden Boy. He's just my big brother.

"I don't deserve this," I mumble, looking at the gelato, which we traditionally buy to celebrate wins. "We didn't win."

"Well, the **Barracudas** didn't win." Henry chuckles, then licks his scoop of pistachio gelato. "But you did score the game-winning goal."

I stare at his goofy, dad-joke grin for a beat. Then I burst into tears.

"Aw, damn it." He takes my cone back from me as it starts dripping chocolate goop onto the car seat. "I'm sorry. It's too soon for jokes."

His arms wrap around me, and I relax into his embrace.

"Henry," I finally say after a bit more crying, hyperventilating, and internal self-flagellating. "I'm never going to be as good as you."

He tsks. "Because you aren't me. You're you. We have entirely different skill sets, and there isn't anything wrong with that. You're awesome just how you are."

I'm not sure I entirely believe him, but my anger and hurt finally fizzle out into exhaustion.

"Thanks for saving me back there." I sniffle, giving the melty gelato a bite at last. "Tía was about to rip me a new one for sure."

Henry laughs. "She's a harsh critic."

"That's a nice way of putting it."

"For what it's worth"—he leans back in his seat—"I doubt myself all the effin' time. So many people expect me to play at Beckham or

Messi's level…but will I ever even be half as good as them? Do I even belong in the big leagues?"

"Of course, you do. You totally do," I say, and I wholeheartedly believe it.

"So, there you go, Hay." His grin reappears. "You'll find somewhere you belong, too. Even if it's not the place you expected to belong, or it takes some time. But I'll always have your back, kiddo."

CHAPTER 22
HAYDEN

I<small>T'S BEEN LESS THAN FORTY-EIGHT HOURS SINCE THE</small> B<small>ARRACUDAS'</small> crushing defeat, and Tía Carmen's mood can only be described as simmering rage.

Luckily, Henry's staying in Miami for the weekend. So, while Papá, Tío Eddy, Dino, and I prepare our weekly Sunday family dinner, Henry and César keep Tía occupied with a discussion about MLS playoff predictions.

Channeling my apprehension into the mojo sauce I've been tasked with making, I bash an orange against a juicer and watch the sweet liquid trickle out.

"Calm down!" Papá pleads as I mutilate the fruit. He stands by the sink, peeling shrimp.

Tía Carmen approaches the kitchen counter and inserts herself into the conversation. "You're too soft with him, Enrique," she admonishes Papá out of nowhere. "He runs away from tough situations instead of dealing with them head-on. What kind of captain abandons his team after losing the game?"

I bite my cheek to refrain from saying something I'll later regret.

Mamma looks up from where she's setting the table with Lela. "Carmen, he's upset about the result."

Tía laughs bitterly. "If he didn't want to be upset, he shouldn't have lost us the game."

"Mom, leave Hay alone." César mumbles from the living room.

Tía's brows shoot into her hairline. "Excuse you?"

"It's not like he was trying to score an own-goal."

I'm not sure why César is jumping in to defend me. He hasn't said two words to me since the game. He's more upset than anyone—especially because I made him look bad in front of the scouts.

"He needs to decide where his priorities lie; that's all I'm saying." Tía Carmen squints at Papá.

"Don't say these things. He's sensitive," Papá whispers to his sister across the counter, as if I'm not standing right here.

When she finally leaves, I turn my attention to tidying the kitchen and pretending I'm completely fine, though what I really want to do is run to Paz's house, eat cookie dough, and watch QUEER EYE.

Tío Eddy adds extra seasoning to the shrimp, then takes me under his arm. "It's okay to be sad." He smiles. "Don't keep it bottled up."

"Easier said than done."

Tío Eddy chuckles. "You need to be gentle with yourself, chiquito. You haven't let anyone down."

Tío was probably a psychic in a past life. He has a spooky way of reading people.

"But Tío," I look up at him, "how am I supposed to be gentle with myself when I'm constantly reminded I'll never be good enough?"

He rakes his fingers through my hair. "You don't have to follow Henry's path, even if it's expected. You're exceptional in your own right."

I'll never understand how Tío Eddy and Tía Carmen make their relationship work. He's the kindest person on planet Earth, and Tía is all jagged edges and disparaging comments. I haven't heard her say a single nice thing since she complimented Lela's eyeliner two years ago.

Thirty minutes later, we sit down to eat. Conversation predictably revolves around Inter Miami and Henry, but I can't exactly complain—I'm no longer the center of attention.

César bombards Henry with questions about Messi, but Henry changes the subject. "Hay. How's Paz doing?"

"He's fine. A little bummed I ruined his Maradona moment."

Henry nods. "That was a spectacular move on his part. Glad you two are still…hanging out." He smiles.

"Hayden, have you told your brother you're learning sign language?" Mamma smoothly interjects, angling herself toward Henry. "He's made a new friend. She's Hard of Hearing."

"You made a friend?" Henry looks surprised. Geez, is it really so hard to believe I can make friends? "Someone I know?" he asks.

"Her name's Casey. She's from Portland," Lela supplies.

"Hipster Portland or Lobster Portland?"

"Hipster."

"Hayden," Tía Carmen interrupts, "do you think it's wise to be adding extracurriculars when you're already struggling with fútbol?"

She couldn't help herself, could she? She had to land another blow.

I cross my arms, trying to stand my ground. "I don't **have** to play fútbol. I **have** to know ASL to communicate with my friend."

A dangerous scowl appears on Tía's face. "You're the captain of the team. You have responsibilities."

Henry's eyes pass between Tía and me. "That's great, Hay. Casey sounds nice."

"Yeah. She totally is," I mumble, avoiding Tía's glare.

César and Dino resume interrogating Henry about the MLS life. I can tell he's embellishing some of his answers, especially given what he confessed at the gelato place. But I don't call him out. Sometimes faking it until you make it is the only option.

After dinner, the Ramirezes head home. One foot out the front door, Tío Eddy stops to give me a warm hug. "You don't have to live in Henry's shadow. You can make your own light." He winks at me and departs.

Scratch the psychic thing—Tío was a poet in his past life. Maybe a psychic poet, straight out of a mid-2000s young-adult novel.

My parents, my brothers, and I cram into our tiny living room to engage in a long-standing family tradition: drinking coffee too late in the afternoon.

Papá studies me, stroking his five-o'clock shadow. "I don't want to drag this out but…" he starts. I preemptively sigh. "Are you having trouble with fútbol?"

I sip my drink, focusing on the way the coffee's bitter notes cut through the sweet condensed milk to distract me from the anxiety triggered by Papá's question.

Were the things Tía said during dinner rude? Yes.

Were they entirely uncalled for? Also, yes.

But they were true. My fútbol skills have deteriorated over the past few months, and I know why.

I've been trying to live life as two completely separate people.

Hayden González-Rossi, team captain, following in his talented older brother's footsteps and bringing fútbol glory to the family name.

And Hayden González-Rossi, musical-theater nerd, who spends his free time memorizing tap routines from NEWSIES and singing every part in HAMILTON'S "Non-Stop."

But only one of those feels right, and I just don't have it in me anymore to keep that other version of me going. I've been letting fútbol-Hayden slip, and my lack of enthusiasm for the sport is finally starting to show on the pitch.

There's only one way to fix this. To be myself.

I have to come clean.

It's time to have my Troy Bolton moment. Here's to you, Paz.

I leap out of my seat. "I need to tell you guys something," I announce.

The room goes still.

The monologue I've been mentally preparing presses the emergency-eject button and exits my brain as all eyes turn to me.

"It's kinda h-hard for me to say this." My voice wobbles as I improvise. "I've been wanting to say it for a long time. But I've never been b-brave enough."

"It's okay, mijo," Papá says, taking Mamma's hand. "We know. And we don't love you any less."

I frown, taken aback. "You...know?"

"We wanted to let you come to us when you were ready to talk about it," Mamma says.

My brothers nod in agreement.

"We'd never treat you differently, Hay," Henry says. "We love you. If Paz makes you happy, so be it. You're still the person you've always been." He gives me a loving smile.

I'm so comforted by his reassuring tone that I nearly miss his comment about Paz. "Wait—what? What about Paz?"

Henry squints at me. "You're...dating Paz?"

"What?!" I slap a hand to my mouth. "I'm not dating Paz! Oh my God! Do you guys think I'm **gay**?"

194

They share a collective look that confirms they do, in fact, think I'm gay.

"Oh my **God**!" I cover my eyes, falling backward into the blue armchair I was sitting in.

"Or bi, I guess?" Dino mumbles.

"Why would you let Paz have sleepovers in my room if you thought we were dating?!"

"You're the most"—Mamma chooses her words carefully—"respectful... out of your brothers. You know how we feel about sex before marriage."

"MAMMA!" I release a hideous grunt-scream.

Dino's horrified expression matches my own, while Henry suddenly looks guilty.

"Honey, your father and I just want you to be smart," she continues. "Do we need to have a talk about protectio—"

"I'm quitting fútbol!" I blurt. "I'm not gay, I'm not dating Paz—or anyone—and I'm **definitely** not having sex. I'm quitting fútbol."

This finally triggers the big reaction I was expecting, though I'm a little surprised nobody really reacted when they thought I was trying to come out. Dino's jaw drops, Papá looks like he's been punched, and Henry freezes.

Papá scoots to the edge of the couch, brows furrowed. "I can talk to Carmen about her methods. She can be harsh, I know."

"It's not because of her." I run a hand through my curls. "I've wanted to quit for a long time. I don't have passion for playing. I'd rather..." I look at Mamma, knowing she'll be the one who reacts best. "I want to be on Broadway," I say, forcing my voice to remain steady and clear. "I've been spying on your lessons whenever I have the chance, stealing the techniques you teach your students."

Her eyes widen. "Why didn't you say anything?" She laughs in disbelief.

"Because I'm supposed to carry on the dynasty. It's all you guys ever talk about!" I reply. "I mean, Abuelo brought a pair of tiny cleats to my baby shower, and ever since, I've just been another step toward fulfilling the family destiny. It was a lot of pressure."

"Oh, tesoro mio," Mamma breathes. "We never meant to put pressure on you." She stands up, sits on the arm of my chair, and gives me a one-armed hug. "We all thought you liked playing soccer. We were trying to encourage you."

"I did like playing at first," I admit. "When it was just Abuelo and Papá and us"—I gesture to my brothers—"messing around in the backyard for fun...But then it became about a legacy and making you guys proud and having my life planned out for me. And I don't want that. I'm sorry I'm not more like Abuelo, but I don't want to play fútbol—I want to follow my own dreams."

From the couch, Papá smiles wistfully. "You're more like your abuelo than you think," he says. "Did I ever tell you that your great-grandparents didn't want Abuelo to play fútbol?"

I blink at him, bewildered. "What? Why?"

"They thought he should pursue béisbol instead. Even when professional sports were banned in Cuba, top-tier béisbol players commanded a lot of respect, and they said fútbol was a waste of Abuelo's time and talent. Back then, fútbol wasn't nearly as big in America as it is now, but your abuelo had faith that the sport would grow, and he believed he would have opportunities here that he might never get in Cuba. It was just one of many things he and his family deeply disagreed on."

"Even so, it wasn't an easy choice—either leave his home to chase his dreams of professional fútbol or placate his family and stay to play a sport he wasn't passionate about."

My small smile mirrors Papá's as I listen to the story. I never knew any of this.

He continues, "I would never force you into a fútbol career if that's not what you want. And I know your abuelo wouldn't either. He would be proud of you for following your heart, just like he chose to all those years ago."

Tears prickle my eyes. I thought having a different dream meant I was the most disconnected of all my family members from Abuelo...but apparently, we have a lot in common. And now I feel more connected to Abuelo now than ever—**because** I'm different from my brothers.

"So...you guys are okay with this?" I ask through a sniffle.

Papá's smile widens. "Siempre te apoyaré, mijo."

"Of course," Mamma assures me. "And honestly, this is very exciting!" Her blue eyes sparkle with endless possibilities. "I can give you proper vocal lessons now! Oh, and next summer we can enroll you in that musical theater camp I teach at! Though, that's almost a year away. Wait—you can perform in the Winter Talent Show next month!" Her hands flutter as she rattles off various ideas. Her Italian is showing.

My eyes widen and I shake my head. "No, no, no! The talent show? N-no way," I choke out. The other suggestions trigger a spike of anxiety, but the thought of singing in front of my classmates and former team-mates? That makes me want to throw up.

Mamma's excited expression fades. "I understand it's a little intim-idating, but singing in front of some high school students and their families will be less nerve-wracking than singing in front of thousands of people in a New York theater."

She's trying to be supportive, but it has the same effect as my family cheering on my fútbol captaincy. It's not helpful; it's just adding unnecessary pressure. Sure, I could try explaining the visceral fear I feel whenever I think about performing in front of an audience, but I doubt my family would understand. I don't even fully understand.

"I'm not ready for that kinda thing," I admit. "But I would like to do vocal lessons, if that's okay?"

Mamma sighs but nods. "I think it'd be good to push yourself out of your comfort zone, but we'll work up to it."

CHAPTER 23
CASEY

"ARE YOU GOING TO TELL US WHY YOU CALLED THIS EMERGENCY MEETING?" Paz sighs from where he's relaxing on the sunflower rug in the middle of my bedroom.

After school on Monday, Hayden sent an SOS message to the group chat he, Paz, and I formed back when we were doing the school project—he said he has something important to tell us, and to meet at my house after soccer practice.

But now that we're all gathered in my room, Hayden isn't saying anything. Instead, he's staring at me and worrying his bottom lip between his teeth.

"What's wrong?" I ask.

Like a snoopy meerkat, Paz sits up and examines Hayden's expression, then turns to me. "He has a confession. That's his confession face."

He glares at Paz but doesn't dispute the "confession face" statement.

"Yesterday, I told my parents and brothers I'm quitting the team to pursue music." His fingers tap anxiously on his leg as he speaks.

"Are you kidding me?!" Paz gasps. "Why didn't you tell me sooner?"

My eyes widen. "Whoa, that was a big step. How'd they take it?"

He smiles sheepishly. "They, uh…they thought I was coming out to them. Actually, they thought I was telling them that Paz and I are dating."

"They thought we were dating? Oh my God. That's hilarious! Can you believe that?" Paz asks me, cackling.

Now it's my turn to be awkward. How the hell did I misread the situation and they aren't a couple? Welp. I might have to take my gaydar to the repair shop. After a beat, I chuckle awkwardly. "Yeah, that's wild. Really…weird."

"Anyway," Paz says, "I'm proud of you." He smiles at Hayden. "Honestly, I'm surprised you worked up the courage to tell them."

"Gee, thanks for the vote of confidence," he scoffs.

"What'd Coach say?" Paz asks.

He goes quiet again. "I haven't told her or my cousins yet. Henry helped me come up with a plan, though. I'm telling them during our family dinner on Sunday."

"Are you nervous?" I ask. I don't know much about his aunt, but based on the intense coaching style I've seen during Barracudas practice, I'm guessing she's not going to welcome the career change with open arms.

"Terrified," he breathes. "She's going to rip me apart."

"It'll be okay." I reach out and take his hand. Paz gives him a one-armed hug. "At least your family knows. They can back you up."

"Yeah. My mom was actually super excited. Too excited," he says with a laugh. "She's going to give me vocal lessons now, which is great. But she also kept listing all these singing things she thinks I should do, like Palmera's Winter Talent Show and some summer camp, and it was kinda overwhelming."

"Palmera has a talent sh—"

"Are you kidding?" Paz interrupts my question. "Hay, you absolutely have to perform at the talent show!" he squeals. "You can let your inner Troy Bolton shine. Track suit and all. I'm with your mom on this one!"

"No, no, no. I could never get on stage by myself," he splutters.

A light bulb appears above Paz's head. "You and Casey can do it together! Oh my God, this is perfect. I am a genius!"

My eyes widen. Unlike Hayden, I have experience with live performances. I did several showcases back in Portland, sang at farmer's markets, and even played Wendy in an eighth-grade production of the musical PETER PAN.

But I haven't performed since losing my hearing. And right now, I think I need more time to rebuild my confidence.

"I don't know if we're ready for that," I admit.

Paz grunts in frustration. "Look, I don't want to pressure you guys, because, you know, consent is sexy, but this is what you want to do, right? Hay, you want——Broadway. Casey, you——killer voice. I've watched——Instagram cover videos. I mean, sure, you haven't performed in a while, but you could pull it off." I fill in the blanks of Paz's rapid speech.

Hayden opens his mouth to reply, but before he can, Paz's phone starts blaring. Paz grimaces as he answers the call. He murmurs into the phone for a few seconds, then hangs up with an eyeroll.

"My dad's making me come home. You borrow some headphones one time and suddenly you're treated like a criminal!" he exclaims. "Hay, I'm proud of you," he adds, squeezing Hayden's shoulder on his way out of my bedroom.

I look at Hayden, but he avoids my gaze and slumps down onto the floor. He leans against my bedframe and starts picking at the fibers of my rug.

I sit next to him and knock my shoulder into his. His whole energy has shifted in the past two minutes. "You good?"

"Yeah. I'm great." His fidgeting fingers and intense eye contact with my floor give the lie away.

"What's going on?" I press.

Tense silence envelops my room. I watch him and recognize the signs of his anxiety swelling: shaky hands, heavy breathing, fidgeting.

Maybe he's freaking out about the idea of a solo performance.

Before I can think about the ramifications for myself, I blurt out, "Performing together could be fun. You wouldn't have to be on stage alone."

But instead of easing his anxiety, this suggestion seems to make it skyrocket. He turns to face me, eyes wild. "No way! How could I possibly get up in front of all those people and sing so soon!? What if my voice cracks? Or I forget the lyrics? Or I get booed? Or…" He ticks off each worst-case scenario on his fingers.

He keeps spiraling for a solid two minutes, growing increasingly upset. "My career would be over before it even starts and—"

"Hayden!" I finally interrupt, placing my hands over his to calm his restlessness. "Nobody is going to force you to perform. It was just an idea, okay?" I reassure him.

He blinks away the tears gathering in his eyes. "Obviously, if I want to be on Broadway, I'll **have** to perform," he emphasizes, "but it's terrifying. I don't know if I can ever do it. What if I'm never good enough?"

I pull him into a side-hug. "You're already good enough! I promise. I wouldn't lie and hype you up if you were a terrible singer. Seriously. I'm not that nice of a person, unfortunately."

This draws a small chuckle out of him.

"You know, I have—er, had—a friend back in Portland who also used to go through this stuff. They're in debate club so they have to get up in front of people all the time, and they always have major anxiety attacks beforehand. Well, I mean, they're dealing with anxiety constantly because of their Generalized Anxiety Disorder, but—"

"I don't have a disorder!" he objects, pulling away from the hug.

I cock a brow. "I didn't say you did…?"

He gulps, seeming taken aback by his own defensiveness.

"Hayden, I wasn't trying to be an armchair psychologist, but I've seen some similarities between you and my friend," I continue, shrugging. "They taught me some of their coping techniques because I got stage fright sometimes. I just thought I could share those with you if you're ever interested. That's all."

"I just…I get jittery sometimes. So what? Everyone gets nervous."

"Sure, getting nervous is normal." I nod. "But you, uh, get nervous a lot."

He looks down, avoiding my eyes again. "Yeah…I do," he breathes. I don't hear it, but I lipread it.

I pat his knee, unsure how to comfort him. He's a better nurturer than I am. "I'm here for you, if you ever want to talk," I finally say.

He cracks the tiniest smile. He touches fingertips to his temple, then lowers a flat hand from his chin: *"I know. Thank you."*

CHAPTER 24
HAYDEN

"HOW'D IT GO?" MAMMA ASKS WHEN I GET HOME FROM CASEY'S HOUSE, looking up from the pasta dough she's kneading in the kitchen. According to her nonna, no self-respecting Italian uses boxed pasta.

I grip the strap on my backpack so tightly my knuckles turn white. At times like these, I resent our house's open floor plan. I would like nothing more than to run upstairs without having to pass Mamma.

"Fine," I mumble, hoping that'll satisfy her. Before she can ask more questions, I escape to my bedroom.

I toss my backpack aside, grab Buñuelo out of his terrarium, and flop onto my bed. Lying on my back, I position Buñuelo on my chest and stroke his scaly head, fingers trailing down his back to the tip of his spiky tail. He wiggles happily and flicks his tongue against my chin.

I exhale slow, steady breaths and keep petting Buñuelo. He's one of the only things that can calm my racing thoughts.

Buñuelo understands me better than most humans.

"You probably don't have any stress, huh?" I ponder aloud. "What do lizards have to worry about? Their heat lamp needing a new bulb? Hah, must be nice."

He blinks his beady reptile eyes at me.

"I know, I know. I'm taking it out on you. Sorry, bro," I mumble. "It's just…I thought after I told my family about quitting the team, I'd be all stress-free and chill! But now it feels like I have five million other things to worry about. I mean, how am I ever supposed to do anything if I freak out over the tiniest things?"

I sit up, lean against my headboard, and stare at Buñuelo. "And now I'm confiding in a lizard." I sigh.

He wriggles closer to me and licks my face again. I chuckle and pat his head. "Thanks. You're a good listener."

Buñuelo crawls off my lap and makes himself comfortable on my bed, apparently deciding he's fulfilled his emotional support iguana duties. I take one more deep breath and feel the last few knots of anxiety untangle. They don't completely go away—because they never do—but they loosen enough that I can focus again.

Now that my mind is clearer, I think back to what Casey told me about her former friend in Portland and how they have an anxiety disorder. Honestly, until now, I didn't even know anxiety disorders were a thing.

Curious, I dig my phone out of my pocket, launch Google, and type in "anxiety disorder symptoms," but I freeze before I can click Search.

Anxiety disorders can't be *that* different from regular, normal-people anxiety, though, right? Right. There's no reason to Google it! Like I told Casey, everyone gets nervous sometimes.

My finger twitches, as if my subconscious is trying to force me to press the button, and I toss my phone away from me. Being a teenager is all about hormones and not having any common sense and growing pains—it'd be more unusual if I wasn't anxious! Every teenager probably flips out every so often. Or every day. Every…hour. Maybe.

Aaand I'm justifying not looking this up.

I glance at Buñuelo and find him shooting me the most judgy look a lizard can muster.

"Okay, okay!" I exclaim, retrieving my phone. "I'll stop being a baby about it! Just…don't look at me like that, bro."

I press the Search button. Immediately, an article on Generalized Anxiety Disorder pops up. A painful lump forms in my throat as I hesitantly click the link and scan the article.

Certain points stand out, striking me as familiar.

It's normal to feel anxious from time to time, but excessive, ongoing anxiety and worry that is difficult to control and interferes with day-to-day activities may be a sign of Generalized Anxiety Disorder…

Symptoms may include:

Constant restlessness…

Fear of making the wrong choice…

Trembling…

Anxiety that seems out of proportion to the situation…

Overthinking worst-case outcomes…

Anxiety attacks…

Sure, maybe some of this applies. But it's totally normal! Everyone goes through this!

Okay, fine, yeah, sometimes my heart beats so violently I think it's going to burst. My lungs don't seem to want to let in any oxygen. The rational, reasonable part of my brain is overthrown by the part that assumes everything will turn into catastrophe…

Crap. Crap, crap, **crap**.

The more I think about it, the more I recognize myself.

I read a bunch more articles, somehow hoping the first, second, and third were flukes, but every single one just further cements the theory I might be struggling with GAD. (I'm not trying to self-diagnose here, but you try reading six articles that sound **exactly** like yourself and tell me it doesn't make you suspicious.)

Eventually, I give up on trying to disprove my newfound suspicion and turn my phone off. The anxiety that reemerged while I was doing research lingers but it's bearable. Somehow, it all feels a little less intimidating now that I might have a term for it.

Like, it's not just me being "sensitive" or something I need to ignore. It's a real thing. And, according to my reading, a thing a ton of people struggle with and have found ways to cope with.

I've never particularly liked using words to identify or label myself because I've already had certain expectations and words attached to me by others—the next step in the legacy, the team captain, Henry's brother. I just want to be **Hayden**, and I want Hayden to be enough, without any other labels.

But the thought of a potential diagnosis that would make sense of my entire sixteen years of life…it makes everything feel a little less lonely.

Scooping Buñuelo up, I slide out of bed and head downstairs for a glass of water. Who knew a heart-to-heart with an iguana could be so dehydrating.

I peer into the kitchen and see Mamma hunched over the counter, reading the cookbook that's been passed down through generations of her family. Her finger traces over the notes in the margins, most of them written in unintelligible, chicken-scratch Italian.

I hope she's engrossed enough that she won't strike up a conversation, but as soon as I reach the bottom of the stairs, she spots me and smiles.

"Good, you're here." She waves me over, then turns away from dinner prep and grabs a piece of paper off the fridge. She extends it toward me as I enter the kitchen, but recoils when she notices I'm cradling Buñuelo. "We've talked about this! Don't bring that thing into common areas, please!"

"Mamma, his name is Buñuelo, and he has feelings. How would you like to be called a 'thing' and banished from family areas?" I rebut, indignant over the ongoing mistreatment of Buñuelo.

She pinches the bridge of her nose and exhales sharply. "Keep him away from the food, at the very least. We don't need lizard flavoring in the Bolognese sauce."

I make sure to keep Buñuelo away from the counters as I pour myself a glass of water. Mamma returns her attention to the paper and holds it up for me to see.

"What do you think?" she asks. It's a poster advertising the Thirty-Fourth Annual Palmera High Winter Talent Show, adorned with small illustrations of instruments, ballet slippers, and even a unicycle.

"It's…a little busy?" I shrug. "Kinda hard to read the date and time of the show with all of the graphics."

"I was worried about that. I'll simplify it." She nods to herself.

I head for the stairs.

"Oh, Hay, wait!" Mamma calls out.

I'm never going to be able to have a nice, cold glass of water in the comfort of my bedroom, am I?

I turn around. "Yeah?"

Mamma motions to the kitchen table, and I take a reluctant seat, setting Buñuelo in my lap so he can't crawl on the tabletop—that might get him evicted. "I know I got overly excited and sprang a lot on you when you told us about quitting the team," she continues, "but I really want you to reconsider the talent show."

I take a long pull of water to buy time while I form a response, but she's not done. "It'll be a great low-stress environment to get some performing experience!" She flashes a wide, encouraging smile.

No matter how much I try, I can't picture performing in public. But I don't know how to explain that to Mamma—it's a terrible thing for a Broadway hopeful to confess, and it's embarrassing to admit to someone who has been singing in front of big audiences since she was a kid.

"Hayden?" Mamma waves her hand in front of me, interrupting my train of thought. "Did you hear me? I said—"

"It's not low-stress, though!" I blurt. "It's still an audience and performing live and having to do a million things at once, like stay in tune, remember lyrics, be charismatic, play an instrument…" I trail off, anxiety blooming in my chest as I think about all the moving parts.

"Stage fright is perfectly normal!" she assures me. "But you'll have to face that fear eventually. I can help you prepare during our lessons." She nods understandingly, but she really doesn't understand.

I'm hyper-aware of my speeding heart and leg bouncing uncontrollably underneath the table. Even ten minutes ago I would have tried to get out of this conversation, but now I have words to explain what's going on.

I take a few beats to regain my composure before meeting Mamma's eye. "I…want to talk to you about something," I admit, my voice small and unsure.

She looks concerned but gives me her undivided attention.

"I don't think it's just stage fright, Mamma." I use my free hand to unlock my phone and click onto one of the GAD articles I read upstairs. "I've been struggling with anxiety my whole life, but it's been especially bad lately."

Memories of recent anxious moments I convinced myself were totally, super, one hundred percent normal come flooding in: Kicking Casey in the library during a moment of panic, jumping to worst-case scenarios after I DM'd her for the first time, having a post-game breakdown in the locker room.

Then I think further back to the time I was ten and had an anxiety attack in the school bathroom because a teacher threatened to call my parents about a bad grade.

Ironically, discussing my anxiety only increases it, but I soldier on. "I think…maybe…I have…a disorder." The last word comes out as a whisper, and I slide my phone across the table.

Mamma looks surprised but remains silent. She takes my phone, and her eyes scan the screen. After a few minutes, she sets the device down.

I speak again before she can. "I want to be a performer, and I want to be able to sing in front of people…but this fear isn't as simple as stage fright. Sometimes, I freak out so much it feels like I'm dying."

"Oh, tesoro mio…I didn't know you were struggling this much." She reaches out and takes my hand. "I should've noticed. I'm sorry."

"It's not your fault." I shake my head. "I've been trying to pretend the anxiety didn't exist because…I dunno. I guess I already felt like I didn't fit in with the family or the team. I didn't want another thing making me different from everyone."

"I'm sorry if I ever made you feel like you had to hide things from me." She squeezes my hand. I don't say anything.

"You know," she continues, "after each of you boys were born, I had intense postpartum anxiety. I couldn't perform live for a long time. I realize that's not the same as dealing with it for your whole life," she clarifies, "but I do know how difficult it can be."

"Really? How did you deal with it?" I lean closer, desperate for any potential solution.

"I learned coping techniques in therapy. Deep breathing, mindfulness, journaling."

Now it's my turn to be surprised. "You went to therapy? I don't remember that."

"I stopped going when Dino was one, so you were only three. It makes sense you don't remember." She chuckles. "It was hard, but it helped me a lot. I had to start with baby steps—I'd sing in front of your dad, and then at church, and finally I was able to sing before a full audience again. I see now it was a mistake to suggest you do the talent show right off the bat. Starting that big would be intimidating even for someone who doesn't have anxiety attacks."

"Mamma, do you…" I pause, biting my lip. "Do you think maybe I could try therapy? I don't know if I can handle this on my own anymore."

Tears well in her eyes. "Oh, of course, honey. You shouldn't have to deal with this alone. I'm here for you, too. You can always lean on me, okay?"

"Okay," I breathe, releasing some of the weight on my shoulders. "Grazie, Mamma."

That night, I try my hardest to focus on my geography homework, but I can't stop mulling over the conversation I had with Mamma about Generalized Anxiety Disorder.

It's hard for me to imagine her being too anxious to perform. She's always been my biggest musical role model (behind Jeremy Jordan)—someone collected and professional, who oozes confidence onstage. I can't picture her having to slowly ease her way back into live singing.

Eventually, I set the homework aside and open Instagram. There's no way I'm getting any work done tonight.

The first post on my feed is a selfie of a grinning Casey next to a highly unamused Jell-O. I smile and double-tap the picture before clicking onto her profile. She's been more active recently, but she still hasn't posted a new cover video since "On My Own."

I scroll down to the video and play it again. As her voice—full of effortless vibrato and perfectly timed emotional inflection—flows through my phone speakers, I think about what Mamma said about taking baby steps.

The thought morphs into an idea, and by the time the video ends, it's fully taken root. Maybe there's a way for me to take a small step toward a live performance and put myself out there.

I open my DM thread with Casey and type a new message.

Nov 7 at 8:02 PM

@HeyitsHayden I researched Generalized Anxiety Disorder…I think I might have it.

@Casey.K.Sings wowza that's a big revelation! are u ok? how do u feel??

@HeyitsHayden Relieved, mostly. I told my mom and we're going to find a therapist so I can get some help

@Casey.K.Sings hell yeah! we stan taylor in this household 😎

@HeyitsHayden Haha. Anyway she used to have anxiety too and told me she had to work her way up to performances

@**HeyitsHayden** I thought…maybe we could record one of our songs and post it on your page? It might help both of us get more comfortable with singing for an audience?

Seen 8:07 PM

@**HeyitsHayden** We don't have to! Just an idea. You don't have to ghost me :/

@**Casey.K.Sings** ughhh you're a menace ☺ but it's not a terrible idea…ok fine. but only if i get to pick the song!

@**HeyitsHayden** Haha sure. You can't post it until after I quit the team though

@**Casey.K.Sings** yep no problem. wanna film on saturday? my ASL lesson was canceled

@**HeyitsHayden** Sounds good. I'll bring Rodolfo :)

@**Casey.K.Sings** wtf. who?? is rodolfo???

@**HeyitsHayden** You'll see…

CHAPTER 25
CASEY

ON SATURDAY AFTERNOON, THE DOORBELL RINGS RIGHT AS I'M EXTRACT-
ing my phone tripod from a pile of still-unpacked boxes. I run to the door
and swing it open.

Hayden smiles at me, wearing his usual outfit: a light pink jersey, cargo
shorts, and hand-me-down Adidas that are literally falling apart. His guitar
case is tucked underneath his right arm, his skateboard under his left.

I smile back and welcome him inside.

"That's Rodolfo," he says, motioning to the guitar case as he props
it against the couch. He scoops Jell-O into his arms, makes his way into
my kitchen, and starts rooting around in the snack drawer with my cat
balanced on one hip like a baby.

"I don't even get a hello?" I scoff.

He shrugs, far more interested in squeeze-pouch applesauce than
in making conversation. "Hi. Nice to see you. You look pretty," he says
over his shoulder. He opens the door to my fridge and reads the orange
juice label with excessive focus.

"You're a real gentleman."

Still cradling Jell-O, he grabs a glass from the cabinet and
one-handedly pours himself juice. "Where are we filming?"

"I thought we could go outside. The lighting is better there." I stand by the kitchen island, hand on my hip, tapping my foot impatiently.

"Okay, okay! Almost ready," he defends. "It's fine, we've got plenty of time. Dino agreed to cover my afternoon shift at El Pollo Cubano so long as I get there in time to help with the dinner rush."

After assembling a snack platter he's satisfied with—string cheese, Doritos, chocolate-covered almonds, and orange juice—he releases Jell-O, grabs his guitar, and we walk outside.

In my backyard, I set up the tripod to hold my phone, then place two chairs in front of it. Hayden sits and munches away as I adjust the angle and film a test video.

Once I'm happy with the angle, I sit in the chair next to his. He places his DIY charcuterie board on the patio table and strums Rodolfo a few times. I do some last-minute warmups, lip trills and vocal sirens I'm sure my neighbors don't appreciate.

I shake two 'R's in the air. *"Ready?"*

He bobs his fist. *"Yes."*

The golden November sun shines in my eyes as Hayden strums the final few notes in "If It Were Us," a new song I had finished writing a few days before he suggested we film together. A sense of calm settles over the backyard.

He flashes a smile. "I think that was the take." He looks to me for confirmation.

I grab my phone and return to my seat. I scoot my chair closer to him and we watch the video. As I predicted, the sunlight washing over us provides the perfect mood lighting for the tender, heartfelt love song.

"How are you so incredible at coming up with accompaniments?" I ask him.

"There wouldn't be any instrumental without your brilliant lyrics." He returns the compliment with a wink.

We watch a few different versions, but the last one is by far the best. "I like it," he says. "We sound good."

I add the last video to my Favorites folder so I won't mix up the six different takes and set my phone on the table. I smile at him. "And it's okay to post this after you talk to your aunt tomorrow?"

He hesitates.

"No pressure." I poke his knee. "If you aren't ready, you aren't ready."

"No, no. It's okay. It's time for me to put myself out there. Send me the video, though. I want to have a copy."

I send him the last take. He picks up his phone to open the message, and his eyes bug out of his head when he sees the time.

"Oh my gosh, I'm late!" he exclaims. He opens his GPS app and calculates how long it'll take him to skateboard to El Pollo Cubano, staring helplessly at the estimated arrival time. "I need to get my driver's license," he grumbles.

I would give him a ride if I had a license, but having one wasn't super practical in Portland, a city with no parking spots and great public transportation.

He panic-scrolls through his contacts and makes a call. He circles the perimeter of my backyard as he speaks to whoever is on the other end of the line. I push the chairs back into the table and break down my tripod.

"César's picking me up." He breathes a sigh of relief and hangs up the phone. "He'll be here in a few."

"How bougie of you to have a chauffeur," I joke as we head inside to wait for César. Hayden stashes his guitar in the coat closet so César won't see it, promising he'll come get it later.

When the doorbell rings five minutes later, he rushes to the door and pulls it open, calling "See you later!" over his shoulder.

"Mm-hmm, see you on—" I fall silent as César walks past Hayden and into my foyer.

"Hey." He nods in my direction.

"Hey?" I lift a brow.

"Hey, hi, hello!" Hayden rushes, trying to pull César back toward the door. "I'm already late for work so can we—"

"Your parents are gone?" César interrupts and cranes his neck to search for Mom and Dad.

"Mm-hmm. They're on their version of a date," I explain. "Shopping for office supplies. Real hot stuff."

"And they're cool with you being home alone with a boy?" He steps toward me.

"Careful, sweetheart. You sound a little jealous." I narrow my eyes at him but find that his awkward smile makes my stomach do a weird fluttering thing.

Okay, what the actual hell?

Sworn enemies are **not** supposed to give you butterflies.

"Um. I'm still here." Hayden clears his throat, breaking the intense eye contact between César and me. "And I'm very, very late for work."

"Yeah, yeah." César waves his hand dismissively. "I just need to talk to Casey for a second."

"Can it wait?" He glances at his phone, checking the time.

"The less you complain, the faster this will be," César snaps. "Can we sit in the backyard?"

"Golly, no! My parents would never approve!" I clutch imaginary pearls, trying to shake off the butterflies and play it cool.

César rolls his eyes and heads toward the backyard. Hayden storms back into the kitchen with an irritated groan.

On the deck, I pull out a chair and sit with my back facing the door. Cautiously, César takes the seat across from me.

The silence builds. Finally, César sticks his hand toward me. "Truce?" he asks. There's a sincerity in his eyes softening his sharp edges.

I squint at him and try to process this unexpected offer of a ceasefire, pinching my wrist underneath the table. I have to be dreaming, right? What else could explain this weird-ass plot twist?

I don't wake up. Damn it.

"No. What?!" I shake my head, pushing his hand away.

César scans the backyard, ensuring no one is around. Which makes no sense, because…we're in my backyard. *"Sorry,"* he signs. "For being——and trying to——so, I'm sorry," he blurts.

"César…I didn't get any of that."

He takes a deep breath, pulls out his phone, and types a quick note. He hands me the device. His cracked screen distorts the message, but I get the gist of it.

"Oh, yeah, you were definitely an asshole. Major asshole. One of the biggest assho—"

"I'm trying to apologize here!" he interrupts with a huff.

I can't help but crack a smile at his annoyance. "I told you I don't want a pity apology."

"I don't pity you. I'm apologizing because you deserve an apology. I made a lot of assumptions about you and blamed you for something that's not your fault. And I'm sorry."

I study him, letting his words sink in. Of course, it's nice to hear César finally apologize—and he definitely has stuff to apologize for. But I guess I've played a part in this feud too, haven't I? I also made assumptions; I was equally petty.

The truth is, the more I learn about César, the less he resembles Victor. He's shaping up to be more of a friend than an enemy.

"I'm sorry too," I say reluctantly. I reach out and grab his hand, giving it a firm shake. "Truce."

A smile threatens his lips.

"You know, you're like a pit bull," I joke. "Everyone is scared of you, but you're actually a big softie, aren't you?"

"I am not," he says, tapping the pale scar on his cheek. "Do 'big softies' get into knife fights?"

My bullshit detector goes off. "Oh yeah? Who'd you get in the fight with?"

He pauses. "Fine. I fell off my bike and my head hit a rock." He leans closer. "But you can't tell anyone. Getting cut by a rock is nowhere near as badass as getting into a knife fight."

I flash a smug grin. "I knew it."

A moment of silence passes between us before he scoots to the edge of his chair and leans closer to me. I freeze, staring at him wide-eyed.

"I also wanted to…thank you."

"Th-thank me?" I stammer, shocked. "For what?"

"Hayden's really come out of his shell since meeting you. He's a pretty reserved kid, but your friendship has clearly been good for him." With an awkward movement, César reaches over and gingerly places his hand on top of mine. His touch is electric, and my heart flips traitorously. He stares straight into my soul with his effin' breathtaking onyx eyes and repeats, "So…thank you."

Uh oh. It looks like my first snarky assessment was right: He's a sweetheart.

Testing the waters, I flip my hand over and widen my fingers. He takes the hint immediately, and his long, rough fingers intertwine with my smaller ones.

We stare at each other for a beat, relishing our truce, which is already more than that. Then he suddenly lurches backward and yanks his hand from mine.

I turn toward the back door and see Hayden standing there, holding a box of Fruit Roll-Ups and wearing an uncomfortable smile.

"Sorry if I interrupted—"

"You did," César snaps.

Hayden blushes. I feel my own cheeks redden too. "Papá and Dino are both going to kill me if I'm not at the restaurant in, like, three minutes."

César sucks on his teeth and squeezes his eyes shut.

"Welp." I chuckle awkwardly. "I'll see you guys on Monday?"

César peers at me. "Yeah. See you then."

Hayden mouths "sorry!" as César drags him out the front door, taking my Fruit Roll-Ups with him.

CHAPTER 26
HAYDEN

CÉSAR PULLS UP TO EL POLLO CUBANO, AND I BARELY LET HIM STOP THE car before leaping out of it and making a mad dash for the restaurant.

The bells on the door jingle violently as it slams shut behind me.

I jog into the kitchen and start washing my hands. Papá exits the storeroom with a huge bag of flour and an unimpressed frown.

"Thank you for gracing us with your presence," he grumbles, setting the bag on the counter.

I look around the kitchen. "Where's Dino and Tío?"

"Eddy is restocking some ingredients. Your brother is helping him, since you went AWOL."

I hold back a frustrated sigh. If it hadn't been for César's flirting, I wouldn't have been so late. "I was with Casey," I explain, securing my apron and hairnet. "We were working on some music."

He doesn't reply, and it instantly puts me on edge. Mamma and I haven't stopped talking about music since my confession, but Papá is harder to make conversation with these days. He's supportive, but our main topic of conversation has been fútbol since I was little. So I'm not sure how he's going to take this news.

"We wrote an original song together," I continue. "It's called 'If It Were Us.' She wrote the lyrics, and I did the accompaniment, and this afternoon we filmed ourselves singing it. We're going to post it on her Instagram and TikTok. We have other songs, too. Like 'Lionhearted Girl' and 'Not Yours.' It turns out we're a pretty good team."

"Are you going to perform them? Besides putting them on the web, I mean." Papá finally speaks as he starts assembling to-go containers next to me.

I suppress a laugh at him calling social media 'the web.' "Mamma wants me to do the Winter Talent Show, but I'm not ready for that."

"Why not?"

"Papá, I haven't even told Tía about all of this," I reply, not wanting to get into this whole talent show conversation for the millionth time.

"You're telling her tomorrow. The talent show is next month, no? Sounds like an excuse, Hayden."

Those kinds of comments are exactly why I haven't told Papá about my (probable) Generalized Anxiety Disorder. What if he thinks I'm making excuses? What if he doesn't understand like Mamma does?

I take a deep breath. "I want to do the show," I admit, my voice barely above a whisper. "But…I'm scared."

He pauses his work and rests a strong, weathered hand on my shoulder. "When I was your age and captain of the team…"

Ah, here we go again. Another fútbol anecdote.

"…I was always scared before big games. Sometimes the things that we love most scare the daylights out of us. Like our children."

Huh. That's not what I was expecting him to say.

I set a bowl of chopped lettuce aside and turn to face him. "What if I'm not good enough? What if I can't make you guys proud?"

"I've always been proud of you." He pats my cheek with a smile. "I'm constantly bragging about you. Did you know, I told a grocery store cashier about you yesterday? I told 'em someday my kid is going to be on a billboard."

"What?" I frown.

"The music chart."

"That's the Billboard Hot 100, Papá." It takes everything I have to not laugh at his cluelessness. "It's not a literal billboard."

He breezes past the mistake. "I *am* proud of you. And I want you to be proud of yourself. That's all I've ever wanted for my boys."

I blink away tears. I don't remember my dad ever being so heartfelt.

"I know it's not your mother's or my decision, but I think you should give the show a try. You'll blow them all away," he adds.

Papá pulls me into a tight hug. We separate when the bells on the door jingle, alerting us to Tío Eddy and Dino's return.

I straighten my apron, Papá gives me a wink, and we get back to work.

"And that's why, Tía, I'm quitting the team." I pause the run-through of my resignation speech with a frustrated grunt. Quitting doesn't feel like the right word.

Staring at my reflection in the toothpaste-smudged bathroom mirror, I tug at the roots of my hair and exhale. My breath causes the glass to fog up.

"I know you're upset"—I gaze into my own eyes and pretend I'm talking to my aunt—"but fútbol isn't my passion. I hope you'll understand—"

The bathroom door opens unexpectedly, and I jump forward in surprise, ramming into the counter.

Dino laughs as he props himself against the doorway, and I glare at him.

"I'm practicing."

"I can see that." He looks past me and into the mirror, fixing his hair.

"Can you not be annoying right now?" I turn back toward the mirror and sigh. "Tía's going to skin me and use my hide as a rug."

Dino gives me a quick hug from behind. "It'll be okay." His lips curl into the most forced smile I've ever seen. He looks like he's filming a proof of life video for his kidnappers.

"I love you or something," he mumbles—a not-very-emotionally-intelligent fourteen-year-old's version of being supportive. "Now stop talking to yourself and come downstairs."

I take one last glance in the mirror before following Dino.

In the kitchen, César and Tío Eddy are chatting with Papá while he puts the finishing touches on dinner. Lela and Tía help Mamma set the table.

Mamma shoots me a supportive smile as she lays out the plates. Tía follows her line of sight and looks me up and down, her judgement seeping into my bones.

I slip into the kitchen and help Papá serve up while eavesdropping on Mamma and Tía's conversation about our church's Christian romance book club.

Everyone sits down as Papá and I bring the food and drinks to the table. Mamma makes small talk with Tío Eddy about yesterday's farmer's market; Dino, Lela, and César bond over their mutual hatred for the ninth grade language arts teacher; and Tía watches me like a hawk. I sit silently, staring at my food and trying to take discreet deep breaths to quell the rising anxiety.

During a stretch of quiet, Mamma nods in my direction. I can't avoid this any longer. It's time.

I scoot my chair out and stand up, but immediately feel strange about standing up, so I sit back down. Which looks even stranger, doesn't it? This is not going well.

"I have something to say." I push my terror into a faraway corner of my mind.

Everyone gives me their full attention.

I mentally run through the speech I practiced, but when I open my mouth, only five ineloquent words pop out: "I'm quitting the fútbol team!"

The room goes still, like someone pressed pause on a movie.

My heart is pounding and pinpricks of anxiety travel through my limbs. "I really hope you don't hate me," I continue, my voice nearly a whisper, "but I don't want to play fútbol. I want to be a singer."

Mamma and Papá smile proudly, Dino gauges everyone's reactions, César stops chewing mid-bite, and Tío Eddy's and Lela's eyes widen.

Tía Carmen is utterly expressionless, which is somehow more intimidating than rage or condemnation. She's not giving any indication of what she's thinking.

The silence is eating me alive. It's literally painful how quiet our dining room is right now. I have no idea what to do so I keep rambling, hoping someone will eventually say something and save me from myself. "It's just…I feel like a little part of my soul dies whenever I play fútbol. And I'd really rather have an alive soul, you know?"

Nothing. Zilch. Nada.

After another eternity of silence, Lela casually reaches over and takes Tía's butter knife, then mouths: "Just in case."

Feeling like I'm about to poke a bear, I timidly ask, "Tía?"

A single muscle in my aunt's jaw twitches, and her nostrils flare ever so slightly. "Music," she says. A statement, not a question. "As a career."

I nod. "Fútbol isn't my passion. It's Henry's and Dino's and César's."

Her eyes darken. "People are counting on you. They expect more than music!" she hisses. "If I had known you were going to treat your position as a joke, I wouldn't have let you anywhere near my team."

Now, she's boiling. Anger burns in her eyes and I can practically see embers drift off her smoldering skin. I take a deep breath and think about what Papá told me about Abuelo—about how he chose fútbol over béisbol, even though his family disapproved. Why would he have taken such a big risk? Why did he put his relationship with the people he loved on the line to chase his dreams?

"Fútbol doesn't make me happy," I say. "Abuelo followed his heart and chose fútbol, because it made him happy; I want to follow my heart and choose music."

Her glare liquefies my insides. "Don't you dare bring him into this. You selfish little—"

"Carmen," Papá interjects, voice firm. "If Papá hadn't been courageous enough to leave Cuba against Abuelo and Abuela's wishes, we wouldn't be having this conversation. Our boys wouldn't be fútbol players. It'd be hypocritical to praise Papá for his bravery but condemn my son for his."

"Yeah, can't we just be happy for him?" Lela adds, smiling encouragingly at me.

Tía considers this for a beat before scoffing indignantly and continuing her tirade. An argument breaks out, Tía's booming, enraged voice jumbling together with words of defense from my other family members.

Across the table, César analyzes me. He hasn't said a word, either to defend me or scold me, and I don't know how to interpret his silence.

My chest tightens so much it's like I'm having a mini heart attack, the same way it felt after we lost against the Sharks. I need to put an end to this fighting or else I'm going to go to a very bad place.

"Stop! Please!" The words are thick as I squeeze them out.

Nobody hears me. The room is filled with sound, but it's like I'm stuck in a pocket of loud, crushing silence. My pleas are buried under the sounds of my family arguing about *my* decision. *My* passion. *My* future.

Hot tears well in my eyes as I look around and realize nobody sees me. I've gone invisible.

César's chair scrapes across the ground as he pushes out from the table. He comes to my side, tucks me under his arm, and leads me to the staircase.

We climb the stairs side by side. I'm slow and rickety, my legs like limp noodles, but he matches my pace and supports my body weight with ease.

We reach my room after what feels like hours. My legs finally give out and I fall onto my bed. I sit on the edge, hands trembling.

"Do you want the lizard?" César gestures toward Buñuelo, who watches me through the glass of his terrarium.

He doesn't wait for an answer, and instead removes the lid from the tank and reaches in. Buñuelo starts scratching his way up the glass walls, trying to get to me. César grabs him with both hands, sets him in my lap, and takes a seat next to us.

"Yeah, there you go." César pats my shoulder with the elegance of a drunkard. "Just pet the lizard. That'll help."

After roughly ten minutes of Buñuelo cuddles, the panic caused by the confrontation starts to wear off.

César starts taking overexaggerated deep breaths and nudging me.

I turn to face him. "What are you doing?"

"I'm deep breathing."

"Why?" I blink at him.

"Because it helps regulate your nervous system or something. I don't know, Hay, I'm not a doctor," he sighs. "But aren't people supposed to take deep breaths when they're upset?"

He's not wrong. Every single article about anxiety attacks I've read mentioned deep breathing. And Mamma did too.

I draw in a long, shaky breath and exhale slowly. After a few repetitions I become less lightheaded and find myself more grounded in the moment. It's wild how something as simple as breathing can help.

Before I register what's happening, César crushes me into a hug. My face is buried in his chest and his crucifix necklace comes perilously close to poking my eye out.

"W-why are you hugging me?" I ask, my voice wobbly. I squirm out of his embrace. "You've hugged me seven times in my entire life."

"Have you seriously kept track of every hug I've ever given you?"

"Maybe." I sniffle. Then, cautiously, I ask, "Are you…mad at me?"

"Of course not. Why would I be mad?"

I shrug. "Because I'm letting the team down."

"No, you're not. The worst thing you could do for the team is keep being captain even though you're not passionate about it. You're doing the right thing by stepping down."

I don't know what to say.

"Do you want to talk about it?" he asks.

I bite my lip. I hadn't planned to tell anyone besides Mamma and Casey about my anxiety anytime soon, but César has had my back since day one. He feels like a safe starting point. Baby steps, right?

"I probably have something called Generalized Anxiety Disorder." I sigh. "It hasn't been officially diagnosed or anything, but Mamma's been helping me with it. I'm going to start therapy once we find a good counselor."

César nods. "I figured."

"W-what?" I splutter.

Did everyone figure out I had an anxiety disorder before *I* even figured out I had an anxiety disorder?

He chuckles. "I didn't know about a disorder, but you've been anxious your whole life, and its only gotten worse this year."

And here I was thinking everyone saw me as the easygoing, chill friend.

"But I'm glad you told me, and I'm glad you're planning to get professional help. Mental health is nothing to be ashamed of." He smiles and musses up my hair. "It's obviously not the same, but I do this when I get nervous before big games, and it always helps me relax. Maybe it'll help you, too?" He takes off his treasured necklace and rubs his fingers against the smooth, shiny metal of the cross, then slips the chain around my neck. "I want you to have it."

I gingerly touch the pendant. Buñuelo starts licking it. "César, I can't take this."

After Tío Eddy's dad passed away, it was all César had to remember his abuelo by. He's never taken it off.

"I always felt loved when I wore it. I want you to feel the same."

Tears blur my vision as I rub the silver cross between my fingers. I can already feel how the cool metal will soothe those red-hot, hopeless moments.

"And I'm here for you, ¿entiendes? Anytime you need me. I'll even give you an eighth hug if you want."

"Thank you, César." I smile and wipe a tear off my cheek.

César throws his arm around my shoulders. "Hey, if we're looking for an upside here…I'm definitely going to be captain now."

"You're ruthless." I give a weak laugh and relax against him. I feel more at peace than I have in a long time.

For once, it seems like things might be okay. I might be okay.

CHAPTER 27
HAYDEN

"Why is the universe so cruel? Woe is me! I am woe!" Paz laments, straight out of a Shakespeare play. He's sprawled out on our usual table at El Pollo Cubano, his dark skin turning golden in the November sunlight that streams through the window.

I don't respond, too accustomed to his antics to care. My focus is trained on the table across the restaurant, where Dino and a freshman girl are having a study date.

"Seriously, though"—Paz briefly drops the melodrama—"how did Dino, arguably the most annoying person to roam planet Earth, get a girlfriend? I feel bad for her."

"Why? Because Dino is unremarkable in every way?"

He snorts. "That, but also because her name is Ruby Rubio."

"Oh, yeah. That's unfortunate." I nod.

As I try (unsuccessfully) to snoop on Dino and Ruby's conversation, I absentmindedly rub the cross that hangs from my neck. It's become a habit over these past few days. César was right—it's oddly calming.

I'm torn out of my poor lipreading attempt when César slams down two plates. Speak of the devil. "Two cubanos. Extra cheese and no pickle on yours." He points to the sandwich near Paz.

Paz drops my hand and peels back the bread to ensure the offensive ingredient isn't in there. "Gracias, Cécé." He smiles coyly. "And if I might be so presumptuous, you look stunning in that hairnet. Or should I call it a bald-net?"

"I hope you step on a Lego every day for the rest of your life," César growls. Instead of heading back to the kitchen, he pulls out a chair and sits, glancing over his shoulder to make sure my dad isn't going to scold him for slacking off. "The Fall Formal dance is tomorrow."

"Correct!" Paz chirps. "He's smarter than he looks, huh?" he whispers to me across the table.

César clenches his jaw but remains composed. He says something else to me, deliberately mumbling.

For all intents and purposes, I'm a César Ramirez grunt translator. But these particular mutterings are out of my area of expertise. I stare at him and wait for him to make a more intelligible noise.

"Is Casey going?" he repeats himself more clearly when he realizes I haven't understood.

"Ooh! Cécé and Casey, sittin' in a tree," Paz singsongs. A scowl settles on César's face as Paz cackles.

"She wasn't planning on going, but she might change her mind if you were to ask her." I smirk.

"What? Why would she ever say yes?"

I shoot César a look. "Are you kidding? I saw you in her backyar—"

He slaps a hand over my mouth and my skin stings from the impact. "Bembelequero," he hisses.

"I'm not gossiping! I'm—"

Another slap.

"Ow! Stop that!"

"Then stop running your damn mouth," César snaps.

Paz glances between us with a sly smirk but doesn't say anything. "Cécé, if we're going to the dance, you're going to need something nicer than a tank top." He looks César up and down. "I'm going to Tan France you."

César leans away from my best friend. "That's not a euphemism, is it?"

"From QUEER EYE?" Paz's eyes roll into his skull. "So uncultured. Ugh, never mind. It doesn't matter. I'm going to QUEER EYE you."

"For the record, I'd prefer to not be…Queer Eyed," César grumbles.

"Too bad," Paz hums. "It's about time for a makeover. You're aggressively straight."

Papá calls to César from the kitchen. César stops near the front counter and turns back toward Paz and me. "Fine," he relents. "You can Queer Guy me."

"That's a different thing altogether," Paz quips, then pulls his phone out and starts scouring Pinterest for suit inspiration.

On Saturday morning, Paz and I wait at my house for César and Lela to pick us up. They pull into my driveway just after lunch, Lela hanging out the passenger window with windblown hair sticking to her red lipstick.

"My brother is whipped!" She howls with laughter as Paz and I buckle into the back seat. "The only thing he hates more than dancing is shopping. I can't believe he's willingly doing both these things!"

César takes the high road, turning on the radio and blasting music as we drive to Casey's house. Lela and Paz act like they're planning a royal wedding, discussing color palette and debating whether they should find outfits that match.

When we arrive, I knock on the front door. Then again. And a few more times. It swings open after the fifth round of knocking.

Casey leans against the doorframe, her eyes darting between the four of us. César salutes her, suppressing a smile. I'd say Lela's 'whipped' assessment was accurate.

"We're kidnapping you." Paz steps forward, his voice raised. "Get in the car."

She quirks a brow. "Sorry guys, today's not a good day to be kidnapped."

"Is it ever a good day to be kidnapped?" Paz muses.

Casey either doesn't hear Paz or chooses to ignore him. "I have ASL class soon. I can't hang out." She looks at me, probably hoping I'll be the voice of reason. "Tomorrow?"

Before I can reply, Mrs. Kowalski appears behind her. "What are you kids doing here?"

"*We want* to take *Casey shopping* for the Fall Formal *dance*," I say while signing what Casey's taught me.

Mrs. Kowalski glances at Casey. "You didn't say anything about a dance! When is it?"

"Tonight," Lela supplies.

"I already told them I have ASL class and I can't go," Casey tells her mom.

Mrs. Kowalski laughs and says, "Sweetie, go have fun with your friends! Dad and I will fill you in on what happened in class later."

César gently pushes past Paz, smiling at Casey, who looks torn. *The dance will be fun. Please?*

"Don't you guys have to work at the restaurant today?" she responds.

"Our parents gave us the day off, since it's a special occasion," César explains.

She looks up at him and carefully weighs her options. After a beat, she sighs defeatedly and signs, *"O-K."*

We pile into César's car and head for the thrift store. The automatic doors whoosh open, and a gust of AC hits us as we enter the building. Lela links arms with Casey. *"I know where* they keep the *good dresses,"* she says and signs with remarkable speed given that she's using her non-dominant right hand.

Lela whisks Casey into an aisle with hundreds of dresses. I'm glad we started the shopping early. Lela has a penchant for haggling, and dragging Paz out of a thrift store is impossible. We're gonna be here for a while.

César, Paz, and I start rifling through racks of suit jackets, boring politician pants, and belts. I stumble across a tweed jacket that fits me perfectly and makes me look smart. It looks like something an English prince would wear for a spot of tea and a game of croquet. (Or whatever English princes do when they're not busy colonizing.)

"What do you think?" I spin, thinking Tan France would be proud.

Paz gags. "That gives off mega dead-grandpa vibes. True fact."

"It does not!" I run my hand over the jacket.

César checks the price tag. "It's four dollars, Hay. Only dead-grandpa coats are four dollars. That's common knowledge."

Paz snorts and high-fives César.

"Since when do you two get along?" I grumble.

"Since you started wearing dead-grandpa jackets," Paz hums.

I reluctantly abandon the tweed and join Paz in rooting through the bins of unsorted clothes, trying to find something I wouldn't be embarrassed to wear in front of my classmates. After twenty minutes, I find a purple plaid jacket. "Surely you can't hate this?" I show Paz.

He scrunches his nose. "Barney and the Brawny Man's illicit love child, in suit form."

"The dinosaur and the paper towel guy?"

"That is correct."

I hang the jacket over my arm. "Better than a dead grandpa."

Paz pulls a fluorescent orange suit from the bottom of a bin.

César looms above us, nose wrinkled in disgust as Paz announces it's his dream suit.

"That's the ugliest thing I've ever seen," César says.

Paz stands, suit neatly folded in his arms. "You've never looked in a mirror before?"

I cough to cover my laughter as César sends a death glare my way.

"Good work, team!" Paz claps as we finalize our outfits. "Now, it's QUEER EYE time!" he squeals.

"Oh yay." César deadpans.

CHAPTER 28
CASEY

"YOU'RE NOT GETTING ANYWHERE NEAR ME WITH THAT THING." I SCOOT away from Lela as she takes an eyelash curler out of her makeup bag.

She smacks a piece of gum, opting to use clunky SimCom so that she can keep chewing. "*You have beautiful* lashes, but they *need a little work.*" She bends over and clamps the medieval torture device onto my eyelashes, then swipes mascara on them. "Voila!" she announces, handing me a compact mirror.

Sparkly gold eyelids. Matte pink lip. Cheekbone highlighter you could see from space. It takes a second to realize I'm looking at myself.

"You're an artiste," I say in a terrible French accent.

Lela adds finishing touches to her own look, which is more dramatic than mine: black and crimson eyeshadow, sharp winged liner, dark red lipstick. I realize I'm staring at her and look away. Someone needs to revoke my chaotic bisexual card—this is too much chaos, even for me.

"I'm nervous about tonight. I haven't been to a dance since I lost my hearing," I admit. "I probably won't be able to hear anyone. The music will be too loud."

"Wow, it's lucky we can sign," she signs, a playful glint in her eyes.

I avoid responding by looking down to scratch Jell-O's chin. She stretches and kneads my bedspread.

Lela touches my arm. "If you get overwhelmed, we'll leave. It's not like we were committed to the dance anyway."

"What do you mean? You guys weren't planning on going?"

She closes three fingers. *"No.* César convinced us to go."

I scoff, throwing a hooked index finger away from my chin. *"Really?* He doesn't strike me as a school dance guy."

"Oh, honey, he's not." Lela smirks, smoothing her black bodycon dress. "Hey, did Hayden ever tell you César got sent home for threatening Marco when he was being a dick about your hearing loss?"

"What? Why would he do that?" I ask Lela, confused. That seems off brand for my dearly beloved (former) mortal enemy.

"Casey. Babe." She stares at me, one brow hiked in a "really?" expression.

I stare at Lela in disbelief. "You're not seriously suggesting he's been pulling my pigtails?"

She heaves an exasperated sigh. "That's an outdated saying that conditions women to accept harassment."

I blink at her.

"But, ignoring that connotation, yes. He likes you. Hello." She nudges me repeatedly, then explains, "César's like a burnt marshmallow. You have to peel away that black, crusty part to get to the sweetness."

I had my suspicions—holding hands in my backyard, anyone?—but having it confirmed by his sister still takes me aback, and I find myself scrambling to change the subject.

"Uh, welp. We should head downstairs! It's almost six thirty!" I hurry toward my bedroom door. Lela follows as I cautiously navigate the staircase, unaccustomed to taking it in heels.

I step off the stairs right as Mom opens the front door, welcoming the boys inside with a beaming smile. César's eyes not-so-subtly slide up and down my body. I wrap my arms around my light pink dress, trying not to fidget.

"You look nice," he signs.

I do my best to ignore Paz, Hayden, Lela, and my mom exchanging looks. *"You too."* I shake a 'Y.'

César wears a crisp white button-up, a pink vest the same color as my dress (unplanned, but absolutely looks planned), and black skinny jeans. A mix of formal and effortless.

"That's hideous, Paz." I divert my attention to Paz's outrageous orange suit. I approach him and run my hands across the velvety material.

"I know! Don't you love it?" Paz strikes a pose.

"He looks like a C-H-E-E-T-O," César signs.

Mom pulls out her phone and steps into our group. She forms the letter 'L' with her thumb and index finger, then crooks her index finger. *"I want pictures!"*

Mom slips into photographer mode, arranging the five of us in optimal poses then attacking us from all angles. My friends accommodate her continual requests to smile wider and switch locations. Eventually, they step aside, leaving César and me standing next to each other.

I glare at the others. They're clearly proud of their ambush. I'm starting to wonder if this was an elaborate setup.

I try to produce a genuine smile, but standing in such close proximity to César distracts me. It doesn't help that Lela is snickering, Paz is making kissy faces, and Hayden is taking his own photos.

"We're going to be late, Mom." I step away from César when it gets too awkward to bear.

My friends start filtering out of the house. I glance at my mom as I grab my purse. From her chin, she tucks her index and middle finger to her palm. *"He's cute!"* She jerks her head toward César. *"Is he single?"*

A shit-eating grin crosses his face. *"Thank you. Yes, I'm single,"* he signs to Mom. His eyes float over to me, and we hold eye contact for half a second too long before he heads outside.

Humiliation floods my cheeks as Mom laughs.

"I didn't know he knew ASL!" she defends.

"You saw him sign when I came down!" I groan.

Mom rubs a fist on her chest, still laughing. "Hey, at least he knows he's cute. I admire a man with confidence."

Outside, I'm absolutely mortified to see César smirking as he opens the passenger door for me. Once I've climbed in, he adjusts his rearview mirror and pulls out of my driveway.

"I like your mom," he says.

"Because she stroked your fragile ego?"

He chuckles amusedly and turns on the radio in lieu of a reply.

By the time we get to Palmera, dozens of students have already lined up in the courtyard. We take our place in the back of the long line.

When it's our turn to buy tickets, I notice that Jessica is running the booth.

"Hey, Casey!" she signs. *"How many tickets?"*

I go to grab my wallet, but César pushes my hand down. He places money on the table.

"Five, please," he signs.

She slides him a strip of five flimsy paper tickets. *"Have fun!"*

We divide up the tickets, then head into the gym. According to César, the gym is called Dihigo in honor of baseball legend Martín Dihigo.

The hand-painted sign hanging above the door informs me that tonight's decor is enchanted forest–inspired, which, it turns out, means fake ivy stuck to the walls with duct tape and an unsightly DIY castle photo backdrop. I'm going to go out on a limb and say the theater kids were in charge of the decor. It screams low-budget Montague vs. Capulet.

Music blares from the speaker system at the back of the room, pulsating through the crowd of students. The dance only started ten minutes ago, but the gym is already packed.

Hayden waves his hand, grabbing everyone's attention. *"Use ASL or type N-O-T-E-S. Casey can't hear well with the music playing."* His lips move while he signs, likely using SimCom, but no sound registers for me. The loud music and chattering make it impossible to hear his voice.

"O-K." César nods.

Lela places her index finger against her chin and pushes her hand forward. *"Sure."*

Paz clumsily bobs his fist twice.

"Thank you." I squeeze Hayden's shoulder.

Paz grabs Lela's hand and drags her to the center of the room, where everyone is dancing. "Don't Stop Believing" by Journey starts to play, and I fight the urge to dance. I don't need to appear whiter than I am, although it's not my fault the DJ selected a playlist full of basic-white-girl songs.

I hang back, hiding in the shadows. The music is audible, but I find myself craving vibrations. Unable to feel the floor through my shoes, I press a flat hand to the wall and smile at the faint reverberation.

"I'm going to get a drink." César motions toward the refreshments table on the other side of the room. *"You want one?"*

I nod.

While César stands in line, Hayden observes the ebb and flow of the crowd, then stops and shakes his head in silent amusement. His object of focus is Dino and a girl I don't recognize, dancing **near** each other, but not exactly together. Oh, to be fourteen and have a crush.

César returns with three red Solo cups. He makes no attempt to converse as we lean against the wall and people-watch.

Hayden catches my attention by flapping a hand in front of me. *"I'm going to the bathroom,"* he tells me. But when he hasn't returned ten minutes later, I excuse myself and go look for him.

I slip through the crowd and into the hallway, heading toward Palmera's front doors. Halfway through the lobby, I spot him near the office and head his way. "Hey. I came to check on you. You okay?"

"Yeah, I'm fine." Hayden nods absentmindedly but stares past me. I turn around and see the talent show sign-up sheet pinned to the bulletin board near us. I meet his eyes and raise a questioning brow. He thinks he masks his emotions better than he actually does.

He takes a deep breath. "I was incredibly anxious about filming songs with you and taking vocal lessons from my mom, but so far those have been fun, so I was thinking…maybe we should consider the talent show? I mean, I'm still super anxious about it…but if you're willing to be my partner, I'd like to do it together."

I stare at him, unable to believe what I'm hearing. (But, hey, when can I ever truly trust my hearing?) "Seriously?"

"Yes," he signs. "Singing with you feels…" he waves his hands around wildly, searching for an adjective. "Ugh," he grunts, "this is why you're the songwriter. I don't know how to be poetic."

Laughing, I rest a hand on his shoulder. "I know what you mean. I feel the same way."

"So?" He sticks his hand out. "What do you say? Partners?"

A cynical voice in the back of my head tells me to say no—to run while I can. It's not too late, the voice says, to just stick to my comfort zone and only post edited videos instead of performing my songs live.

But what kind of a life would that be? Running from performing when it's one of the only things that makes me happy?

No. I refuse to be silenced any longer.

I shake his hand, feeling terrified, resilient, and inspired all at once.

"Partners," I agree.

Hayden grabs the pen hanging from the sheet, and with another deep breath, scribbles our names onto the paper. "This means we have to write a new song!" I exclaim as he turns back around. "Oh God, how are we going to pull that off?"

"We can always do a cover," he suggests. "Or an old song."

"No way!" I scoff.

Me performing for the first time since becoming Deaf-Hard of Hearing plus Hayden's first performance **ever** is a momentous occasion. We can't use recycled material for it. We have to sing something special.

He gives me a quick hug, then readjusts his purple suit jacket. *"Don't worry,"* he signs. "We'll figure it out. But right now, let's just enjoy the dance."

Back in the gym, we go our separate ways. Paz drags Hayden out onto the dance floor and they start awkwardly doing the Dougie. I sidle up to César with a small smile, pull out my phone, type a note, and pass him the device: **how weird would it be if i took my heels off?**

He smiles and hands my phone back with a new message.

personally i wouldn't walk around barefoot in a high school gym but to each their own

I crouch and wrestle my feet out of the godawful stilettos I borrowed from Lela. It's a relief to take them off, and it's nice to feel the music through the soles of my feet.

Suddenly, everyone starts partnering up. Couples lean against one another and gently sway to the music. It's too soft for me to hear, but I can safely assume it's a slow song. (Unless this is an elaborate prank and everyone is slow-dancing to "Cotton Eye Joe.")

César dons a nervous smile as he swings an upside down 'V' over his upturned left palm, brings his knuckles together with extended thumbs, points to himself, and pulls upturned, clawed hands toward his body. *"Do you want to dance with me?"*

He offers his hand and I consider him for a beat, then allow him to lead me to the dance floor. I lean against him as he sways back and forth, hands hovering above my hips. I appreciate his polite conduct but decide to gently push on them. He lets them relax against the curve of my waist.

"I wish I didn't take my heels off," I say, looking up at him. "I wasn't so short when I had them on."

César removes one hand to sign. *"You're perfect."*

My face heats up—even full-coverage foundation can't conceal the wild blush spreading across my cheeks. What is this boy doing to me?

I get closer and hide my face in his pink vest. My arms slip around his waist and rest on his low back; his grip grows tighter, pulling me into an embrace.

We continue swaying and I try to avoid acknowledging the butterflies fluttering between us.

CHAPTER 29
HAYDEN

THANKSGIVING IS A WHOLE ORDEAL IN MY HOUSEHOLD.

Papá spends all day in the kitchen, basting the turkey, peeling ripe plantains, and supervising the annual all-hands-on-deck culinary project.

This year he's extra stressed because, at the last minute, I asked if we could invite the Kowalskis, which sent Papá spiraling into professional chef mode. He's been rushing around and barking orders at my brothers and me all morning like we're unpaid lackeys. Which, now that I think about it, *is* what we are.

"Hayden, stop dawdling!" Papá chides as he gives the raw turkey an overly sensual massage, rubbing spices into its pink skin. "I need you to stuff the turkey."

I crinkle my nose. "Stick my hand in the turkey hole? No, thank you!"

He narrows his eyes. "Hayden."

"Okay, okay." I roll up my sleeves and grab a handful of sweet plantain stuffing. I close my eyes and shove my hand into the turkey, obediently filling it. When I'm finished, Papá pours orange and garlic marinade on the outside.

"Hay," Tío Eddy distracts me from the bird carcass, his knife thumping against a cutting board as he chops sweet potatoes. "Lela told me you've been doing Instagram and...clock talk...videos?"

"TikTok," Lela corrects with a sigh as she helps Tío chop.

"And they've racked up six thousand followers," Henry chimes in.

"I bet ninety-nine percent of those are fangirls," Dino teases. "Chicks love curly hair, freckles, and charming personalities. Hayden has two of those things." I stick my tongue out at him.

"I used to be in a punk-rock band in high school," Tío continues.

"Seriously?" I ask, startled by this confession. Tío Eddy doesn't strike me as a punk rocker.

"Sí. Coiffed hair, leather jackets, the whole nine." He sighs, overtaken with nineties nostalgia. "I'm happy for you, chiquito. You're following your own path."

From the dining room, Tía Carmen shoots me a withering look. Clearly not everyone shares Tío's sentiments.

A few hours later, while Papá carefully monitors the almost-cooked turkey, Henry and I drag a heavy, rectangular fold-up table outside and set up an outdoor eating area. The main table will be overwhelming for Casey, with all the overlapping conversations, so I figured eating outside would be best.

"I've been sharing your videos on my Stories," Henry says while we set the table.

"I know. I've seen them." I set a pitcher of lemonade in the center of the table and head to the other side to give Henry a quick hug. "Thank you."

Henry's support really does mean a lot to me, even if I'm not good at verbalizing it. I feel like I'm getting to know him again, like I'm getting my older brother back.

The sliding glass door squeaks open and Dino pokes his head outside. "Casey's here."

"I'll finish up." Henry musses up my hair before nudging me inside. Casey's family stands by the front door. Mrs. Kowalski compliments our house while Mr. Kowalski chats with Papá and Tío Eddy.

César plants himself by Casey's side, signing something that makes her laugh. My lips curl into a sly smile. César has not yet mastered the art of subtlety.

"Hey!" I greet Casey in ASL and give her a hug. "We're going to eat outside."

After some mingling, we walk toward the back door, but César blocks Casey from opening it and insists on doing it for her. Outside, he pulls her chair out with a suave grin, then claims the seat next to her.

I sit across from them, wanting the best vantage point to observe César's clunky flirting. I pour lemonade for everyone while Lela settles into the chair next to me.

César grazes a hand across Casey's shoulder to get her attention. He alternately rotates his pointer fingers toward his body, then fingerspells "Thanksgiving." Then, with downturned eyebrows, he presses his knuckles together and rotates his thumbs. "How do you sign T-H-A-N-K-S-G-I-V-I-N-G?"

This launches them into a long-winded conversation. I catch some of the signs, but their hands dart around like race cars. I've been getting faster every day, but I can't keep up.

Dino interrupts, announcing that dinner is ready. We grab our plates and shuffle indoors. I pile my plate with food, taking extra servings of Tía's baked mac 'n cheese and Papá's star anise-infused cranberry sauce.

In the backyard, we tuck in. Dino devours his drumstick like a rabid dog, turkey juice dribbling down his chin. Lela flaps her hand at Casey. "Enjoying your first Thanksgiving in Miami?" she asks.

She smiles widely. "Absolutely. This sweet potato is amazing." She takes a big bite of Tío's casserole.

"He might give you the recipe if you ask nicely," Lela chuckles. "Or you could help him make it next year—" She stops herself, suddenly remembering this is Casey's first and last Thanksgiving in Florida.

The table goes quiet.

"So, what are you guys performing for the talent show?" César scrambles to change the subject as Casey pushes food around her plate with a frown.

A different new subject would've been better, but hey, he tried. 'A' for effort. Casey sighs heavily and looks to me for backup.

"We're working on a new song," I supply.

What I don't tell him is that Casey has her heart set on writing a new original song, but we've been struggling to come up with fresh material. I'm still trying to convince her to do a cover, or one of our old songs, since time is ticking, and we'll have to have something prepared once rehearsals start.

Thankfully, nobody presses for more information, and Thanksgiving dinner passes without further incident.

While the adults chat over glasses of wine in the kitchen, my friends and I gather in the living room.

I plop into my favorite blue armchair and Lela relaxes into the chair next to mine. "He's *giggling*. I haven't heard him giggle in my entire life," she whispers, leaning over.

César and Casey are crammed onto one cushion on the couch opposite us, both grinning as they sign to each other. Sure enough, César is releasing sporadic schoolgirl laughs.

"Oh my gosh." I clasp a hand over my mouth in genuine shock. It feels wrong to be observing the exchange, but I remind myself they're in my living room. It's not exactly private.

"It seriously doesn't bother you?" She motions toward them. "He's swooping in on your girl."

"Casey's not 'my girl,'" I groan. "And why is there such emphasis on romantic love anyway? Platonic love is just as valid and meaningful. I'm happy just having you guys—my family and friends. My music."

She reaches over and lovingly pinches my cheek like a grandma, which somehow feels right even though I'm four months older than her. "Just promise me you won't end up being an old cat lady."

"An old lizard man, maybe."

"Ugh! What on earth am I going to do with you?" She rubs her temples with a sigh.

CHAPTER 30
CASEY

IT'S T-MINUS THREE DAYS UNTIL THE START OF OFFICIAL TALENT SHOW rehearsals, and Hayden and I still have nothing prepared.

Usually, when we're working on a new song, I send a video of myself singing lyrics to Hayden and he creates an instrumental to go with the tune I wrote. This time, we've decided to work in reverse order.

He's doing the accompaniment before I've provided—or made substantial progress on—the words. We're hoping I can conjure up some lyrics by listening to his melody.

We head into his bedroom, and he digs Rodolfo out from his closet. He settles on his bed and strums as I lean against his headboard, staring at the measly five words I've written down:

I AM NOT BACKGROUND NOISE

Thirty minutes of staring later, Hayden pulls me out of my lyrical crisis. "Do you like this melody?" he asks.

I slam my leatherbound notebook shut and rest my hand on the body of his guitar.

He closes his eyes as his fingers slide up and down the fretboard. I close mine too. The notes to the song roll in like a heavy tide. The vibrations shoot up through my fingers and into my arm, spreading through my body.

A heavy exhale escapes my lungs as the song ends. The last note hangs in the air. When I open my eyes, Hayden is smiling at me.

"Did you like it?"

"It was perfect."

"Then why do you look like someone just punched you in the face?"

I grunt in frustration and hand him my journal, turned to an empty page that's supposed to be full of lyrics. "I have all of these ideas in my head, but whenever I try to write them down...they disappear."

"I like what you have so far." He smiles. "I am not background noise," he sings the words to the tune he wrote. It fits like a glove.

"This song would be Grammy-winningly perfect if I could do my damn job."

"You're starting to sound awfully self-critical. That's a very me thing to do," he muses.

I roll my eyes. "Can you play it again? If I listen to it a few times, maybe something'll shake loose up here." I tap my temple.

He brings Rodolfo into his lap and his slender fingers pluck the strings. The room fills with gentle, barely audible strumming. I lie down on my stomach and bury my face in his pillow.

By the third repeat of the lyricless song, I'm experiencing Bella-Swan-in-NEW-MOON-level depths of despair.

I groan loudly. The music stops, and Hayden's hand comes to rest on my back. "Hey, it's okay. You'll figure it out," he soothes.

"We have three days left to write this song." I sit up and stare at him.

He sighs, running a hand through his curls. "How about this?" he says after a moment of pondering. "We perform an old song during rehearsals and keep working on this one in the meantime. If you can't finish the lyrics before the show, we'll do the other one. But if you do finish, we'll sing the new one. That gives us a little more time."

I grunt again. "Stop making sense. It hurts."

He chuckles. "How about 'Lionhearted Girl'?"

I glance at my empty notebook. "Fine."

He starts playing his guitar with a satisfied smile. I place my hand on the instrument and begin singing the familiar lyrics.

I leave Hayden's house thirty-seven times less frustrated than when I arrived.

His suggestion has already lifted a weight off my shoulders. If I'm not able to scrounge up usable words, craft a story, and fit it all into Hayden's melody, we'll still have something to perform.

After Dad picks me up, we stop to buy a take-home pizza and return to Coral Grotto. Mom is working late (again), so it's just the two of us tonight.

At home, I run upstairs, plug in my phone, and slip into my Geordi La Forge shirt and R2-D2 pants, my go-to lazy clothes. Then, I head back down to the living room, where Dad is queuing up season five of STAR TREK: THE NEXT GENERATION. The smell of cheese and pepperoni wafts from the oven.

I flop onto the couch; Jell-O abandons Dad's lap and scurries onto mine. It's hard to tell if she loves me more than Dad or just likes my fuzzy pants. Either way, I'll take it.

Dad presses play, and the cheesy, late-eighties CGI appears on screen. Jell-O's purring reverberates through my leg. I press my hand to her rib cage and feel her buzzing with contentment.

Halfway through the episode, Dad pauses the show to take the pizza out of the oven. I nudge Jell-O off my lap, earning myself some serious feline evil eye.

"Hey, Dad?" I take a seat at the kitchen island as Dad slices the pizza.

He peers over his glasses, gears churning. I see the meaning behind his intense focus when he signs to me. *"Yes? What?"* He tilts his brows up.

I raise my brows too, then dramatically lower them, showing him the proper expression for asking WH-questions. He always forgets.

"Ah." He adjusts his brow placement by furrowing them. *"What?"*

I squirm on the barstool, tapping my fingers on the counter. "Do we have to move back to Portland after a year? Or…can we stay?"

The question has been rattling around my brain like a ball in a bingo cage for weeks now. I'm not sure when exactly it happened, but my desire to move back to Oregon stopped a long time ago.

"I do not know, moja droga." Dad sets the pizza cutter aside with a sigh. "Don't you miss your friends back home?"

I reach over and steal a piece of greasy pepperoni. "I haven't talked to them since a week or two after we moved. They don't get it. They never even tried to get it."

Dad slumps, resting his elbows on the counter. "Your hearing loss?"

"Mm-hmm." I nod. "Hayden's the best friend I've ever had, and I've only known him for three months. The people I've known since kindergarten didn't care enough to accommodate me, but a bunch of strangers did."

Dad smiles understandingly. "When I came to America and fell in love with your mother, I knew I had found my home. She was my home. I wanted to stay in America forever." He presses a kiss to the back of my hand.

"Is that a yes?!" I cross my fingers under the counter. "Proszę, Tata!? Please?"

"Nie dziel skóry na niedźwiedziu, moja droga." Another Dad-ism: he's urging me not to get ahead of myself. My shoulders slump.

Dad comes around to my side of the counter and pulls me into a bone-crushing hug. His sturdy hands comb through my hair. "I will talk to Mom about staying," he says, pulling away so I can see his face. *"O-K?"* he signs.

"Thank you." I release the breath I was holding.

"Now, zjedzmy. Let us eat."

CHAPTER 31
HAYDEN

"This is exciting!" Mamma says for the hundredth time today. We're sitting at a table near the entrance to the gym, welcoming students to the first rehearsal for the Winter Talent Show.

Greg, Palmera's choir teacher (who thinks he's much cooler than he is because he lets students call him by his first name), has overseen the school's performance events since sometime in the late nineties, but Mom's been helping out with the talent show since Henry was a freshman. Greg almost exploded with glee when he found out his parent volunteer had a background as a professional singer.

"Exciting? I was thinking disastrous," I mumble. "We've barely practiced."

"I could be wrong, but I believe the purpose of rehearsals is to practice, hm?" she teases.

"I dunno. I'm not a dictionary."

"Oh, tesoro mio. You'll be fantastic. You and Casey make a great team. Hey, heads up." She motions to the group approaching us.

I start writing name tags for the ASL Club as they stop in front of our table.

"Hello, Jessica!" Mamma smiles.

"Hi." Jessica beams. "I love that color of lipstick!"

Mamma holds up the line talking with Jessica. I hand out badges as they chatter.

"What are you performing this year?" Mamma asks.

Every year, the ASL Club signs along to a song. I've been told it looks like an interpretive dance, but I've never gone to our talent shows so I haven't seen the act.

"An Ed Sheeran song." Jessica takes her name tag from me before she and the ASL Club all enter the gym.

My hand starts cramping after writing my twenty-fifth name badge. Luckily, Casey is number twenty-six. I give her a name tag and let Mamma take over.

Casey and I snag two of the fold-up chairs that are arranged in a huge circle on the basketball court. I pass her a piece of paper with handwritten chords and lyrics for "Lionhearted Girl."

"Any progress on a new song?" I ask as she reads the DIY sheet music.

"Still the same five words," she admits with a defeated look. "I promise I tried. But I can't get past my writer's block."

"That's why we have this." I tap the paper. "This is an epic song. Don't stress out about it."

We briefly discuss our plan while the rest of the students file into the gym. Once everyone has arrived, Greg launches into a welcome speech from the center of the chair circle.

"I'm honored to be here, dear friends. Helping your inner self shine. Raising you to new creative heights. Aiding in your rebirth as an inspired soul."

Greg drones on and on, drawing bizarre parallels and using metaphors that make no sense.

Casey pokes my leg. *"What's he saying?"* She points to Greg, touches a pointer finger to her chin, and shakes an upturned hand.

"Um…" I wiggle my fingers while I think. How do you sign "a middle-aged man wants to hatch a bunch of high schoolers like baby birds, and regurgitate creativity into us"?

"That is why, dear students, I encourage you to look within yourselves and ask: Do I want to be a meteor—a piece of space junk? Or do I want to be a star, the true pinnacle of art?"

Scattered applause passes around the circle. Casey claps slowly, every bit as confused as I am.

"Thank you, thank you," Greg clasps both hands over his heart. "And now, Ms. Rossi, if you would." He motions Mamma forward.

"He said—" I attempt to interpret, but Casey waves her hand, urging me to drop it.

"What's your mom saying?"

I easily keep up with Mamma, who talks in a way that makes sense to mere space junk like myself.

She angles herself toward other students but remains in a place where Casey can hear her better. "This afternoon, Greg and I will be observing your routines and arranging the acts in a suitable lineup. Now, please find a space in the gym to practice."

I finish my rough translation, proud of how many signs I knew.

Casey and I grab a spot at the back of the gym where it's quieter. I unzip my guitar case and she ties her hair up. "Are you warm?" she asks, referring to vocal warm-ups.

I bob my hand. I point to her and raise my brows.

"Mm-hmm, I warmed up before I came." Her eyes float around the room as the other students begin to practice. The acts range from politically incorrect comedy routines to nails-on-a-chalkboard singing to tap dancing.

I know the other students will be focused on their own acts, not watching us, but a buzz of nerves travels through me at the thought of practicing in front of everyone.

I instinctively take deep breaths and rub my cross necklace.

Casey's eyes land on the necklace. "Does that help?"

"Yeah. Kinda. It was actually César's. I told him about my anxiety, and he gave it to me," I explain. "He said rubbing it helps calm him when he's nervous before games."

"Wow. That was nice of him." She smiles.

"I **told** you he's nice," I emphasize jokingly.

She rolls her eyes. "Well, anyway, we've got this," she says.

"Right. We've got this," I parrot with fake confidence.

Pushing aside my unease, I strum Rodolfo's strings once, testing to see if he's tuned. He has a bad habit of slipping into untuned territory, but the sound has to be perfect if Casey's going to rely on the vibrations.

Rodolfo is a bit pitchy today, so I alternate between twisting his tuning pegs and plucking his strings while Casey watches. "Hayden?" she asks suddenly, "can you teach me how to play guitar?"

I pause and look at her. "I don't think I'm qualified," I say loudly enough that she can hear me over the noise.

She chuckles. "I'm helping you learn sign, and I'm not a professional."

Touché.

"Okay. I suppose." I smile at her.

Once I'm finally satisfied with Rodolfo's sound, I spread the sheet music in front of us. "*Ready?*" I shake an 'R.'

She comes closer, placing one hand on the body of the guitar and the other on her throat. "Ready."

In this song, the first few notes are the hardest. There's no singing, just me on guitar, which leaves little room for error. I steady my nervous hands enough to start playing. Once I get into the rhythm, I unclench my jaw and allow memory to guide my strumming.

Fifteen seconds into the intro, Casey begins singing. Her facial expressions are sincere and powerful, her tone silky and bright. She's a natural performer.

She reaches over as she delivers her last phrase and rests her fingertips on my throat.

Mamma's voice plays on a loop in my head as I work through my solo, telling me to lift my soft palate, breathe with my diaphragm, and enunciate each word. Juggling the moving parts makes following the chords difficult, but I manage. A few lyrics get skipped over when I forget them, but for the most part, I'm performing decently.

Not at a pro level yet, but good enough for the talent show.

Casey joins me for the last part of the song, blending our voices. I lose myself in the waves of raw emotions, high and low voices, and resonant strumming.

I pay close attention to my breath support as we sing the last elongated note. My lungs slowly deplete as we end.

Tuning into my surroundings, I realize Greg is standing in front of us. He starts clapping vigorously. I offer a shy bow and Casey chuckles.

"You two have a gift!" Greg proclaims. "You've successfully sowed seeds of inspiration within your souls!"

Casey and I glance at each other, holding in our laughter.

"Thank you, Greg," I reply. He gives another round of applause and wanders off to observe another act.

We laugh out loud once he's out of earshot.

"That went better than expected." Casey motions to my guitar and the sheet music.

"I'm good with performing this, and not worrying about a new song," I smile at her. "What do you think?"

I know how it feels to pressure yourself. I've been doing it my whole life. And I'm starting to learn that we need to set limits for ourselves. To acknowledge when there are things we can't handle. If she can't work past her writer's block, so be it. It's not earth-shatteringly important we sing a new song.

She stares at me, deep in thought, then says, "I guess." She returns her hand to the body of the guitar with a shrug. "Let's go again."

I leave the conversation hanging in midair and restart the song.

CHAPTER 32
CASEY

"SORRY I'M LATE!" MOM SAYS AS SHE HANGS HER COAT BY THE FRONT door after yet another Saturday spent at work. "My client couldn't choose a color palette to save her life."

I fork a bite of mac 'n cheese into my mouth and wave a greeting.

"Do not worry about it, najdroższa," Dad says. "Come eat." He motions toward the pot we're eating directly out of.

Mom scrunches her nose in disapproval as she sits at the table. "No vegetables? Really, Stan?"

I snicker softly. Mom's been working overtime most nights and isn't here to lecture Dad and me about GMOs or eating a balanced meal. Which has resulted in a lot of takeout food and mac 'n cheese. We take advantage of her absence whenever we can.

"Oh, tell your mom about rehearsal." Dad diverts the attention away from his vegetable deficiencies.

"That's right! Rehearsals started today! How did that go?" Mom asks excitedly. She borrows Dad's fork and starts eating.

I put off responding by shoving another huge forkful of noodles into my mouth. Mom gets scatterbrained after a long workday, so I'm hoping she'll move on to a different topic if I wait.

Unfortunately, she's still watching expectantly when I'm done chewing.

"It was fine." I shrug.

"Fine?" She frowns. "Did something happen?"

"No. It went well. We sounded good."

"But?"

Ugh. Why do all moms come equipped with mind-reading technology? Not cool.

Mom can always tell when something is bothering me. But tonight, it's not something I can verbalize or make sense of.

I thought I was at peace with our decision to perform "Lionhearted Girl." It seems like the smart move. But the smart move isn't always the right move, is it?

There are so many unexpressed emotions inside me, so many truths waiting to be told. But I don't know how to say the things I need to say. I don't know how to paint a mural using my true colors, without baring my soul—something I've been so vigilantly protecting.

"Everything's fine," I assure Mom. I can tell she doesn't believe me, but she doesn't pose any follow-up questions.

My parents chat about their days while I pick at the remaining noodles. When we're finished, I rinse off my fork and head for the stairs.

Jell-O trots behind me as I drag myself up the staircase and into my room. Mom tracks my every move, but she remains quiet.

Once I'm alone, that all-too-familiar silence descends, curling around me like poisonous vines. I look around for a distraction. My eyes land on my backpack by my desk and I grab it, slumping onto my floor.

Jell-O curls up next to me and kneads my rug while I dig through my backpack to find the homework I've been ignoring. I pull out a crumpled wad of paper at the bottom of the bag, separate the pages, and smooth them out.

Tangled up with the homework sheets are the pamphlets the school counselor gave me after the ASL Night debacle. I must've forgotten to toss them.

I cast aside the one about cyberbullying but linger over the other one: SO, YOU'RE GRIEVING: COPING WITH GRIEF AND LOSS.

I frown. Back in her office, Colleen seemed to pick these two pamphlets very intentionally, but now I wonder if she made a mistake. Why would she give me a pamphlet about grief? Nobody died.

Scratching Jell-O's head with one hand, I flip open the brochure to reveal three panels brimming with information. I skim through everything at first, but in a section about what can trigger grief, my attention is caught by "a sudden diagnosis or health issues."

On my second, more careful read-through of the brochure, an odd mixture of recognition and curiosity takes root in my chest. The more I read about the emotional impact that losing something important to you can have, the more I start to see myself and my recent experiences reflected in the pamphlet.

When I get to the last page, I find a resources list, including various websites about grief. I grab my phone and type in the link to an article, then start reading.

STAGES OF GRIEF:

Denial – You can't believe this person is truly gone.

Anger – You're upset this person is gone.

Bargaining – You try to figure out if you could've changed the outcome.

Depression – You're sad this person is gone.

Acceptance – You understand this person is gone and try to get back to normal as best you can.

Everyone goes through the stages of grief in their own way. You may experience them linearly, go back and forth between them, or skip one or more stages altogether.

A description from another article—one about grieving a newly acquired disability—also stands out to me:

You may experience loss of self, as if the person you were before your diagnosis and the person you are now are different; Isolation, feeling cut off from loved ones who can't understand what you're going through; Anger or frustration as you struggle to come to terms with your diagnosis; Worrying about the future—how you'll cope or how your life may change.

Holy shit.

As I read more about the grieving process in relation to becoming Disabled, a puzzle piece clicks into place.

Until this moment, I had never considered that someone could grieve something that wasn't a death. But everything makes so much more sense now. My volatile emotions, the loneliness, the not feeling like myself.

I've…been grieving.

How can a single article and one very determined school counselor make sense of the past six months, when nothing else has?

As if on cue with my epiphany, my bedroom light flickers on and off. I look up and see Mom standing in the doorway holding a pint of Phish Food and two spoons. She takes a seat next to me on the floor, opens the ice cream tub, and offers me a spoon. I take it and she puts an arm around my shoulder as we start eating.

We started this—ice cream therapy—when I was a little kid. Tonight, it's exactly what I need. Mom's maternal mindreading superpowers are amazing.

"Did you know you can grieve things besides someone dying?" I mutter after my fifth or sixth bite.

Mom glances at me and nods. "Sure. I grieved when I got laid off from a company I'd worked at for seven years."

"Well, I didn't know it." I sigh and eat another bite of ice cream. "I think that's sort of what's been happening since I lost my hearing. But I didn't know what was wrong with me."

"Nothing is wrong with you, Case."

"Mm-hmm. I guess not. But it felt like things were finally stabilizing, and now I've taken a step backward. One second, I'm writing lyrics at lightning speed; the next, I can't get down a single word. And my emotions are still all over the place, like I'm riding the worst roller coaster ever."

Mom sets the ice cream on my bedside table and drags me into a hug. "You're a fighter," she says, pulling back. "But sometimes, you fight the wrong person."

"You?"

"Well, yes." She laughs. "But I meant yourself."

I frown at her.

"You've been through so much recently. More than a lot of people face in their entire lives. You're allowed to be emotional. Actually, I'd be worried if you weren't emotional," she says. "I suspect you've been suppressing those feelings instead of letting them happen. Even when emotions hurt, you should let yourself feel them. You shouldn't try to outrun them because they'll always catch up sooner or later."

I stare down at my hands and process her insight. Like most teen-agers, I hate to admit when my parents are right…but she's right.

I've been beating my feelings into submission because it's easier than dealing with them. Who willingly lets themself be angry? Who allows their heart to break?

"Be gentle with yourself," Mom continues, "but let yourself feel."

Using her calm reassurance as a starting point, I release everything I've kept pent up—bitterness, grief, even hope—with a long, shaky breath.

"Thank you, Mom," I sign tearily.

She kisses the top of my head and smiles. "I'm here for you, sweetie."

After Mom leaves my room, I turn to my songbook.

The small act of granting myself permission to hurt, to laugh, to **feel** has opened the floodgates. I hum the new tune Hayden created and write as fast as my hand will allow.

I write every word I wish I'd had the courage to say. I write like I'm going to run out of time. I write until the early morning sun peeks through my curtains and I have a semblance of a song.

Reading through ten pages of unedited lyrics with tired, bloodshot eyes, I sing out words while playing the backing track Hayden recorded. And it fits.

Hayden's guitar combined with my lyrics make for one hell of an original song. I'll have to trim it down—I don't intend for this to be the next "Bohemian Rhapsody"—but at least I have actual words to work with. It's easier to edit what you have than start from scratch.

I grab my phone from my nightstand and send a slew of frenzied messages to Hayden, hoping he's awake. He takes a while, but finally replies to the last one.

Dec 4 at 6:13 AM

@Casey.K.Sings i did it! i freaking did it dude!!! 😭

Dec 4 at 6:49 AM

@HeyitsHayden And what exactly are you doing at 6am?

@Casey.K.Sings i wrote our song! it shook loose

@HeyitsHayden Wait, a new song? So, we aren't singing Lionhearted Girl?

@Casey.K.Sings can u meet up today so we can talk abt it?

@HeyitsHayden Yeah. How about this afternoon? BTW I'm proud of you. You know that?

@Casey.K.Sings aw shucks😊 see u later

CHAPTER 33
HAYDEN

"I HAVE A SURPRISE FOR YOU!" MAMMA ANNOUNCES AFTER DINO AND I finish washing dishes on Sunday night. We exchange a look.

It's been a busy day of dinner with the Ramirezes and working on the new talent show song with Casey, and the last thing I want is to be dragged along to another holiday craft fair—which was what Mamma's holiday "surprise" turned out to be last year.

"Let's go!" She grabs her car keys. Papá tells us to have fun from his spot on the sofa, where he's absorbed in a Concacaf fútbol match.

"Shotgun!" Dino catapults himself toward the passenger's seat as we head outside.

"Oldest gets the front," I argue.

He replies by shoving me aside and jumping into the front seat.

I watch the blur of Christmas lights as we drive through our neighborhood. The holiday decor, palm trees wrapped in twinkling lights and colorful plastic displays in yards, with afternoon heat still hanging in the air makes me think of a Hallmark movie. Something along the lines of "A Christmas in Paradise."

After a short drive, Mamma pulls into the parking lot of a strip mall and exits the car, bouncing with excitement. I scan the storefronts, trying to figure out where we're going. The strip mall has a supermarket, a pet store, a Thai restaurant, and several discount stores.

She leads us toward the supermarket. Dino whispers to me, "Is this her way of making us go grocery shopping with her? Because that's not a fun surprise."

"Hey, she didn't say it was a **fun** surprise." I chuckle.

We reach the entrance of the store, but Mamma veers left and heads farther down the sidewalk. I quicken my pace to catch up to her. "Where are we going?"

My question is answered when she stops in front of a music store. "I'm buying you a new guitar for the talent show!" She beams, proud of herself for hatching this plot. "Let's call it an early Christmas present."

"But…I already have Rodolfo. You don't have to buy me a new guitar." I shoot a wistful glance at the storefront. I've needed a new guitar for a while, but getting an upgrade feels like cheating on Rodolfo.

"Your guitar is acoustic. You can't plug it into an amp. And, honestly, it's a bit…weathered." She chuckles. "I couldn't be prouder of you, honey. I know I'm giving you vocal lessons, but I want to support you in every way I can. And that includes this." She motions to the store.

I consider for a moment. "Okay." I smile. "Grazie mille, Mamma! You're the best mom a guy could ask for."

Dino frowns. "How is this a surprise for both of us?"

"Dino, be happy for your brother," Mamma chides.

"Wow, Hayden! I am legitimately, one hundred percent, **so** happy for you." He smiles sarcastically.

Inside, rows of guitars hang from the back wall in all different shapes, sizes, and colors. When I bought Rodolfo, I had no clue what I was doing. I was perusing a garage sale, looking for old records or maybe a bike, when he called out to me like a siren luring a sailor to his death—but, you know, with less death.

An employee approaches me. "Can I help you find anything?"

"I'm looking for an acoustic-electric guitar." I scan the options, but they all look the same to me.

Mamma joins us as the employee leads me toward a sleek, black Fender. He removes it from the wall and places it in my arms.

I close my eyes and let my subconscious take over. My fingers begin plucking the strings to the tune of "Wonderwall." The fear of judgement slips away as I get lost in the song. The strings on this guitar are tight and snap against the body with each note.

I get why Casey is obsessed with vibrations. Feeling music reverberate against you is intoxicating.

"That sounded incredible," Mamma says as I finish. "But this is a little over budget." She taps the price tag on the guitar.

I check the tag, and gulp when I see four digits. "Right. Something cheaper would be better."

We leave the store an hour later. I cradle my new Yamaha APX600, who I named Geoffrey, like a baby. His shiny, bright blue varnish sparkles in the moonlight.

Dino rushes to claim the front seat again, carrying my new portable amp. I roll my eyes at his stereotypical youngest-sibling behavior and climb into the back.

"Don't you want to put your guitar in its case for the drive home?" Mamma asks.

"No way. He's ridin' with me." I set Geoffrey on the floor, propped against my knees. I buckle up and run my fingers along his tuning pegs.

I can already tell I'm going to need a two-bedroom place when I move out someday: one for Buñuelo and me, one for my future army of guitars.

On the drive home I have an idea. Although I'm attached to his beat-up, stickered charm, I think it might be time to find Rodolfo a new owner. Luckily, I know just the person—someone who will love him as much as I do. (And who will grant me visitation rights.)

CHAPTER 34
CASEY

I'VE ALWAYS BEEN A CHRISTMAS PERSON. THE SNOW, THE UGLY SWEATERS, the twinkly lights, all of it. But my favorite thing about the holiday is our family tradition of renting a cabin near Mount Hood at Christmastime. Mom's siblings, my grandparents, and my cousins always get neighboring cabins and we create our very own holiday village.

I don't miss much about Portland anymore, but I do miss winter. So I'm thrilled when Mom announces she's finagled a "working vacation" and last-minute cabin rentals. We'll be leaving Miami the day after the talent show to spend a couple of weeks in Oregon.

But taking our annual trip means I'll miss my only chance to celebrate the holidays with my new friends. I've asked Dad about staying in Miami several times since our heart-to-heart, but he always says he and Mom are "still discussing it." As it stands, this time next year we'll be back in Oregon. Permanently.

"No hard feelings about Christmas, right?" I ask Hayden for the umpteenth time.

He laughs. "You're spending the holidays at home with your family. What kind of friend would I be if I got upset about that?"

"I know," I say. "But I was looking forward to celebrating with you guys."

He sets his guitar on the bed, signaling the end of today's practice session. "That's why we're doing a gift exchange today. So you won't be missing out!"

"Speaking of which," I glance at my phone: 5:28 p.m. I flip the screen toward him. "Everyone's going to be here soon."

Hayden has joined Mom's last-minute-plans club. When I told him I would be in Portland for Christmas, he organized a gift swap for the group. He had us draw names and told us to have a gift ready in time for this evening.

He hurries to his feet, scoops Buñuelo out of my arms, and places him in the tank. Buñuelo starts licking the glass.

"Does Buñuelo get gifts?" I ask as we head downstairs.

"Bok choy. He goes nuts for it."

Just as we get downstairs, Paz bursts through the door, kicks off his shoes, and belly flops onto the couch.

"¡Oye!" César barks as he enters behind him, his biceps bulging as he carries an armful of gifts. "Ever heard of knocking?"

"I don't need to knock. Do I?" Paz smiles at Taylor, who stands in the kitchen.

Taylor chuckles. "No, Paz. You're welcome anytime."

"Merry Christmas!" Lela pushes past César and engulfs me in a hug. I admire her shirt as she pulls back, a red crop top that reads SANTA'S FAVORITE HO.

César sets the gifts on the coffee table, glaring at a sprawled-out Paz. I take a seat next to Paz on the couch and investigate the presents on the table.

"Is this what you consider gift wrapping?" I raise a brow at César, gesturing to an El Pollo Cubano takeout bag with a sticky note covering the chicken logo, reading: **MERRY XMAS.**

"Like yours is any better?" He eyes the present I brought as I pull it from my backpack. It's wrapped in plain brown paper with a red burlap ribbon tied around it.

"It's eco-friendly, sweetheart." I flash a smug smile.

Paz cackles from beside me. "Casey's saving turtles, while innocent baby seals will probably choke on that plastic bag someday, Cécé."

"Murderer," Lela signs. Somehow, I'm not surprised she knows the sign for murderer.

César shakes his head, fed up with our teasing. *"I barely had time to——don't give me——did my best."* He attempts to use SimCom but it's harder than it seems and some of his gestures aren't actually ASL. He notes my confusion. *"Did you understand that?"* he signs.

I swallow the sour feeling bubbling up. A simple statement is about to turn into a drawn-out conversation just so I can grasp what was said. "Uh, no. But it's fine."

César studies me, then concludes that's not an acceptable answer. He grabs his phone, types a message, and hands the device over.

I almost didn't have time to get a gift. Normally I'm capable of wrapping things

I return the phone. "Welp. It certainly has…character!" I smile.

Taylor enters the living room with a tray. She hands us each a mug of hot cocoa. "I put the AC on full blast," she says. "Hopefully it'll cool down in here soon."

Her comment triggers a reaction in Paz, who launches forward and grabs my hands. "Do you get snow in Portland?"

"Yep. At least in the mountains. Ugh, I miss cold weather."

"I've never seen snow." He sighs dramatically. "Take me with you, please!"

"Unfortunately, we only have three plane tickets."

César sips his cocoa then smirks through a whipped-cream mustache. "He's small enough to fit in the overhead."

I try to hold back a laugh, but a small giggle escapes. Paz recoils at my treasonous behavior.

After Hayden's parents leave for date night, we drink the rest of our cocoa and I answer questions about Portland and my family. I tell my friends Jell-O will be staying at a cat hotel. Which, I have to explain, yes, is a real thing.

After cocoa refills, Paz declares it present time. He sets a golden box in Hayden's lap and hands me a sparkly white gift bag. "Merry Christmas!"

"Um, Paz?" I clear my throat. "You know you're only supposed to give one person a gift, right?"

"I was going to give you these anyway. Today just happened to be perfect timing." He waves his hands, urging us to open them. "Go on!"

Hayden unwraps the box and I remove tissue paper from the bag. I pull out my present first: a light green crop top with a pink embroidered palm tree on the chest pocket. I look up from the shirt and laugh as Hayden holds up a pair of pink satin shorts with a green palm frond pattern.

"Ta da!" Paz grins ear to ear. "They're for the talent show! I sewed and embroidered them myself!"

Hayden eyes the clothing warily. "Matching outfits weren't exactly what we had in mind..." He trails off, frowning as Paz's gleeful expression begins to fade. "But these are great!" He forces a laugh. "Super great! I love it. So cool."

Hayden looks in my direction, wordlessly asking me to go along. I lean over and give Paz a quick hug. *"Thank you,"* I lower a hand from my chin. "We'll look fantastic."

After that, Lela gives Paz a DVD of YOUNGBLOOD starring Rob Lowe, and Lela gets neon green and orange lipsticks from César.

I smirk to myself as I give César the eco-friendly present I brought. He tears into it and sighs heavily, brandishing a copy of the book COMMUNICATION FOR DUMMIES. Paz snorts while Hayden and Lela fight laughter.

"I thought it'd be useful," I say through a chuckle. César just blinks at me. After I've had my fun teasing him, though, I lean down, grab his real gift from my backpack, and hand it over.

He eyes the small black box suspiciously, likely expecting another gag gift. But when he finally opens it, and takes a silver necklace out, his expression softens.

"I figured you needed a new one, since you gave Hay yours," I explain. "It's Saint Luigi Scrosoppi, the patron saint of soccer." I gesture to the pendant hanging on the chain, depicting St. Luigi holding a soccer ball.

César's lips tip into a gentle smile. *"Thank you,"* he signs. *"KissFist."*

He slips it over his head, and I mirror his smile. I was hesitant to spend money on the super expensive overnight shipping for the necklace, but César's reaction is worth every penny.

The pile of presents is now depleted, but Hayden jumps up, buzzing with excitement. *"Close your eyes, Casey,"* he uses SimCom. "I'm going to get your present."

He takes off toward the stairs. I obediently close my eyes.

Moments later, his voice breaks through the silence. "Okay, you can open them!"

276

My eyes flutter open. I blink as I readjust to the brightness of the room. "Hay…" I gape at him in disbelief.

"Merry Christmas!" He signs with one hand, using the other to place his beloved, sticker-covered guitar in my arms. "My mom got me an acoustic-electric guitar, so I want you to have Rodolfo. Now, during our lessons you'll have your own."

"You're giving her a thirty-year-old guitar? That's an extreme case of regifting." Paz comments.

"It's more like fifty years," Hayden murmurs.

Paz rolls his eyes. "That is not helping your case."

"Shh, Paz," I breathe. "I love it." I set the guitar aside, stand up, and wrap my arms around Hayden. "Thank you," I say into his shoulder, the sound muffled.

He pats my back when I refuse to let go. *"I love you,"* he signs as I head to the couch. I return the sign.

"This is the best Christmas ever," I say. "Portland ain't got nothing on you guys."

By the time the cooling system finally kicks in, we're on our second cheesy and extremely heteronormative made-for-TV Christmas movie. This one has an identical plot to the first one, but it takes place in a different fictionalized small town, and the characters are exes, not childhood friends.

Hayden sets a plate of cookies on the coffee table, and everyone converges. I grab some cookies and tap César's shoulder.

"Can you hand me a blanket?" I ask, using ASL so I don't disturb the watch party.

César crawls toward the cabinet underneath the TV. He pulls out a knitted quilt.

"Yo, grab me one!" Paz shouts, crumbs spraying out of his mouth.

"And me!" Lela adds.

César grabs two more and chucks them toward Paz and Lela, then returns with my blanket and gently drapes the fabric over my lower half. He glances at the others before making eye contact with me. He scratches the back of his neck and teeters nervously.

Paz, Hayden, and Lela pretend to watch the movie, but their heads are tilted in our direction, more interested in our subplot than the one onscreen.

I fold the blanket in half and clear a César-sized space on the couch. With a small smile I ask, "Do you want to sit with me?"

He grabs his cookies and settles into the spot next to mine. I cover him with the blanket and scoot closer. When we reach the plot twist, where Ms. Broken-Heart discovers Mr. Ex-Who-Broke-Her-Heart is her dad's oncologist (whatever *will* they do?), César sticks his hand under the blanket and finds mine. He laces our fingers together and his thumb strokes the back of my hand.

I smile to myself and lean my head against his shoulder, giving his hand a squeeze.

I guess I'm pretty invested in this subplot, too.

CHAPTER 35
CASEY

THE DRESS REHEARSAL FOR THE TALENT SHOW IS **CENTURIES** LONG, AND by the time I'm home, I'm tired in ways I didn't know a person could be tired.

I immediately plant myself on the couch for a STAR TREK marathon with Dad, and I'm determined to stay there until bedtime, but a few minutes after we start the first episode, Dad suddenly pauses the TV.

"*Doorbell.*" He mimics ringing the bell, then points to the door.

"Why do I have to get it?" I groan.

"Because I said so." Dad's quintessential parent line triggers another groan.

I hop off the couch and hurry to retrieve our pizza. "Thanks," I offer automatically as I open the door.

"You're welcome?" César says uncertainly.

I freeze and mentally dissect his outfit: black skinny jeans, red Converse, black Inter Miami hoodie, and the necklace I gave him hangs from his neck. I can't help but smile. Besides the Fall Formal, this is the most "dressed up" I've seen him.

"Are you free? I was hoping we could go for a drive." He jerks his head toward the street, where his car awaits.

With zero hesitation, I call to Dad over my shoulder, "I'm going to hang out with Cés—uh, my friends! I'll be back before curfew!"

I dash inside and grab my phone and a pair of boots, then meet César by his car before Dad has a chance to ask follow-up questions. Whatever's happening right now doesn't seem like a follow-up question situation.

César holds open the car door and I slide into the passenger's seat. I'm suddenly grateful I hadn't yet changed into pajamas.

"You love kidnapping me, don't you, sweetheart?" I ask. The nickname I once used to annoy him slips out naturally, but this time it's more of an endearment. I observe César's profile as he exits Coral Grotto, streetlights illuminating his amused smile.

He glances at me. "You're very kidnappable."

"Good to know?"

He navigates us onto the highway, breezing through the residential parts of town. We watch the night pass us by in comfortable silence.

Two, five, ten minutes pass without a word. Soft smiles, beating hearts, warm air. He rests his right hand on the center console, palm facing up. Without a second thought, I place my hand in his. His dark eyes stay trained to the road as his fingers wrap around mine.

He only moves his hand away when we pull up to a shopping mall. He parks, turns off the ignition, and darts to my side of the car to hold the door for me.

I lower a hand from my chin, but he misses my gratitude, busy rooting around in the back seat. When he re-emerges, he thrusts a pink hoodie at me. Inter Miami's logo is printed on the chest.

I raise an incredulous brow. As a Floridian, he might consider seventy degrees to be sweatshirt weather, but I most certainly do not.

"Trust me," he signs.

Reluctantly, I pull the hoodie over my head. He chuckles when he sees how huge it is. It hits past my knees, swallowing me. Worst (or best) of all, it smells like César. Grumpy, gorgeous, ex-sworn enemy César.

I take his hand and we head into the building.

Inside is a huge Christmas village. Children of all ages line up to have pictures taken with Santa, and two teens who seem not to have embraced a joy-to-all mentality hand us candy canes as we pass.

"You said you missed winter," César explains. "I know it's not quite the same as Portland, but this is about as close as Miami gets."

I laugh as we approach an ice rink in the middle of the mall.

After César pays for our tickets, we lace up our skates and waddle toward the rink, holding hands when we step onto the ice.

We do a few slow laps, then pick up speed, whizzing past other couples and little kids wearing helmets. César lets go of my hand, skates ahead of me, and attempts a small spin but doesn't stick it; instead of executing a graceful move, he lands flat on his butt. I slap a hand over my mouth to contain a cackle. With an embarrassed blush, he hoists himself up and dusts ice off his pants.

I finally chuckle as he returns to my side. "It's lucky you're good at soccer, because I don't think figure skating would be your sport."

He takes my hand and smiles amusedly. "Shit. I would've looked damn good in a bedazzled leotard."

Before stepping off the ice, César spins me around, pulling me close when I stumble. We laugh, return our rented skates, and head for the hot cocoa stand.

"Successful kidnapping?" he asks as we settle in an empty corner of the mall, next to a photo booth, to drink our cocoa.

"I'd say so." I move closer and he tucks me under his arm. After a few minutes of silence, I stand up and toss my empty cup into a garbage can. "Okay, c'mon," I haul César to his feet, "we're commemorating tonight." I drag him toward the photo booth.

We cram ourselves inside and I pay, then press the start button. César eyes me uneasily. "I'm not a photo person."

"Too bad. You're doing CHARLIE'S ANGELS with me." I press my back against César's and make a finger gun. He chuckles and copies my move.

For the second round, we pull the weirdest faces imaginable, laughing as the photo pops onscreen. When the ten-second countdown starts over, I take César's hand and smile directly at him. He rests his free hand on my knee, giving it a gentle squeeze. The shutter snaps, the moment captured.

César maintains eye contact, raises his brows to indicate a yes or no question, and slowly brings all the fingertips of his right hand together and touches them to his lips, then presses it to his left fingertips, which form the same shape. The sign for kiss.

My breath halts but I manage to nod. Possibly too enthusiastically.

He smiles and cups my jaw. I wrap my hands around his neck and César pulls me close. The countdown ends, and the distance between us disappears. The light from the camera flashes as our lips connect.

César's hands run down my back, his lips inviting. When his tongue brushes mine, I catch a taste of peppermint hot chocolate. I tighten my grip on his neck and kiss him harder. Heat rushes to my stomach as he works his fingers through my hair.

Finally, we break apart. "I've been wanting——you're so——long time," he breathes.

I don't ask him to repeat himself. The look in his eyes says everything. I press a lingering kiss to his cheek, savoring the moment. I check the time on the photo booth screen and groan. "I should get home. The talent show is tomorrow…"

"Yeah. It's late."

Neither of us moves.

"Maybe a few more minutes?" I suggest, after a prolonged pause.

He grins wickedly. "Couple more won't hurt."

CHAPTER 36
HAYDEN

THE FIRST THING I DO IN UNFAMILIAR SOCIAL SITUATIONS IS PLAN MY escape. I locate all possible exits and brainstorm excuses.

"I'll miss curfew." "I got food poisoning." "My lizard choked on a grape and needs emergency surgery." These are all excuses I've used in the past.

I've always clung to the familiar and avoided uncharted territory—it's scary. And making a debut performance in front of three hundred students and their families is crap-your-pants-level scary.

But today there's no exit strategy. No plausible excuses. No backing out.

Because right now Casey and I are in the hallway outside the gym, lined up with the other talent show acts, waiting for our turn to perform. I force myself to take a few deep breaths as my anxiety rises, my hands wrenched in the fabric of my shirt.

"Dude." Casey grips my shoulders and tries to break me out of my panic spiral. "It'll be okay. We'll be great."

I shake her off. My nervous energy sends sparks flying. I steady my hands as I sign. *What if I forget—*

"Hayden." Her expression is stern but grounding. "We've practiced this song five bajillion times. We'll be okay, I promise."

I wipe my sweaty palms on the pink shorts Paz made me. *"But—"*

"We're going to do great," she says, then signs, *"I believe in us."*

I can't tell if she's comforting me or herself. Either way, it's nice to know I'm not alone.

The ASL Club walks past us through the hall and enters the gym to do their number. I triple check that Geoffrey is properly tuned. His strings are far tighter, and the sound is much clearer, but I miss Rodolfo.

An Ed Sheeran song blares through the gym doors, and I strain my neck to see how many acts are in front of us. Tap dancing girl, Jacob Miller with his juggling routine, and Emily Cole, who'll sing "Blackbird" by the Beatles.

I take one last look at the sheet of guitar chords. My fingers strum the air as I go over the various progressions. Though I could play this song in my sleep, there's a gnawing feeling in my gut telling me everything is going to go wrong.

As more acts go on, the feeling spreads, an anxiety pandemic.

Greg calls Emily's name and she steps into the gym.

"Casey?" I press myself against the wall. "I don't think I can do this."

She takes the paper from me and tucks it into her jeans. "Hay, deep breaths."

I feel the urge to bolt. "I'm scared," I whisper.

"What?" She stares at my lips.

I peek through the window in the gym door and see Emily strumming her ukulele. *"I'm scared."* From either side of my body, I throw both hands in front of my chest and let them hover there for a second, trembling.

"Me too," she admits, shaking a 'Y' between us. "I know it's scary right now, but we'll be okay."

Casey guides me through deep breathing. She raises her arms with each inhale and lowers them with exhalation. I focus on the pattern of the exercise and find solace in the familiarity. In and out, in and out. Her composure helps calm me.

"Hayden, Casey," Greg claps his hands together. "It's showtime!"

She smiles at me and heads toward the gym doors. I hear our names being announced as if I'm a long distance away.

Next thing I know, I'm pushing my way through Palmera's front doors and sliding onto the hot pavement, the sun shining directly into my watering eyes. Without warning, my chest heaves.

Every system in my body begins to fracture in a nuclear meltdown. My lungs struggle for air, my limbs go numb, pain twists my chest into a knot.

The doors swing open. I hear the sound of Casey's army boots coming toward me. She sits cross-legged next to me, hand resting on my shoulder.

"I'm s-sorry," I choke out, running my fingers along the smooth metal of César's crucifix.

She wraps me in a hug. "There's nothing to be sorry for, Hay."

I lean my head against her shoulder and stifle a sob.

"I'm right here," she breathes. She starts quietly humming "On My Own," which brings me back to the first time I heard her sing, watching her Instagram video from my hiding spot in El Pollo Cubano's kitchen. So much has changed since then, but one thing feels the same—anxiety still rules my life with an iron fist.

A few minutes pass. Casey's fingers rake through my hair, I fiddle with the necklace and take deep breaths. Eventually, the storm of anxiety calms, and the contents of my stomach stop violently sloshing. Hopefully, once I start therapy and learn some coping mechanisms, it won't take as long for me to calm myself, but I'm still thankful it eased up.

I sit up straighter and sniffle, wiping away tears. "I want to do the performance," I say.

She watches me carefully. "Are you sure?"

"*Yes.*" I bob my fist. "I feel like…I dunno." I shrug, sending a watery smile in her direction. "I feel like I can do anything when I'm with you. You make me strong."

Now it's her turn to get emotional. She scrunches her nose to keep from tearing up, trying not to ruin the makeup Lela did for her today. "God, you're sappy."

We both laugh. Then hug. And laugh while hugging.

In her embrace, the last of the fear washes away. And—for some reason I may never fully comprehend—I'm oddly confident.

"Let's do this," I say, wiping my sweaty palms on my shorts.

We stand and head inside, hands entwined.

The four acts after us performed while we were absent, but Greg takes pity on my tear-stained cheeks and wobbly voice and allows us to perform out of turn. The show must go on!

As we step into the gym, I tighten my fingers around the neck of my guitar, and Casey links our arms. She squeezes my wrist, wordlessly assuring me she's here. She's got me.

Forget about Buñuelo—Casey is my emotional-support human.

Hundreds of eyes are trained on us as we head for center court, where a portable stage is set up with a purple, pink, and orange ombré backdrop that reminds me of sunset. I plug my guitar into the amp next to my stool. Casey lowers the microphone several inches. I tell myself not to look at the crowd—I can't guarantee I won't have an EXORCIST moment and projectile vomit all over the basketball court if I do. But against my better judgment, my eyes float to the bleachers.

The seats are at max capacity, but a cluster of familiar faces in the middle of the crowd catches my eye: the Kowalskis, Paz, Dino, my parents, my cousins, Tío Eddy, and…Henry!

For once, Henry's presence doesn't feel like added pressure. Instead, I feel accepted. I send a thankful smile toward Henry as our families cheer and clap for us.

From the bleachers, Jessica leaves the ASL group and stands a few feet away from us. I shoot Casey a confused look. "I asked her to interpret for our performance," she explains.

I drop a flat hand from my chin and Jessica gives me a thumbs-up. Casey glances at me. *"Ready?"*

I take a deep breath, align my fingers on the strings, and give her a quick nod.

"Hi everyone," she says into the microphone. It squeals loudly, but she carries on, unable to hear the feedback. "I'm Casey Kowalski and that's Hayden González-Rossi"—I wave timidly—"and today we're going to be performing an original song called 'Background Noise.' It's about feeling like an outsider who fades into the background of everyone else's lives."

I start the intro as Casey takes off her shoes so she can feel the vibrations through her feet. She rests one hand on her throat. My shaky fingers miss a note, but I recover. Casey's angelic, pitch-perfect voice helps calm me. The lyrics to her solo flow smoothly and powerfully.

Can you hear me? I've been calling out your name.
Are you listening? You just looked the other way.

And I'm afraid, I'm afraid I'll never be the same again.
They speak, they speak but I can't hear a word.

Her confident singing washes over the audience as they look on, mesmerized.

Jessica keeps pace with our singing. Her signing is melodic and matches the song. It makes me wish I had seen the ASL Club's performance.

I get so carried away listening to Casey's solo that I miss my first line and subsequently trip over the accompaniment.

Casey chuckles as I scramble to save myself. I play an additional interlude before starting my verse.

Can you see me? It's like I'm invisible.
Are you out there? I don't want to be alone.
And I'm afraid, I'm afraid they'll never understand.
They expect, they expect me to play the part.

Partly to make up for my mishap, partly because I have a strange urge to show off, I toss in a few ad-libs here and there. We start our duet and I smile in Casey's direction.

Our amplified voices swirl together, the meeting of two worlds. We're two people from very different backgrounds, with different skills, coming together to create something inimitable. Something beautiful.

They try to tell us who to be. They try to tear us down.
We will rise victorious against the silent sound.
I am not background noise. I'm not a game to play.
I am not background noise. I won't be ignored.

Casey looks over as we reach the final line. Our eyes lock, and we hold the note until the last guitar string has stopped vibrating.

We turn back to the audience and find the onlookers doing jazz hands—clapping in sign language. I asked Paz, Lela, and César to spread the word about it, but I didn't think many people would follow through.

Clearly, I was wrong.

Everyone in the audience is doing jazz hands, except for our family members, who wave enthusiastic "I love you" signs.

My heart tumbles in my chest. I unplug my guitar and swing it around to my back, then crush Casey into a hug. Her arms wrap around my neck, and I lift her off the ground, laughing and fighting off tears.

We join hands, face the crowd, and take a bow before climbing the bleachers and squeezing in next to our families. We're immediately encased in hugs and congratulations. Both of our moms are crying. We sit next to each other and watch the rest of the show, still buzzing with the thrill of the performance.

Casey elbows me. I look at her and she holds up her hand with her middle and ring fingers tucked to her palm. *"I love you."*

I beam at her, repeat the sign, and press it against hers, my heart fuller than ever.

CHAPTER 37
HAYDEN

"CONGRATULATIONS!" HENRY BELLOWS THE MOMENT I STEP INSIDE EL Pollo Cubano later that afternoon. My family insisted on closing the restaurant for the show and a post-show celebration.

He crushes me into a hug, then pulls away with a grin. "Next up is an Oscar! No, wait, that's for movies…an Emmy?" He gestures toward the cheap gold trophy I'm cradling like it's my firstborn child. César slings an arm around Henry's shoulders as he joins us.

"I think you mean either a Grammy or a Tony," Paz chimes in from behind me.

I simply smile at the first place trophy for the Thirty-Fourth Annual Palmera High Winter Talent Show. "Thanks, but I've got a long way to go."

Henry waves off my modesty. Mamma, Tío Eddy, Paz, and Lela descend to shower me with compliments and congratulations.

For most people, winning a flimsy, ten-dollar trophy isn't a huge career achievement. But for Casey and me, it marks a giant step. It's proof that we're embracing our love of music and being brave enough to chase our dreams.

Hugging the trophy a little tighter, I check the time—the Kowalskis are supposed to be here soon to join the festivities. I'm going to give

Casey the biggest hug when she gets here because we did it. We actually **did it**.

"—and I want you to know…Hayden?" Papá's voice pulls me out of my thoughts.

He's standing near the Wall of Fame, one hand behind his back. With his free hand, he motions me closer. I walk over to him, feeling uneasy. My eyes scan the frames, and I linger on my abuelo's picture before looking to Papá.

"When I put these pictures up, it was because someone in our family had worked hard to wholeheartedly pursue their passion," he explains. "So, I put this here"—he taps the framed photo of me in my Barracudas jersey—"when you earned your captaincy. I was very proud of you." His lips curl into a wistful smile.

My stomach twists and I bite the inside of my cheek. This is the opposite of what I want him to say right now. I want Papá to congratulate me and tell me I performed well, the way he does after Henry or Dino play a good game. Hearing him reminisce about how proud he was when I was on the team, when I was miserable but doing what was expected of me, shatters the confidence I gained from killing it in the talent show.

"But this photo doesn't belong here anymore," Papá continues, and the trophy almost slips out of my clammy hands. He takes the picture off the wall. The empty space where the frame used to hang feels like a gut punch.

"Because it doesn't represent your passion," he explains. He hands the photo to Tío Eddy, who winks at me. My eyes dart back and forth between my family members, all of them wearing similar proud expressions. César and Henry both flash me brotherly smiles.

I barely have a chance to wonder what the heck is happening before Papá removes his other hand from behind his back and presents a new framed photo. "This is who you are," he says as he hangs the picture on the wall.

I take a closer look at the photo and my heart skips a few beats. It's a screenshot from one of the Instagram videos Casey and I filmed—complete with the app's logo, Casey's username, and part of the comment section.

"Papá, you couldn't have cropped it? Seriously?" Dino groans.

"Hey, hey, I don't know all these photo editing tricks you kids do. Cut your old man some slack," Papá chides.

"You can literally just do it once you screenshot—"

"Oh my God, Dino, teach him how to screenshot later!" Paz hisses. "This is not your moment, hon." He glares at my younger brother.

I sniffle and look between the wall and Papá. "Y-you really think I belong up there? Next to all of you?" I ask him, my voice small.

"It's our wall of pride, mijo. And we're so proud of you, Hayden. All of us." He motions to our family, and everyone nods in agreement.

"Extremely proud," Mamma adds, squeezing my shoulders from behind me. I turn to look at her and she beams, tears welling in her eyes.

I rush forward to give Papá a hug. His strong arms wrap around me, and he plants a kiss on my curls. "Just promise to call us even when you're off in LA or New York or wherever."

I chuckle and nod, glancing at Henry. "Yeah, I've recently learned how important communication is, so I promise."

"Okay!" Papá claps, signaling the end of the heart-to-heart. "Let's get to work. The food isn't going to cook itself!" He ushers Dino, César, and Lela into the kitchen while Mamma and Henry push tables together to create a larger one.

"Damn, I wish I had my food handler's license. I would totally help. It's so unfortunate, really," Paz sighs. "I guess I'm destined to a life of being waited on." He situates himself at the table by the window.

I chuckle and go to join him while we wait for Casey to arrive.

"Hay, can I steal you for a moment?" Tío asks before I can sit down. He leads me to a quiet corner. "I feel honored to have been able to watch you grow into an incredible young man and such a talented artist," he says. "And your papá is right. Everyone is proud of you."

"Everyone?" I raise a skeptical brow.

Tío smiles sympathetically. "Your tía will come around. Someday she'll be just as proud of you as the rest of us and all of this will be ancient history."

"What, in like twenty years?"

"Maybe fifteen, if you're lucky," he jokes. "But truly. I don't want you to underestimate how happy I am for you. You're following your own path and being true to yourself for the first time—and who you are couldn't be more wonderful."

"Ah! Everyone needs to stop being so heartfelt!" I hide my face in my hands. "I've already cried way too much today!"

Tío's cheery laughter fills the restaurant, and he gives me one last hug before heading to the kitchen.

I sit next to Paz, and he leans his head on my shoulder.

"Hay, I—"

I slap a hand over his mouth. "Don't say anything sappy! You people keep being all nice and proud and ooey-gooey!"

He chuckles and gives my hand a quick squeeze. "Okay, fine. Consider me sapless."

Sunshine streams in through the window. The familiar low whir of the industrial mixer and the feeling of César's necklace between my fingers put me at ease. I look at the Wall of Fame, my focus shifting from generation to generation, until I land on the poorly cropped screenshot.

Today was full of ups and downs—heck, so was this whole semester—but in this very moment, I'm not panicking over what the future holds.

I just feel happy.

And even if a day from now, or an hour from now, I'm sucked into another hopeless anxiety spiral, I promise myself that I'll always remember this moment and the people who supported me every step of the way.

CHAPTER 38

CASEY

As I exit Palmera with Mom and Dad, I'm still so hyped up from our kick-ass performance I practically do a happy dance as we walk.

Hayden and I haven't had a chance to talk since we performed. We sat together to watch the last few performers who went after us, but we got separated when the show ended, each of us swept up into our own group of cheerleaders and well-wishers. And I don't think I can wait much longer to gush about how **unbelievably fucking amazing** we were. I mean, I'm not trying to sound cocky, but if we hadn't had won first place, I would've been sure the show was rigged.

I pull my phone out of my pocket to text Hayden that we're on our way, but Mom grabs my wrist.

"Hang on, Case," she says. She swaps a look with Dad before leading me to one of the benches in Palmera's courtyard and motioning for me to sit down between them.

I eye my parents. "We're supposed to meet everyone at El Pollo Cubano for the afterparty," I remind them.

"Moja droga, before we go to the restaurant, Mom and I need to talk to you," Dad says, patting the bench.

My heart plummets into my stomach. Nothing good has ever come from that phrase. Nothing.

I take a reluctant seat between them, my body tense. *"What is it?"* I ask using SimCom.

"Casey, sweetie," Mom starts, "after you became Deaf-Hard of Hearing…it felt like you were so lost. Dad and I had no idea how to help you, and, admittedly, we made some missteps.

"We were incredibly worried about making this cross-country move in the middle of all of this, but you've flourished so much in Miami." Mom chokes up, staving off tears. "We can see that the friends you've made here are irreplaceable. They've given you so much support and helped you regain your confidence, and it's clear how happy they make you."

She peers over my head and shares another conspiratorial look with Dad. He winks at her then pats my knee lovingly.

"We do not want you to lose this confidence and joy," he says. "We were going to wait until Christmas to tell you this, but celebrating your talent show victory seems like the perfect occasion. So…" he mimics a drumroll on his legs for added suspense.

"Tata, proszę! Hurry up!" I urge, unable to stand it anymore.

He chuckles. "Your mother and I have decided to stay in Miami until you graduate high school!" He and Mom both do jazz hands.

My jaw drops. "Say that again?!"

He beams, displaying an indecent level of glee for any respectable Pole. "We are staying in Miami, moja droga."

"Are you serious? *True biz!?*" When they laugh and nod, I pull them into a group hug, tears of happiness forming in my eyes.

We hug each other and cry-laugh together for several minutes until the news sinks in: I'm staying in Miami!

Holy shit!

I free myself from my parents' embrace. "I have to tell Hayden!" I exclaim. Mom and Dad hug me one more time before we get in the car and head to El Pollo Cubano.

During the drive, I brainstorm the best way to share the news. I eventually land on announcing it as soon as I walk through the door because I might combust if I have to keep it secret any longer than that. But when I finally walk into the restaurant, César hurries over to me, holding a bouquet of flowers, and every thought I've ever had disappears.

He hands me the flowers, a huge smile on his face, dark eyes impossibly sparkly. *"You sing beautifully,"* he signs.

"Thank you," I lower a hand from my chin and try to ignore the fact that everyone's stopped what they're doing to watch us.

He takes a step toward me and I automatically respond by standing on my tiptoes and kissing him. It's far more chaste than our kiss in the mall photobooth, but to be fair, we're in the middle of his dad and uncle's restaurant in front of our whole families.

When I pull away, his eyes are wide. "I, uh, was going for a hug. But okay," he mumbles.

Mortification floods my entire system. "Oh my God, yeah, no. I just assumed…you…I—"

He interrupts me by planting a soft kiss on my cheek. "Shall we?" He nods toward our friends, who are watching with a mix of horror and amusement.

"Trzymaj się…wait a second! When did you get a boyf—" Dad starts, but Mom smacks his arm and leads him to where Hayden's parents, older brother, and uncle are drinking coffee.

I swallow my embarrassment as César takes my hand and we walk to the table. We sit together and he wraps an arm around my shoulder. I guess the cat is officially out of the bag.

"You didn't get **me** flowers," Hayden scoffs. César rolls his eyes and grabs a buñuelo from one of the baskets on the table.

"Oh, I have news!" I blurt, suddenly remembering what I was going to say before César turned my brain to mush.

At the same time, Lela says, "I have a confession." She eyes me. "I'll go first," she decides. I doubt whatever she's going to say is as exciting as my news, but hey, I'll be the bigger person. I take a bite of buñuelo as Lela pulls up Instagram. She places her phone on the table, sharing the screen with everyone.

I see my username and a new post on my feed. My eyes bug out of my head. I wipe powdered sugar off my hands and pick up Lela's phone.

"Lela, you posted our performance? On **my** account?"

"Yes." Lela nonchalantly bobs her hand. "And you've already gotten two thousand views. I'll accept gratitude in the form of cash or credit."

"Wait…how'd you know my password?"

Lela smirks. *"I know everything."*

Paz swallows a bite of buñuelo, sugar sticking to the lower half of his face. "You guys are going to be rolling in dough soon! With the kinds of views you're pulling in? You could move to LA and live in an influencer house or whatever."

I sign out of my account from Lela's phone and make a mental note to change my password. "We're hardly influencers," I snort. "But…" I look at Hayden, an idea coming to me.

"But what?" he asks using SimCom.

"We should take this to the next level. Like, maybe we should try to book some local gigs. And someday maybe we could record an EP!"

"*I don't know…*" He throws a flat hand away from his temple. "Would we even have time? With school and everything?"

I shrug. "For once, Paz may be right. We should explore where this takes us."

Paz rolls his eyes. "I'm always right."

I can see Hayden weighing the options, but it's not long before he cracks a smile.

"*O-K,*" he concedes. "But only because we're the greatest team there's ever been. Even better than Inter Miami. Oh, but promise we aren't going to do bubblegum pop?"

"Of course not." I crinkle my nose. "The only bubblegum bands that have rights are One Direction and DAYDREAM."

"Amen!" Paz applauds my choices.

"So…we're doing this?" I extend my hand.

"I suppose we are." Hayden shakes my hand with a laugh.

"In that case," I smirk, "it's a good thing we have until graduation to hone our craft."

The table falls silent. Everyone looks confused.

"Oh my god, how clueless can you guys be? I'm staying in Miami!" I announce.

Hayden blinks at me. "Miami, Florida?"

"Hay, in the context of this conversation, what Miami do you think I'm referring to? Really."

His jaw drops. "Holy crap. No way. No way!"

Lela starts chattering excitedly, Paz bombards me with questions, and Hayden just beams at me. Through the chaos, César taps me and removes his arm from around my shoulders to sign. *"True biz? That's amazing!* But you won't get overheated? Sunburned?"

"Very funny." I roll my eyes. "I'm more worried that you'll get sick of me."

"But you're perfect in every way," he jokes and presses a soft kiss to my lips. "So that's impossible."

"Okay, scoot over! Best friend coming through!" Hayden exclaims, moving his chair to my side of the table and creating a space between César and me. César playfully scowls at him but doesn't protest.

Hayden gives me a one-armed hug. "You really mean it? You're not moving back home to Portland?"

I freeze, struck by the sound of him calling Portland my home.

I look at my friends—people who were strangers only a few months ago, but who I now feel like I've known my whole life—and then glance out the window. Palm fronds sway in the breeze and the hot Miami sun is shining, strong as ever even in December.

"Home?" I breathe, thinking about what the word really means.

What I've learned this year is that home has nothing to do with geography. It's about people. The people who love and accept you—who don't treat you like an inconvenience.

I think about Hayden's unconditional friendship, Paz's theatrics, Lela's shameless yet entertaining gossip. The way César kisses me like the world is ending. Taylor helping me find my voice again. These things are home.

Home is salty air, sign language, and smiling until it hurts.

"Portland isn't home anymore." I say, turning to face my friends. "Home is you guys. Home is us."

ACKNOWLEDGMENTS

It truly takes a village to "raise" a book, and I'm extraordinarily lucky to have had the most amazing village help me make THE LOUDEST SILENCE a reality. I am eternally grateful to everyone who played a part in getting this book on shelves!

To my superstar agent, Emily Forney: from day one you've been not only an unbelievable champion for this book and for me, but also a hilarious and cherished friend, and I'm so thankful for you.

Thanks to my editor, Alex Aceves, for seeing the importance of this story; my copy editors, Maya Myers and Leigh Ann Cowan; and designer Chelsea Hunter. A massive thank you to Jaqueline Li, who illustrated the gorgeous cover and brought Casey and Hayden to life!

I'm beyond grateful to my mom who read hundreds of draft versions and gave the best feedback. I couldn't have done any of this without you. Thank you to my brother, Cam, for helping me fact-check soccer scenes; my service dog, Boss; and my regular dog, Rusty. Your cuddles got me through some tight deadlines and frustrating plot holes. And thanks to my incredible friends, Nona, Toby, and Noah, for cheering me on every step of the way. I love y'all!

And to Grandpa B: you always joked you'd buy dozens of copies of my books. Your support meant the world to me. I miss you every day. Ich liebe dich.

I'd be remiss to not give a huge shoutout to my ASL teacher, Briana Garry, and former vocal coach, Taylor Gonzaga. You two have been so influential in my life and I'm forever grateful for you.

In the 4+ years I've been in the publishing world, I've made so many incredible, once in a lifetime friends: Cass Biehn, Sarah Street, Elanna Heda, Kelly Andrew, Birukti Tsige, Autumn Kohler, Aiden Thomas, Anna Sortino, Amanda Woody, Birdie Schae, Sophie Gonzales, Greg Saunders, Bethany Matson, Liana Solomon, Zoie Konneker, Tiara Blue, Camille Lerner, Elle Gonzalez Rose, CJ Ellison, Nadia Noor, Rosiee Thor, Sabrina Lunavong, Kyla Zhao, Sujin Witherspoon, Elle Grenier, Olive J. Kelley, and Nicoletta Poungias. I feel so lucky to have met you! Thanks for putting up with my chaotic DMs.

Thank you to my fellow members of Signed Ink—a coalition of D/deaf and Hard of Hearing authors and illustrators. You guys' insight and advice along the way has meant a lot to me!

I truly wouldn't have made it this far without the mentorship (and friendship) of Meredith Tate, Amparo Ortiz, Christina Li, and Justine Pucella Winans. Having you guys in my corner and hearing your advice on all things publishing has meant so much to me.

To my "Big 5" group chat, Famke Kim-Thy Halma, Layla Noor, Victoria Wlosok, and Ann Zhao: you guys have always given me so much support. "Big 5" forever!

And my 2024Ever Debut Buddies: Christen Randall Young, Clare Edge, Kalie Holford, Wen-yi Lee, Kamilah Cole, Erin Baldwin, Marissa Eller, Colby Wilkens, Matthew Hubbard, Anthony Nerada, Hayley Dennings, Elba Luz, and Megan Scott. I'm honored to be debuting with such a talented line up.

Big thank you to my authenticity readers, Stephanie Weber and C. A., whose insightful feedback helped me ensure accurate representation, and Miriam Cortinovis, who helped out with the Italian.

Shoutout to Disney Channel for HIGH SCHOOL MUSICAL, which altered my brain chemistry and was my first theater-kid awakening; to One Direction, specifically for releasing "Strong," which was one of the only songs I could listen to for a year while revising; and to Kim Seungmin for doing a cover of "Ghost" by Justin Bieber, which was also on repeat for *a year*.

Lastly, thank YOU, dear reader! Thank you for reading THE LOUDEST SILENCE, for briefly living inside Casey and Hayden's world, and for letting me share this deeply personal story. I am forever grateful.

RESOURCES

D/deaf and ASL Resources:

Signed Ink: A list of D/deaf authors + illustrators and D/deaf resources

Online ASL dictionaries and lessons:

    Lifeprint

    Handspeak

    Gallaudet University (ASL Connect page)

Mental Health/Anxiety Resources:

The Trevor Project (Resources for Mental Health Support page)

Nemours TeensHealth (Anxiety Disorders page), also available in Spanish

Queer Teen Resources:

The Trevor Project

Planned Parenthood (Info and Resources for LGBTQ Teens and Allies page)

It Gets Better Project

Links to these resources can be found on my author website: **www.slangwrites.com/the-loudest-silence.**

Disclaimer: these resources are included for informational purposes only. Author is not responsible for the content, accuracy, or applicability of resource websites' information or materials.

PRAISE FOR
THE LOUDEST SILENCE

"Hilarious and heartfelt, Langford has crafted a story that will mean so much to so many readers. A story of friendship and loss that will tear your heart to pieces before stitching it back together. A stunning debut from a much-needed voice." **—Mason Deaver, author of *Okay, Cupid***

"Comforting, authentic, and at times laugh out loud funny, *The Loudest Silence* deals with facing your fears and finding your people through music and language. Langford handles themes of friendship, acceptance, and grief with a deft hand, delivering both a poignant look into the Deaf experience and a compelling depiction of platonic love. The distinct voices of this dual-POV debut make for a heartwarming read—one that is not to be missed by fans of contemporary YA." **—Kelly Andrew, author of *The Whispering Dark***

"Witty and full of heart, *The Loudest Silence* is a genuine portrayal of what it's like to become disabled at the same time you're trying to find your way in the world. Langford approaches the narrative and their characters with an abundance of empathy that is present in every page. A lovely debut." **—Lillie Lainoff, author of *One For All***

"Exploring expression through language and song, *The Loudest Silence* will make your heart sing. Sydney Langford crafts a delightfully captivating story that doesn't shy away from the realities of grief and change."

—Anna Sortino, author of *Give Me a Sign*

"A witty and nuanced debut! *The Loudest Silence* is an extraordinarily crafted love song to language, grief, vulnerability, and finding community. With a captivating voice and poignant storytelling, Sydney Langford is destined to become a new favorite for many readers."

—Julian Winters, award-winning author of *Right Where I Left You*